What people are saying about …

THE OZARK MOUNTAIN TRILOGY

"*Not by Sight* is nonstop tension and danger, young love, and conflicts of faith that make it a not-to-be-missed experience. Another winner for Kathy Herman!"

Lorena McCourtney, author of the Ivy
Malone Mysteries and the Cate Kinkaid Files

"Just when you think *Only by Death* is over, it's not … and the tension mounts. Young Jesse is brave, spunky, and lives out his faith. I want to be like Jesse when I grow up!"

Roxanne Henke, author of the
Coming Home to Brewster series

"Prepare yourself for a roller-coaster ride. Kathy Herman's latest suspense doesn't deliver just one mystery but many twists and turns that will keep the pages flying! And all in another picturesque location. Don't miss this wild ride!"

Lyn Cote, *USA Today* bestselling author

"As a longtime Kathy Herman fan, I know I can expect a top-notch mystery that will grab my attention from the very first page."

Carol Cox, author of the Arizona
Territory Brides series

"Readers of all ages will readily identify with the protagonist in *Only by Death*. This highly engaging read is not your typical murder mystery."

Eric Wiggin, MsEd, speaker, author
of *The Gift of Grandparenting* and *The Hills of God*, rewritten as *The Recluse*

"*Only by Death*, book 2 of Kathy Herman's Ozark Mountain Trilogy, is filled with action, suspense, and surprises, as well as thought-provoking questions about what it really means to live the Christian life."

Julianna Deering, author of the
Drew Farthering Mysteries

"*Only by Death* is one of Kathy Herman's best so far, especially in the faith thread. It will challenge you at a deep level, making you question where you would stand if the same things happened to you. I highly recommend it—truly a must read."

Miralee Ferrell, award-winning author of
Runaway Romance, also a TV movie

A
TREACHEROUS
MIX A NOVEL

OZARK MOUNTAIN TRILOGY

KATHY HERMAN

BESTSELLING
SUSPENSE NOVELIST

A TREACHEROUS MIX

A NOVEL

DAVID C COOK

transforming lives together

A TREACHEROUS MIX
Published by David C Cook
4050 Lee Vance Drive
Colorado Springs, CO 80918 U.S.A.

Integrity Music Limited, a Division of David C Cook
Eastbourne, East Sussex BN23 6NT, England

The graphic circle C logo is a registered trademark of David C Cook.

The website addresses recommended throughout this book are offered as a
resource to you. These websites are not intended in any way to be or imply an
endorsement on the part of David C Cook, nor do we vouch for their content.

This story is a work of fiction. Characters and events are the product of the author's
imagination. Any resemblance to any person, living or dead, is coincidental.
All Scripture quotations are taken from the Holy Bible, NEW INTERNATIONAL
VERSION®, NIV®. Copyright © 1973, 2011 by Biblica, Inc.® Used by permission.
All rights reserved worldwide. NEW INTERNATIONAL VERSION® and NIV®
are registered trademarks of Biblica, Inc. Use of either trademark for the offering
of goods or services requires the prior written consent of Biblica, Inc. Quote in
chapter 35: "The Invisible Effects of Sex before Marriage," Moral Revolution,
accessed October 25, 2017, https://moralrevolution.com/the-invisible-effects-of-
sex-before-marriage/. See ref. material: Caroline Leaf, *Switch On Your Brain: The
Key to Peak Happiness, Thinking, and Health* (Grand Rapids, MI: Baker Books,
2013); and Joe S. McIlhaney and Freda McKissic Bush, *Hooked: New Science
on How Casual Sex Is Affecting Our Children* (Chicago: Northfield, 2008).

LCCN 2017964688
ISBN 978-0-7814-0805-9
eISBN 978-0-8307-7550-7

© 2018 Kathy Herman
Published in association with the literary agency of Alive Communications,
Inc, 7680 Goddard St., Suite 200, Colorado Springs, CO 80920.
The Team: Alice Crider, Jamie Chavez, Amy Konyndyk,
Nick Lee, Jack Campbell, Susan Murdock
Cover Design: Kirk Douponce, Dog-Eared Design
Cover Photo: iStockphoto.com

Printed in the United States of America
First Edition 2018
1 2 3 4 5 6 7 8 9 10
053118

To Him who is both the Giver and the Gift

ACKNOWLEDGMENTS

The Ozark Mountains of northwest Arkansas provide the backdrop for this series and many of the images I describe in this story. However, Sure Foot Mountain, Angel View Lodge, Raleigh County, and the town of Foggy Ridge exist only in my imagination.

During the writing of this book, I drew from several resource people, each of whom shared generously from his or her storehouse of knowledge and experience. I did my best to integrate the facts as I understood them. If accuracy was compromised in any way, it was unintentional and strictly of my own doing.

I owe a special word of thanks to Retired Commander Carl H. Deeley of the Los Angeles County Sheriff's Department for taking time (even while on vacation!) to answer my questions. In this book, perhaps more than in any other, I realized the need to understand more about the FBI and CIA and their various functions. While these two agencies do not comment at all regarding their operation, Carl's firsthand experience with them over the years was extremely valuable in helping me to craft a believable scenario. Carl, from the bottom of my heart, thank you for answering my emails when my deadline required quick replies in order for me to continue. You are a blessing and a friend.

I'm deeply grateful to moralrevolution.com for the wealth of information you make available online. Your professionally presented facts support what I knew in my heart but found difficult to articulate. I hope my readers will visit your website and be enlightened by the science that supports the wisdom of keeping sex within the confines of a marital relationship. God bless you for boldly speaking the truth.

A special thank-you to Nancy Godsey, Betty Mix, Martha Shelton, Sharon Mayville, Buzz Adams, and the staff at the Waterton Inn in Tyler, Texas, for respecting my night-writing, day-sleeping schedule. You will never know how much I appreciated you guarding my time so I could finish this manuscript.

I'm immensely grateful to my faithful prayer warriors: my sister Pat Phillips, dear friends Mark and Donna Skorheim, Susan Mouser, and Susie Killough; and my online prayer team: Pearl Anderson, Judith Depontes, Jackie Jeffries, Joanne Lambert, Diane Morin, Kim Prothro, Kelly Smith, Carolyn Walker, Deanna Tyler, and Sondra Watson; my friends at LifeWay Christian Store in Tyler, Texas, and LifeWay Christian Resources in Nashville, Tennessee; I cannot possibly express to you how much I value your prayers.

To my agent, Lisa Jackson, at Alive Communications for being an advocate for this series. I never have to wonder if you're looking out for my best interests.

To my editor, Jamie Chavez, for being such a delight to work with. I love the rhythm we've developed and hope we get to work together again in the future. Your wit, insight, gentle nudging, flexibility, and encouragement were so appreciated. It's been a privilege working with you!

To Cris Doornbos, Dan Rich, Alice Crider, and the amazing staff at David C Cook publishers for believing in me and investing in the words I write; thanks for all you've done to support my writing ministry, and for giving me the opportunity to finish this series. Over half of my writing career has been spent working hand in hand with your professional staff, who share my heart for wanting to bring people closer to Christ. I deeply cherish the years I had as a part of the Cook "family," and pray that God will continue to bless your faithfulness.

To my sweet Paul, whose voice of wisdom still echoes in my mind, I cherish all the times you were a sounding board for my ideas, my storylines, my characters, and my hopes and dreams for what the Lord could do with the words I write. I miss you with every breath, but never more than when I birth a new book. Your DNA is on every page.

And to my Father in heaven, thank You for the privilege of writing stories that touch hearts and draw them closer to You. I pray that this story will give us all a glimpse of the heavenly Bridegroom and a deeper understanding and reverence for marriage and all You intended it to be.

"This is the message we have heard from him and declare to you: God is light; in him there is no darkness at all. If we claim to have fellowship with him and yet walk in the darkness, we lie and do not live out the truth." 1 John 1:5–6

PROLOGUE

Brody Armison leaned against a rock formation and held the binoculars to his eyes, pretending to watch the sailboats on Beaver Lake, but never losing sight of the young woman who sat on a patchwork quilt, her sleek dark hair tossed about by the playful breeze.

She looked both innocent and seductive, barefoot and dressed in a pink sundress, her smooth ivory skin caressed by the sun. Her dark eyes were almond shaped, her cheeks the color of the roses that grew around his grandmother's front porch. Posed against a distant backdrop of white sails and rippled water the color of blue topaz, she might have made the perfect subject for an Impressionist's canvas.

What could a classy lady like her possibly see in the rugged, unlikely companion who sat beside her, trying to look cool in his Walmart sunglasses, his hairy arm casually draped over her shoulder like a cheap handbag? The man was definitely not in her league—denim versus fine linen—and yet the joy she wore needed no interpretation. She was smitten, wholly absorbed in the moment. And judging from Denim Boy's tender touches, it was mutual. Lucky dog!

Brody turned his gaze away from the couple and onto the reason for his being there—the sailboat races on Beaver Lake. He'd never watched them from up this high on Sure Foot Mountain, but every year the crowds that gathered close to the water had made him more and more claustrophobic. He had driven up the mountain and some distance beyond Angel View Lodge and spotted this rock formation at the top of a grassy slope. He got out and really liked the view of the lake from there, never thinking that he would be invading anyone's space.

He spied again at the couple. She looked like an angel, smiling peacefully, her face kissed by the sun. She just might be the most beautiful woman he had ever seen. Hopefully Denim Boy realized what he had.

Brody heard a funny sound and looked up just as a drone, similar to one his cousin Dennis owned, flew over his head. He watched it through his binoculars … a really cool-looking hexacopter drone, its six propellers making it look like a flying spider. It descended the hillside in the direction of the couple and then hovered about ten feet above them.

Brody chuckled. "Smile. You're on *Candid Camera*." He wondered if the couple was even aware that they'd been caught on film by some local Bubba wanting to play with the latest technology.

In the next instant, something resembling a reddish vapor fell on them, and then the drone disappeared behind the trees. Both the man and the woman began coughing, their hands to their throats. They seemed to be struggling to breathe, and then they just fell back, motionless on the quilt.

Horrified, Brody started to climb down from the rocks, thinking once his feet hit the grassy slope, he wouldn't have to run more than fifty yards or so before he reached them. He heard deep voices and put the binoculars to his eyes. Two men wearing gas masks and black coveralls ran out of the trees. One quickly picked up the woman and put her over his shoulder, while the other rolled her lover over on his side and picked up the quilt the couple had been sitting on only a few minutes ago. Then they ran back toward the trees.

Brody kept his gaze on them, his binoculars held tightly to his eyes. The men ran toward a huge house visible through the trees. He hadn't noticed it before. A plain white truck the size of a large U-Haul was parked out front. A black Suburban sat in the drive-way, but he couldn't see the license plate. The men quickly slid the woman into the back of the Suburban and closed the door. Other men dressed in black coveralls and black caps—six in all—came out of the house and got into the white truck, then both vehicles drove away.

Brody's knees almost buckled, and he fell back against a rock. What had just happened? Who were those people, and where were they taking the woman? Was she alive? Was her lover? It seemed like something out of a movie. Obviously, this was planned. Carefully calculated. Whatever "this" was, it certainly wasn't harmless.

He turned and looked down the grassy slope at the body that lay motionless. He resisted the urge to go check to see if the man was breathing. What if someone else was coming to pick up the man's body? And what if the drone had gotten a picture of *him*? Brody shuddered to think what would happen to him if the men who did this caught him there. Or found out he'd gone to the authorities. He couldn't tell anyone about this, not even Sheriff Granger.

If he could just muster enough leg strength to climb down from these rocks and make his way back to his truck, he would drive straight home and bolt-lock his doors. But after what he'd just seen, he doubted he would feel safe anywhere. If they wanted to find him, they would.

CHAPTER 1

Hawk Cummings felt an excruciating pounding in his head, like a sledgehammer was breaking his skull. He seemed to be spinning round and round at a dizzying speed and swatted the air for something to grab on to before finally clutching the grassy ground with his left hand, perspiration running off his face. What was happening? Where was he?

Kennedy's! He wasn't sure whether he'd blurted it out or merely thought it. He remembered telling his family he was going to the sailboat races by himself, since Laura Lynn had to work. They had no idea he was having an affair with Kennedy Taylor, and he intended to keep it that way.

He remembered coming to Kennedy's home just after sunup. Climbing the stairs to her room. Crawling under the softest, most luxurious comforter he'd ever felt, and sharing an entire morning of lustful bliss. Afterward, Kennedy fixed them bacon and waffles and they ate out on the deck. Then they decided to watch the sailboat races. They grabbed a quilt to sit on, and walked over to the grassy hillside, high above Beaver Lake, where they had an unobstructed view. From that point on, nothing was clear in his mind. He remembered dreaming that he and Kennedy were caught in a web and a giant black spider spewed venom on them. He remembered struggling to breathe and thinking he was going to die. He remembered hearing voices. And feeling someone push him on his side, then pulling the quilt out from under him. Was all that a dream?

Hawk rolled over on his back, then groped the grassy ground on either side of where he lay and didn't feel Kennedy or the quilt they had spread on the ground beneath them. This was too weird.

He opened his eyes and peeled off his sunglasses. A kaleidoscope of blazing pink and purple pieces slowly came into focus. *Sunset?* He pushed the button on his watch and squinted: 8:32 p.m., Saturday, June 3. The last time he remembered checking the time was just before three. Had he been lying here all that time?

He sat up, the pounding in his head subsiding slightly, and stuffed his sunglasses into the pocket of his cargo pants. He stumbled onto his feet and stood a moment until the dizziness faded a bit, then walked slowly toward Kennedy's house. The lights were on! He hurried his pace until he reached the kitchen door. He knocked, then turned the handle and cracked the door.

"Kennedy? Are you in here …? Kennedy …?"

Hawk pushed open the door and sucked in a breath. Every piece of furniture, every accessory, and every wall hanging was missing from the kitchen and adjacent dining room. He walked down the hall to the living room—stripped bare. He hurried upstairs to Kennedy's bedroom—completely empty. He opened her walk-in closets—even the hangers were gone.

Hawk, his heart racing with questions, then went from room to room on both levels of Kennedy's house. The place was huge.

And completely empty. If she intended to dump him, why would she have invited him over? One thing he knew for sure: it took organized planning to strip a house in a matter of hours. She couldn't have done it, so who did?

Hawk felt another wave of dizziness and fell back against the door, noticing a pale red spatter on the front of his shirt. Was it possible he hadn't been dreaming? He couldn't explain the giant spider he saw, but the red substance was proof that someone or something must have sprayed some kind of chemical on them. What else would have made him feel so disoriented?

Maybe Kennedy didn't leave of her own free will. Maybe she was a victim. But of what? What did he even know about her? She told him she was an only child who inherited a fortune after her parents died. He thought it was odd that she talked very little about herself but figured maybe the pain was too fresh. But what she lacked in verbal communication she made up for in physical expression. And despite biblical admonitions regarding premarital sex, he could hardly think of anything else. Except making sure each sensuous rendezvous remained their private business.

What now? There was no way he could report what had happened today and sound credible unless he admitted to Sheriff Granger, to Laura Lynn, and to his family that he'd been having an affair. An affair so intense and shallow that he hadn't taken time to get to know the woman he'd been involved with. How would they react?

Hawk suddenly felt hot all over. It was one thing to have immersed himself in the pursuit of pleasure, but another to confess it openly. How could he admit to them that he'd let lust control his

actions? That he'd betrayed Laura Lynn? That he'd broken the vow
he'd made to the Lord not to have sex until he married?

Hawk glanced out the window at the last vestiges of the sunset.
Why tell them anything? He couldn't undo his actions. Or give the
sheriff even one reliable fact about Kennedy Taylor, which probably
wasn't even her real name. All he wanted to do was go home and take
a shower and wash this nightmare down the drain. He felt as if he
were living in the twilight zone—only this was *real*.

❧

Kate Stafford sat arm in arm with her husband, Elliot, on the porch
swing of their log home, savoring the sights and sounds of nightfall
on Sure Foot Mountain.

"It's glorious out here tonight," Kate said. "June is my favorite
month. I hope the guests are enjoying the cool breeze after being out
in the sun for the sailboat races."

Elliot smiled. "I saw a whole crowd of them out on the back
deck of the lodge when I walked up here from the marina. Someone
had a guitar and they were all singing. The kids were down by the
gazebo, chasing lightning bugs. Compared to this, Riley might find
Camp Evergreen downright disappointing."

"It's just for a week. But Angel View does feel different without
her chatty little self charming the guests. They get such a kick out
of her. *And* Jesse's hummingbirds. I want our guests to have a great
time, but I've never been comfortable mingling with them. Micah

was the one who loved being out front. I was better in the business office."

Elliot kissed her cheek. "I'm sure he's smiling down from heaven at the way you've kept this place going. And, after all these years, you should know that *everyone* has a wonderful time at Angel View."

"Well, it doesn't happen without someone keeping an eye on details." Kate gave Elliot a gentle jab in the ribs with her elbow. "I'm glad you talked me into promoting Savannah to general manager. You were right. It was much easier to replace my head waitress than it would've been to hire and train someone to manage this place."

"Especially when you already had someone who understands the operation." Elliot smiled wryly. "Doesn't hurt that her husband is probably the best chef the lodge has ever had."

Kate laughed. "I must say you've taken more of an interest in Angel View Lodge than I ever expected."

"Well, I've gotten to know the owner intimately."

"Is that so?" she said playfully, combing her hand through his salt-and-pepper hair.

"Indeed. Now I find myself completely enmeshed in the entire operation. I'm even crazy about her family, as if they were my own."

"Sounds serious."

"Very." Elliot picked up her hand and slid his thumb across her wedding ring. "To tell you the truth, when I'm with her, I'm more at home than I ever was in that sprawling old house of mine. I love living at Angel View, in this log house that Micah built, on this property that God provided, with my ready-made family that I loved from afar. It's what I was made for."

Kate laid her chin on Elliot's shoulder and looked up at him. "Do you ever wonder if you need your head examined?"

"Every day." He laughed. "But there's nowhere else on earth I'd rather be."

Kate heard a car door slam and sat up. "That had better be Hawk."

"It is. May I suggest you remember he's twenty-four years old and not give him the third degree as if he were still in high school? Just sayin'."

Kate took a deep breath. Elliot was so good for her.

Hawk Cummings walked up on the porch. "Hey, you two. Any of that spaghetti left?"

"I saved you two helpings," Kate said proudly, "which is no easy task with Jesse rummaging through the fridge around the clock. So how was your day?"

"So-so. No great shakes. Sailboat races were cool."

"Did you catch up with your friends?" Elliot said.

"Everyone was there. Except Laura Lynn, of course. She got off at seven, so I drove by her place on my way home. Think I'll go take a shower and put some aloe on this sunburn. Then enjoy some of Mama's spaghetti."

"Savannah brought over quite a list of customers signed up for tomorrow's Jeep tours," Kate said. "I put it on your dresser."

"Thanks." Hawk bent down and kissed the top of Kate's head. "I love you, Mama. You're the best."

Kate looked up at her firstborn, aware that she was being charmed, but unable to resist. "I love you too."

Hawk took Elliot's hand and they did the fancy handshake known only to the two of them, and no words were necessary.

Hawk opened the front door and went inside.

Kate nestled closer to Elliot. "How'd I do?"

"Perfect. I'm proud of you. You didn't even mention that he'd spilled something on his shirt."

"It's hard to accept that Hawk's an adult," she said. "That's so strange, too, considering he tried to be the man of the house all those years Micah was missing, and I let him. Now that he's actually grown up, I find it hard to think of him as an adult."

"I wonder if it's because he's still under your roof."

"Maybe," Kate said. "But since he's running the Jeep operation, it has worked out well for him to live here. You know what an invaluable help he's been to me and Dad, not to mention a great big brother to Abby, Jesse, and Riley."

"I know, darling. It makes perfect sense. I'm just saying it might be why you find it hard to see him as a grown man."

"I just know that it'll be difficult when he finally does move out. The younger kids think he hung the moon." She smiled sheepishly. "I suppose a part of me does too."

Hawk pulled off his yellow polo shirt and looked in the bathroom mirror at his uneven sunburn, made weirder looking by his short stubble beard. The left side of his face and neck, his left arm, and the outer side of his left leg were badly burned. He must have lain on his side for a long time.

After examining the spatter on his shirt, he took his sunglasses out of the pocket of his cargo shorts and held them up to the light. They were sprinkled with the same red substance. Upon closer inspection, so were the denim shorts. He rummaged under the vanity and found a box of thirteen-gallon trash bags he'd bought for a camping trip. He plucked a bag, opened it up, and stuffed his shirt, shorts, and sunglasses inside and tied it. Until he could figure out what had happened, he would find a safe place to hide these for evidence.

He turned on the water in the shower and waited until it was just right, then stepped in and let the water pour over his head and down his back. The hot water didn't feel good on his sunburned skin, but he took the bar of soap, worked up a lather, and washed away the sweat, grit, and whatever chemical had been used to render him helpless. If only it were that easy to wash away the confusion, fear, and guilt.

He couldn't stop thinking about Kennedy just vanishing like that. If she wanted to break off the relationship, all she had to do was stop inviting him back. He could only wonder if she was a victim too—he knew he certainly was. He was left with many questions and no answers. And a huge secret he was afraid to report. Not that he could really tell the sheriff anything for certain—other than he had sold his soul to revel in carnal pleasure with a beautiful woman who either had disappeared on purpose, or might be in grave danger. Or was dead. Or not.

Hawk turned off the water, stepped out of the shower, and wrapped the bath towel around his waist. He wiped his feet on the mat and stepped over to the sink to look at his reflection in the mirror. His eyes appeared dark and empty. He knew his heart was.

How could he have put on blinders and let himself be lured into a web of deceit? Something Pastor Windsor had said at the men's retreat came rushing back to him:

"Just remember you can't have it both ways. If you walk in the pure light of God's Word, you know the truth. But if you start compromising what you know is right, your truth becomes an ugly, watered-down shade of gray. It's a treacherous mix."

Hawk gripped the sink and hung his head. He knew he should have run the minute he laid eyes on Kennedy. She was so beautiful. So desirable. So available. He walked into that trap with his eyes wide open and his conscience on mute. He'd used her. Looking back, she gave herself to him as if he were all that mattered. Unselfishly. Unashamedly. As if she were letting go of all her pent-up feelings. What was she hiding?

Hawk's heart sank. He would probably never know what had happened to her, and that would haunt him the rest of his life. But he was different after that intensely intimate experience. He had partaken of the ecstasy God intended for marriage, pleasure he had no right to, and it had changed him. He wasn't sure exactly how, but he wasn't the same man.

Tomorrow he had to muster the courage to tell Laura Lynn that he was breaking up with her, that he'd been sexually involved with someone—but without revealing Kennedy's name or that the affair ended only because she disappeared. He did not look forward to hurting Laura Lynn, and was deeply sorry for the betrayal he knew she would feel. Maybe one day she would be able to forgive him. But he doubted it would be tomorrow.

CHAPTER 2

Hawk was up with the sun and put in a full day, taking guests at Angel View Lodge on Jeep tours across Sure Foot Mountain. He hadn't had much time to rehearse what he was going to say to Laura Lynn when he met her at Coffey's after work.

After saying good-bye to the last of the guests who had signed up for the day's Jeep tours, Hawk went home and showered. He took a couple of Tylenol that he doubted would dull the nagging headache that had plagued him all day. He didn't know if it was stress related or a by-product of yesterday's bizarre mystery. He just wanted it to stop so he could think straight.

"You missed spaghetti night." Jesse Cummings stood in the bathroom doorway, munching a cookie. "*And* church this morning."

Hawk smoothed his hair and looked over at his little brother, who was holding several cookies in his hand. "What are you, my conscience? I can't always be home for spaghetti night. And I had to do Jeep tours today because I switched days off with Connor so I could go to the sailboat races."

"I miss you, that's all," Jesse said. "I haven't seen you much lately. We should go fishing. We always have a great time."

"We do, Jesse, but I only get one day off in the summer, and part of that is spent in church …"

"And the other part is spent with Laura Lynn. I know." Jesse's countenance fell.

"Can't you get Elliot to go with you?"

"We do other things. He's cool. He's just not a fisherman."

"What about Dawson? I know he fishes."

"He loves it, but he's got football training camp, church camp, and then he's going to Washington DC with his grandparents."

"What about Grandpa Buck?"

Jesse raked his fingers through his fine, dark hair. "We catch bluegill at the marina, but it's too hard for him to hike along the riverbank to where the bigger fish are."

Hawk turned to his brother and looked into his pleading eyes, remembering the long hours their dad had to put in at Angel View when Hawk was thirteen, and how Grandpa Buck had always been available to take him fishing on the river. "Okay, sport. I'll go with you next Sunday after church—if you'll get the bait and have our tackle ready to go. Deal?"

"Deal!"

Hawk bumped fists with Jesse, noticing for the first time how he was losing his boyish features and looking more like a teenager. "Now let me finish getting ready."

"You going out with Laura Lynn?"

"I'm meeting her at Coffey's."

"You must be tired. You don't sound very happy about it."

Hawk turned Jesse around and gave him a shove. "Good night, Dr. Phil."

Jesse laughed. "Bye. I'm going over to Timothy's and watch a movie on Netflix. I'll see you when I see you."

Hawk stared at his reflection in the mirror. He didn't even look the same. After tonight, Laura Lynn would never speak to him again.

Hawk drove slowly past Coffey's Grill House and saw the festive, colored lights strung in the trees around the back patio. The place was busy for a Sunday night—mostly with locals. It was too far off Main Street to attract many tourists. What made him think this was a good place to bare his soul?

He saw someone waving and realized it was Laura Lynn. He pulled his Jeep into the space next to hers, suddenly feeling sick to his stomach. He could do this. He had to do this.

"There you are," Laura Lynn Parks said.

She came up to his Jeep, still dressed in her pink-and-white uniform from Bella's Bakery, her long blonde hair tied back in a ponytail, her facial features delicate and feminine. He remembered how attracted he was to her the first time he laid eyes on her, and how he had agonized for weeks before he'd had the courage to ask her out. How could he have ruined everything?

"You don't look very happy to see me," she said.

"Sorry." Hawk got out and took her hand. "I'm just tired. Would you mind if we took a walk instead of going inside right now?"

"All right. It's beautiful out tonight."

As they walked toward Timberline Avenue, Hawk held tighter to Laura Lynn's hand than he had intended. He just couldn't make himself start the conversation.

"Hawk, is something wrong? And please don't tell me no. You haven't been yourself for weeks now. I'm feeling very insecure about this relationship. We haven't seen each other in almost a week, and you look more like you're going to a funeral than on a date. Is it me?"

Hawk shook his head. "I promise it's not you. You're remarkable. I, on the other hand ..."

"You, on the other hand, *what*?"

Hawk sighed. He stepped over to the barbershop window and leaned his back against it, facing Laura Lynn. He looked around to make sure they were alone. "I've done a terrible thing, babe. I've struggled to find an easy way to tell you, but there just isn't one. I've been seeing another woman for a while now." Hawk looked down at his shoes. He could hear his heart pounding in the agonizing moments that followed. *Come on, Laura Lynn, say something.*

"How long is *a while*?" she finally said.

Hawk lifted his head. "About six weeks."

"No wonder you've been avoiding me. Do you have feelings for her? Is it serious?"

"I'm not in love with her, if that's what you mean. But it's serious on another level." *Just say it before you can't.* "I—I've been sleeping with her."

Laura Lynn held her hand over her mouth and whimpered. "How could you, Hawk? We made a vow to God not to have sex until we marry. What were you thinking?"

"Obviously, I wasn't. I let my guard down. I'm not proud of it. I don't know what else to say."

She threw her hands in the air. "There's absolutely nothing you can say. *Once* is letting your guard down, and that's bad enough. But six weeks? That's a deliberate slap in the face. Does anyone else know?"

Hawk shook his head. "No, I wanted to tell you first. I'm so sorry. I know this must be devastating—"

"Do you *think*? This changes everything ..." Laura Lynn started to cry. "I can't—no, I won't—build a future with a man I can't trust. What's this woman's name?"

"It doesn't matter. You don't know her."

"Are you going to continue seeing her?"

"No, it's over," Hawk said firmly. "She's left town."

"You can't possibly think we can continue seeing each other after this."

"No. I let you down. Let God down. Let myself down. I don't deserve to be in any relationship until I can understand why I let this happen."

"Seems clear to me: your libido was stronger than your commitment. I can never trust you again." Laura Lynn looked dazed. She took off her promise ring and held it with her thumb and forefinger. "I guess that's it. This is good-bye."

Hawk sighed. "I wish we could at least stay friends, but that never seems to work while the pain is so fresh."

Laura Lynn seemed trapped in a long pause. Finally she said, "Tell me something. Not that I would have done it ... but why didn't you even try to get *me* to sleep with you? Am I not desirable? Is there something wrong with me?" Laura Lynn's eyes brimmed with tears.

Hawk swallowed the emotion that was just under the surface. "I respected you too much, babe. I never let down my guard with you. That's the way it's supposed to be. You're a beautiful and extremely desirable woman, and an incredibly kind and giving human being." He wiped her tears with his thumbs. "Someday the man God intended for you to marry will come into your life. He'll appreciate that you saved yourself just for him."

Laura Lynn took his hands and pushed them away. "I wanted *you* to be that man."

"So did I," Hawk said. "I'm sorry. I'm not the first man to be blinded by lust. I just want you to understand that what happened was my choice, my undoing. It was not a reflection on you as a woman."

Laura Lynn's face turned stone cold. "Doesn't matter. I couldn't feel any less significant than I do at this moment."

"I never intended to hurt you."

"I could almost believe that, if it had happened just one time. But you deceived me for six weeks. Did you even feel an ounce of remorse? Obviously, you were more interested in satisfying your lust than in protecting my feelings or this relationship."

Hawk couldn't think of anything to say in his defense. She was right. "I'm so sorry. There's no excuse for what I did. If I could go back and change it, I would. I know your heart is broken, and I know what we had is over. But I hope someday you'll be able to forgive me."

Laura Lynn put her promise ring in his hand without replying. The prolonged silence that followed was excruciating.

"Just so you know ..." Hawk finally said, his voice cracking, "I'm not planning to tell anyone else about the affair, other than

Mama and Elliot, and Grandpa Buck. I'd like to spare us both the humiliation."

"What are you going to say if someone asks why we broke up?"

"I'll say we came to the mutual realization that we were growing in opposite directions, and it seemed best to end it."

Laura Lynn nodded. "That's true enough. I really don't relish the thought of having to tell our friends what you did, though killing you has some appeal." Her half-hearted attempt at humor just produced more tears. "Despite everything, you're not an easy person to hate."

"Well, if it's any consolation, I hate myself enough for both of us." Hawk stood up straight. "Come on, I'll walk you to your car."

He started to take her arm and she put her hands in her pockets. They walked up the block, side by side, without talking.

When they got to her car, he put his hand on the door so she couldn't open it. "Laura Lynn, please look at me. I can't let you go without saying one last thing."

She spun around. "What is there left to say?"

He looked into her eyes and saw the sweet, tender soul who had won his heart. "You are my first love, and no one else can ever be that. There were so many positive things about our relationship. Despite everything, I'll never forget that. I hope you won't either."

Laura Lynn's eyes glistened. She turned around and waited for him to move his arm, then quickly opened the door, her hands shaking, and slid in behind the wheel. She started the engine, backed out, and drove away, without saying a word.

Hawk sat at the kitchen table with Elliot and Grandpa Buck, staring at his hands and enduring the extra-loud clanking of pots and pans as his mother grabbed them from the dishwasher and shoved them into the proper cupboard. It was her way of letting off steam. And it was easier for him to deal with than having her go off on him after his gut-wrenching confession.

Finally, Kate came back to the table and sat next to Elliot. She breathed in slowly and exhaled, and then looked over at Hawk. "I don't think I have to tell you how disappointed I am, as much for the pain it's causing Laura Lynn as anything else."

"Of course you don't," Hawk said. "I knew you would be. I'm beyond disappointed in myself."

"What hurts most," Kate said, "is your blatant dishonesty. You've been with this woman numerous times in the past six weeks, and you told us you were with Laura Lynn."

"I didn't exactly say that, but I did let you think it."

"Which is the same as lying," Elliot said.

Hawk ran his hands through his hair. "I know. I was ashamed. I didn't want you to know what I was doing."

"Especially while you had no intention of ending it," Kate said sarcastically.

"We've all made bad decisions." Grandpa Buck took off his glasses and set them on the table. "But so help me, boy, this one takes the prize. That girl was the best thing that's ever happened to you. Why were your eyes rovin' in the first place?"

Hawk sighed. "I wasn't *looking*, Grandpa. I was leaving Salisbury's market and saw this gal fumbling to hold on to a busted sack of groceries that were falling all over the pavement, so I went over to help. We got to talking. She was new to the area and said she was having a hard time making friends. I couldn't imagine why. She was drop-dead gorgeous and easy to talk to. Before I knew it, I'd offered to take her on a Jeep ride—not here at Angel View, but on my own time. The rest is history. It's a moot point anyhow. She decided not to stay in Foggy Ridge. She's moved. It's over."

"Thank God for that," Kate said.

Hawk started to say something and then didn't. "Before you judge her, there's something I think you should know. Though the time I spent with her was morally reprehensible, nothing about it was sordid or sleazy. And in fairness to her, she had no idea I was already in a relationship. Despite what you're probably thinking, she was a very nice person. Under different circumstances, you would have liked her."

Kate raised an eyebrow. "So does this 'very nice person' have a name?"

"Her name isn't important," Hawk said. "It's over. She's gone. Let's leave it at that."

"Don't be surprised if it isn't that simple," Elliot said. "There are often far-reaching consequences to sin we haven't even thought about."

"What could be more far reaching than losing Laura Lynn? It's going to affect me for the rest of my life."

"Hawk, have you given any thought to how your deceitful behavior has affected the rest of us?" Kate glanced at Elliot and Grandpa Buck. "I don't think you realize that you betrayed us too. I, for one, have always been able to trust you with anything. *Anything.* You kept this family together when your father and sister were missing and it was all I could do to get up in the morning. And suddenly, I wonder if I even know you and if I'll ever be able to trust you …" Kate's voice trailed off, and she struggled to keep her composure.

"Mama, please don't think that. I'm the same person. You *can* trust me. I'll never lie to you again."

"How would I know?" Kate dabbed her eyes. "You pulled off this whopper without any of us suspecting a thing. Can you understand how unsettling that is?"

"Your mother brings up a good point." Grandpa Buck hooked his thumbs on his suspenders. "Our love for you is free, Hawk. But our trust in you isn't. And it doesn't come cheap. You're gonna have to earn it back, for however long it takes."

Hawk sat back in his chair, his arms folded across his chest, and looked over at Elliot. "I see what you mean. I guess it's not that simple."

Elliot put his hand on Kate's. "Consequences never are."

CHAPTER 3

Hawk awoke with a start, soaked in perspiration, his breathing rapid, his head aching with that relentless pounding he couldn't get rid of. That was the third time he'd had that crazy dream involving Kennedy and him, and a huge black spider that didn't bite but spewed venom. So real and yet so vague. It was creepy.

He threw off the covers and let the air from the ceiling fan cool his sunburn. Why was this dream recurring? The spider couldn't have been real, and yet the reddish substance on his shirt was. It must have been a drug or some kind of chemical because he'd been having miserable headaches ever since. What if it was affecting his health?

Hawk reached over to his nightstand and grabbed the bottle of extra-strength Excedrin he had picked up at the drugstore after breaking up with Laura Lynn. He shook two tablets into his palm, picked up his water bottle, and washed them down. That should at least take the edge off so he could go back to sleep.

Thoughts of Kennedy returned to him, and he wondered for the hundredth time who she really was, and whether she was still alive. He didn't have to wonder where he stood with Laura Lynn, though.

His encounter with her earlier tonight was less explosive than he had imagined. But their relationship was definitely over—instantly shattered by his confession of betrayal. How sad for them both.

He could imagine how special it would have been on their wedding night, had Laura Lynn been the first. Instead, Kennedy Taylor—a woman he didn't know at all and yet knew intimately—would forever hold that place in his memory. One more way he would pay the consequences of his actions.

He wanted to stop thinking about Kennedy, but her mysterious disappearance consumed his thoughts. If he chose to tell his family the entire truth of what had happened, they would insist he go to the sheriff and report it. Then it would become public—a *case* probably involving numerous law enforcement agencies. Kennedy was likely involved in criminal activity, or was a victim herself. Of one thing he was sure: it was complicated, and reporting it could put him under a microscope. On the other hand, Kennedy might be in trouble, and he her only life preserver. Was he really so intent on protecting his family's privacy and his own reputation—and the fact that he hadn't reported it right away—that he would take that chance?

If he did report it, he would be interviewed over and over again by law enforcement people asking embarrassing personal questions about every aspect of his involvement with Kennedy. Or worse yet, they would try to implicate him in her disappearance. And if it turned out she *was* a criminal, wouldn't that make him look like a complete moron for not having a clue?

Hawk turned on his side and pulled the top sheet up to his waist. He had hoped after he confessed his wrongdoing that he would be able to let it go. But telling only half the truth had actually made it worse.

Halo jumped off the windowsill and crossed the room. She hesitated a moment, and then jumped up on Hawk's bed and rubbed against him. He pulled her close to his chest, and she nestled next to him and started to purr. Comforted by the sound and the closeness, he also bemoaned the fact that she was the only female who wanted anything to do with him at the moment.

Laura Lynn would never forgive him. His mother would, but not without making him feel guilty until she could deal with her disappointment. Even the clerk who had sold him the bottle of Excedrin was abrupt with him, as if she knew what he'd done.

Hawk rubbed Halo's chin, glad when she purred even louder. For the first time in a long while, he had no plans for the future. What kind of fool trades the most precious relationship in his life for a few weeks of sleeping with a stranger? And now, even after owning the affair and losing Laura Lynn, he was still caught in a web of deceit. The mystery surrounding Kennedy's disappearing act hung around his neck like a giant question mark.

The next morning, Hawk decided to eat breakfast at Flutter's and avoid any unpleasant encounters with his mother or Elliot.

He sat along the wall of windows facing the hummingbird garden and waved at Jesse, who was already outside filling the feeders. Several guests were watching, fascinated at the swarm of hummingbirds around Jesse.

"Well, look who's up with the sun." Abby Cummings stood at the table, holding a fresh pot of coffee. "You look like you could use some caffeine."

"Restless night," Hawk said, holding up his mug. "I wouldn't be up this early, especially on a Monday, but I've got a seven-thirty appointment at Armison's to have my Jeep serviced."

Abby poured him a cup of coffee, glanced around the café, and then pulled out a chair and sat next to him. "I've got a few minutes before this place gets busy," she said. "Tell me what's going on. I came home last night and heard Mama, Elliot, and Grandpa talking in the kitchen. I heard your name mentioned. But when I walked in, they got quiet. Being the nosy sister I am, I wanted to know what was going on. They got all flustered and tongue tied, and said it was personal. So I'm asking you."

"It *is* personal." Hawk felt his cheeks get hot. "I would rather not get into this now—or ever."

Abby folded her arms on the table. "Listen, you. We've never kept secrets from each other. Since when can't you trust me?"

Hawk pursed his lips. "Okay, I'll tell you. But you can't tell anyone."

"I tell Jay everything," Abby said. "You know that."

"All right. But no one else."

"Fine," she said. "Tell me."

Hawk looked at his sister's innocent face and hated that she would never again look up to him. "I'm not proud of myself, okay? I did something really, really stupid." Hawk sighed. "I didn't plan it, but I got involved with another woman. I mean, *really* involved."

Abby just stared, her eyes big and round. Finally she whispered, "You slept with her? Are you out of your mind?"

"It's over. She's left town. I told Laura Lynn last night, and she gave back the promise ring. We're done."

Abby sat back in her chair. "She must be devastated."

"Thanks for stating the obvious. Look, I really don't want to talk about this right now. I just destroyed the most important relationship I've ever had and the person I love the most. I'm feeling about as low as a person can get."

"Who was she? Someone I know?"

"No, you didn't know her," Hawk said. "But since she's left town, it's a moot point, and I don't want to talk about her."

Abby's eyes brimmed with tears. "I'm just sick. I love Laura Lynn like a sister. Once Jay and I set a date, I was going to ask her to be my maid of honor."

Hawk hung his head. *One more consequence of my actions.* "I'm sorry, Abby. But you don't need to change your plans because of me."

"You idiot. Jay was going to ask *you* to be his best man. You ruined everything." Abby stood and picked up the coffeepot. "I need to go take care of the guests. Take your own order."

Hawk sat for a moment, heat radiating from his cheeks. He took a couple of Excedrin out of his pocket, popped them into his mouth, and drank a few gulps of ice water. He waited until Abby was across the room, her back to him, and then left by the side door.

Hawk stuffed the last bite of a doughnut into his mouth and washed it down with coffee, his hunger satisfied, but his heart heavier now that he was carrying Abby's disappointment on top of everything else.

He left the Foggy Ridge city limits and saw the blue-and-white sign for Armison's Body Shop up ahead. He turned his Jeep into the gravel lot just as someone in a late-model red Mustang spun his wheels and pulled onto Highway 62, leaving Hawk in a cloud of white dust.

Dennis Armison, a red bandana tied around his head, waved him into the open garage.

"Hey, Hawk Man. Good to see you. I apologize for my cousin's rude exit."

"I didn't realize that was Brody." Hawk got out of the Jeep and brushed the dust off his black T-shirt. "So what's his problem *this* time?"

"Aw, it's a long story. I'm worried about him, though."

"How so?" Hawk went over to a table in the corner and poured himself a cup of coffee.

"Remember back in high school when Brody said he saw a UFO and it turned out to be a huge flock of blackbirds?"

Hawk smiled. "Yeah, but that was no big deal. It was kinda funny."

"Well, this isn't." Dennis lifted the hood on Hawk's Jeep. "He needs to go talk to his shrink before it gets out of hand."

Hawk blew on his coffee, took a sip, and just listened.

"I'm afraid he's losing it. He hasn't told anyone else the stuff he's been telling me. Says he's afraid people will think he's nuts." Dennis arched his eyebrows. "And believe me, they will."

"Come on, you don't really think he's crazy. Brody's always marched to the beat of a different drummer."

There was a long pause. Finally, Dennis said, "Hawk, no one in his right mind would believe the stuff he's telling me."

"Like what? I'm all ears."

Dennis hung a light from under the hood and glanced over at Hawk. "Just between us? Says he saw a hexacopter drone—you know, like the ones I play around with—flying up on Sure Foot Mountain the day of the sailboat races. Only this drone flies right over his head to one of those grassy slopes where a man and woman are sitting on a blanket. It hovers over them and then covers them with a cloud of something red that makes them cough like crazy and then pass out cold. The drone flies off, and a few seconds later, two ... Should I assume by the look on your face that you've already heard enough?"

"Not at all. I'm fascinated. Go on." *So it wasn't a spider, and I wasn't dreaming!* Hawk's heart pounded so hard he wondered if Dennis could hear it.

"A few seconds later, two men dressed in black wearing gas masks came running out of the woods. One picked up the woman and put her over his shoulder, and the other picked up the blanket they were sitting on. They ran back into the woods where a huge house was almost hidden in the trees. Brody saw a black Suburban in the driveway and a plain white moving truck parked out front. He couldn't make out the license plates, but the two men put the woman in the back of the Suburban, closed the door, and got inside. Six other men, also dressed in black, but with black caps on their heads, came out of the house and got in the white truck. Then they all drove away. That's it. He swears it happened."

"But not enough to go to the sheriff and report it?"

Dennis laughed. "Of course not."

"But if he believes it, why not?"

Dennis took the air filter out of the Jeep and set it aside. "He's scared. I mean *really* scared. The drone could have easily taken a picture of his face, and he thinks the men who took the lady may be trying to find him. He's superparanoid now—much worse than usual."

"Did he say what happened to the man?"

"Brody thinks he was dead. He wanted to go check on him, but was afraid they might be coming back to get his body. So he got out of there."

"Well, did he get a good look at the guy?"

"Hardly at all. He'd been checking out the lady with his binoculars. Said she was gorgeous and sexy and very classy—a real looker. The man was wearing sunglasses, and his back was to Brody most of the time. But he appeared to be earthy and casual—a regular Joe. He seemed way out of his league."

You have no idea. "It's been two days," Hawk said. "Has anyone reported either of these people missing?"

"Not that I know of. I've watched the paper and listened to the news."

"So you think Brody imagined the whole thing?"

"Don't you? I mean, nothing fits."

"How can you be sure, since the man and woman are missing? I'd at least want to go up there and check it out."

Dennis shot Hawk a sheepish look. "Okay, I did go with Brody to where he saw the drone and where the woman was taken and the man was left. There was no body. We went to the nearby house where he swears the woman was put in the Suburban. There's a for-sale sign in the front yard. I called the real estate company and asked if the house was occupied. Get this: they said it's been vacant for months. Pretty insane, huh?"

"It's weird, all right." *The twilight zone!* Hawk wiped the per-spiration off his lip. "But it seems extremely detailed, not what I'd expect to hear from the head of a guy who was really disturbed."

"But there's no other explanation, right?"

"I don't have one," Hawk said. "It does bug me that no one has reported either person missing. How well did you search the grass where the couple was supposedly covered with the red stuff from the drone?"

"I didn't get down on my hands and knees, if that's what you mean. But I didn't see anything on the grass. I'm telling you, man, if he's imagining that kind of stuff, he needs help."

"Well, at least it's over now."

"Think again." Dennis lifted his head out from under the hood. "The reason Brody left mad this morning is because I cut him off before he was through talking and said I'd heard enough."

"There's more?"

"Oh yeah. Now he's convinced he's being followed. Did you see anyone else when you pulled up?"

Hawk shook his head. "No. No one."

"Well, Brody's scared to go to work. Scared to go home. I'm thinking about calling my aunt and uncle and seeing if he can move home until they can get him an appointment with his shrink. Maybe he needs his medication increased."

CHAPTER 4

Hawk drove past Kennedy's house and saw the for-sale sign in the front yard, just as Dennis had told him. He dialed the phone number on the sign and let it ring.

"On the Spot Realty, this is Hilda Schneider, how may I help you?"

"Yes, ma'am, this is Johnny Smith. I'm inquiring about the house for sale at 101 Mountain View Court in Raleigh County. The mailing address is Foggy Ridge. I'm sitting out front now, and there are no flyers. I was wondering if you could fill me in."

"One moment, please ..."

Hawk looked in his rearview mirror and all around him. He didn't see any other houses nearby, though it looked like some of the lots were being cleared.

"Hello, Mr. Smith?"

"Yes, I'm here."

"That's the gorgeous cedar home with a stone front. I would be happy to go through all the features with you. Or you could just go to our website at onthespotrealty-dot-org and take a virtual tour of the home and see if it's a good fit. The price is two million two-seventy-five but is negotiable."

"Is it currently occupied?" Hawk said.

"No, sir. It's been vacant since October of last year when we got the listing. However, the owner has kept it maintained inside and out, so it's move-in ready. It's really quite spectacular."

Hawk glanced up at the house. "Do you know if the owner lives in this area?"

"I see here it's owned by the FAMPRO Corporation out of Little Rock."

"All right. I'll look up the listing on your website. Thanks. You've been very helpful."

Hawk took out his phone and pulled up the website, then found the listing. He read the description and watched the slideshow. The house had six bedrooms, five and a half baths, a formal living and dining, a family room, a kitchen fit for a chef, a media room, and was sixty-five hundred square feet. Two million, two-hundred-seventy-five-thousand dollars … he smiled without meaning to. Not even that beautiful estate house of Elliot's had sold for that much.

It was clear that Kennedy had lied about having bought the house with her inheritance money. The real estate company lied about the house having been vacant since October. Someone was definitely hiding something. He had a feeling the FAMPRO Corporation might have the answers. What if it was a front for the people behind Kennedy's disappearance? Did he dare start nosing around when he had no idea what he was dealing with? Brody's account of what had happened seemed to fit, and Dennis said that Brody was scared he was being followed. If whoever was behind this thought they had left

Hawk for dead, the last thing he wanted to do was draw attention to himself.

The loud cawing of a crow echoed through the trees and caused him to look up, his pulse racing. A cold chill slithered up his spine.

He started the Jeep and headed down the mountain toward Angel View Lodge with an eerie, unsettling feeling that he was being watched.

Hawk worked all afternoon and into the evening, taking guests on Jeep tours across Sure Foot Mountain. While he was working, he'd been able to focus on making it a fun adventure for the guests and forget about the black cloud of unanswered questions that just kept growing.

But the minute he headed to the house and opened the front door, he was all too aware of both the affair he'd confessed and the secret he was keeping to himself. He took a shower and changed clothes, dreading dinner with the family.

Jesse appeared at the bathroom door. "Dinner's almost ready. We're having pot roast. Mama's in a mood and so is Abby. Women are sure hard to figure out."

"Tell me about it." Hawk took a towel, rubbed the fog off the mirror, and combed his wet hair. "Better get used to it. It's one of the mysteries we guys live with."

"Elliot's not cranky, but he's really quiet. Grandpa too. Is there something going on I should know about?" Jesse said.

How could Hawk possibly explain his situation to his thirteen-year-old brother? Yet the way Jesse was always eavesdropping, he was bound to overhear something. Better to nip it in the bud.

Hawk went over to his bed and sat. "Come here. There *is* something you should know."

Jesse plopped down on the bed.

"I'm going to speak man to man about something private. But I think you can handle it, now that you're a teenager."

Jesse smiled. "Cool."

"Laura Lynn and I broke up," Hawk said. "It was all my fault. I was seeing another woman behind her back. I knew it was wrong, but I let my strong attraction to this other woman cloud my judgment. I allowed things to happen with this other woman that I promised I wouldn't do until I got married. It hurt Laura Lynn—a lot. It was a betrayal. Do you understand what that means?"

"Isn't it like doing something the other person never expected of you, and it really hurts them?"

"Yes. And it changed me. I can't explain how, but I've robbed myself of something special, and I can never go back and undo it. Does that make sense?"

Jesse nodded, his cheeks flushed.

Hawk looked into Jesse's eyes. "Listen to me. I'm ashamed of what I did, and I hope you'll have better sense. There's a reason the Bible instructs us to wait until we're married to get involved that way. It complicates everything."

"I get it. We talked about that in youth group. I'm sorry you and Laura Lynn broke up. I really liked her. Is she mad?"

Hawk sighed. "More like devastated. I hate that I've hurt her so much. Mom and Abby are really upset and disappointed in me, so don't be surprised if they get emotional. Grandpa and Elliot are disappointed too, but they seem to shut down and not say anything.

I'm not sure which is worse. One thing I *am* sure of is that no one is more disappointed in me than me."

"I understand how that feels," Jesse said.

Hawk patted Jesse's knee. "I know you do. I'd appreciate it if you'd keep this just between us. I haven't told anyone outside the family, and I'd like to keep it that way. It'll be humiliating for Laura Lynn if people start talking about what I did."

"I won't say anything. Thanks for trusting me. That means a lot."

"What it means is you're growing up. Okay, sport"—Hawk pulled Jesse to his feet—"let's go eat."

After dinner, Hawk didn't know what to do with himself. There was no place to go and no one to be with, so he walked down to the gazebo on the back lawn of Angel View and decided to find out more about the FAMPRO Corporation. He took his phone out of his pocket and logged on. He googled the name, then read the business description.

"FAMPRO Corporation is located in Little Rock, Arkansas. This organization primarily operates in the Business Activities at Noncommercial site business/industry within the Business Services Sector. The organization has been operating for approximately ten years. FAMPRO Corporation is estimated to generate $10,103,000 in annual revenues, and employs 6 people at this single location."

Hawk swatted a mosquito. That didn't tell him anything that meant anything. He wrote the contact's name, the street address, and the phone number on the palm of his left hand, though he had second thoughts about looking into anything related to Kennedy's disappearance. But after what Brody said he witnessed, there could be no doubt that she didn't leave of her own volition. Hawk could no longer pretend it was none of his business.

But what if he was dealing with the mob? Or a drug cartel? Or some other criminal force? They had already left him for dead once. To go digging for answers on his own was dangerous. To report it to the authorities could be even more dangerous. And he had no way of knowing whether Kennedy was still alive.

Lord, I can't believe the mess I'm in. I know it's my own fault, but I don't want to do the wrong thing and cause something tragic to happen—to me or to Kennedy, or to anyone else. I need You to show me what to do. Lord, give me wisdom and don't let me doubt it when You do. In Jesus's name, I pray.

"Okay if I join you?" Grandpa Buck stood at the bottom of the steps.

"Sure," Hawk said.

Buck came up the gazebo steps and sat next to Hawk. "I guess it was a little too icy at the dinner table, eh?"

"Pretty much," Hawk said. "I don't blame anyone but myself, though. It'll take time for everyone to get over the disappointment. But it's not just that, Grandpa. I'm a little lost right now. My life's changed dramatically. There's really nowhere to go, and no one to be with."

"Oh, I wouldn't worry too much about that. It'll change soon enough. Maybe it's good you have a little time to reflect. Make some adjustments."

"That's all I seem to be doing."

"Hawk, you need to give it time. This isn't going to just blow over."

"I know. But the more I think about it, the worse I feel. I learned my lesson. I'm never going to let something like this happen again."

"Well, there's more learnin' involved than just deciding what you won't do. You might want to consider what you will do. Such as, going out of your way to win back your mother and your sister. I'm not sure you realize how personal this feels to them as women."

"So now I have to worry about all the females in the family ganging up on me? Like I don't already feel guilty enough?"

"They're not ganging up on you, Hawk. They love Laura Lynn too. We all do. They just have more empathy for her pain than for your remorse. They'll come around a whole lot quicker if you don't get your defenses up."

"What defenses? I didn't say a word at dinner."

"Well, believe me, women read between the lines." Grandpa shot him a crooked smile. "What I'm tryin' to say is don't be afraid to let them see your pain. They may never understand the temptations a man faces, or how a man can get involved the way you did. But they can sure relate to how much you're hurtin' and how sorry you are, if you just don't try so hard to cover it up."

Hawk cracked his knuckles. "Is that what I'm doing?"

"I've known you all your life, Hawk. You can hold back on showin' your true feelings as well as any man I've ever known."

Hawk nodded. "I guess that's true. I've never been good at letting my feelings show. I wait until I'm alone."

"And that's fine," Grandpa said. "But I promise you, those two women need to *see* how sorry you are. You might start by not avoiding eye contact. And if that makes you uncomfortable, just go with it. The important thing is to be real."

How real can I be when I've only told half the truth?

CHAPTER 5

On Tuesday morning, Hawk woke up with a throbbing headache, but he was glad that he'd gotten through the night without a repeat of that awful spider dream. He sat up on the side of the bed and took two Excedrin, acutely aware that the reality of the spider drone was much worse than the dream.

He glanced at the clock. It was ten minutes to seven. He showered and dressed and quietly left the house.

He drove into Foggy Ridge and bought a copy of the weekly newspaper from the machine in front of the post office. He got back in the Jeep and scanned the lead article about the sailboat races. Then he scanned each subsequent page. No missing persons reported. No sightings of a mysterious drone. It was as though it had never happened. Only it had. The awful headaches were proof enough for him, especially after Brody had filled in the blanks. But his sunglasses, shirt, and shorts with the red spatter were tangible proof.

As he put the newspaper on the passenger seat, he thought he saw someone duck behind the drop-off mailbox across the street.

He froze, the beating of his heart almost audible. He looked up and down the sidewalk but didn't see anyone. The only business open before nine a.m. this far off Main Street was the Sweet Butter Café half a block up the street.

"Hello?" Hawk said. "Who's there? No point in hiding. I saw you."

Hawk reached down on the floor, picked up the ball bat he'd never gotten around to putting away after the church softball game.

"Why are you following me?" Hawk said. "Show yourself. Let's talk."

Hawk hopped out of the Jeep and crouched down behind it. He could hardly breathe. Was he crazy? Whoever was hiding could have a gun. He was tempted to run up the street to the café but didn't want to risk getting a bullet in his back.

"Tell me what you want!" he shouted. His words were met with silence.

Hawk cowered behind his Jeep for what seemed an eternity, the bizarre events of recent days bombarding his mind. Finally, his anger boiled over. He jumped up, let out a war whoop, and charged the mailbox with the ball bat ready to start swinging. He slowed as he reached the side of the mailbox and then stopped abruptly when he could see no one was hiding there.

He listened for the sound of feet pounding the pavement, all the while looking up and down the street. All was quiet except for the low hum of early morning traffic.

Feeling both foolish and furious, Hawk hurried back to his Jeep. He climbed in, started the motor, and pulled onto Sweet Butter Street. He was starting to act as paranoid as Brody.

He turned right onto Shelby and drove several blocks until he came to Main Street, still feeling the sting of having acted like an idiot. His cell phone rang just as the traffic light turned red. What could Dennis want this early?

"Hey, Dennis."

"Something terrible's happened! Brody tried to tell me, and I blew it off—"

"Slow down, man. What's wrong?"

"Brody's dead."

"*Dead?* Good grief! What happened?"

"My uncle called and said that Brody spent the night with him and my aunt. He went to bed around ten o'clock, but slipped out the window in his room and went for a drive up the mountain. He misjudged a curve and went off the side of the road and down a steep embankment. A couple in an SUV must have come by right after it happened and noticed the twisted guardrail and a cloud of dust. They spotted his Mustang smashed headlong into a huge hardwood tree about a hundred feet below and called nine-one-one. It took a long time to get to him. My uncle called Brody's cell phone, but he didn't answer. When they finally got to his car and pulled it up, Brody was dead. Apparently it was horrific. The deputies wouldn't let my uncle see him."

Hawk's heart was practically beating out of his chest. "So the authorities think it was an accident?"

"Yes, but I'm sure it *wasn't*! I don't know if the skid marks will prove anything, but in my gut, I know someone ran him off the road. I should go talk to the sheriff."

Hawk's mind raced with the implications. "Have you talked to anyone besides me about what Brody told you?"

"No. I told my aunt and uncle that Brody had been imagining things and acting more paranoid than usual, and that maybe he needed to see his shrink."

"Hold on a minute." The light turned green, and Hawk pulled into a convenience store and shut off the engine. "Dennis, you still there?"

"Yeah, man."

"Don't say another word on the phone. You remember where you were when you got up the nerve to finally ask Jillian to go out?"

"Of course I do. What does—"

"Meet me where we parked the car that night—as fast as you can get there. This is life-and-death serious. If you have to cancel appointments, do it. I'll wait as long as it takes. Just say you'll come."

"All right. Let me make a few calls and I'll leave."

"Before you head this way, take the battery out of your cell phone. I'm going to go get prepaid cells the two of us can use to communicate."

"Hawk, you're creeping me out, man."

"Hurry."

⚜

Kate hung up the phone and let out a loud sigh.

"Honey, what's wrong?" Elliot said.

"That was Connor. He wanted me to know that he's going to fill in for Hawk this afternoon, and that he hopes Hawk's headache gets better. Why didn't Hawk tell me himself? And where is he? If his headache is that bad, he should be home in bed. I'm really worried about him."

"We all are. I imagine he's stressed to the max over his breakup with Laura Lynn, not to mention the load of guilt he's carrying."

"He doesn't act that sorry to me," Kate said.

"Why do you say that?" Elliot pushed aside the bowl of eggs he was whipping for omelets and wiped his hands. He went over to the kitchen table and sat facing Kate.

"I don't know," she said. "He acts cold and removed, almost like he's annoyed with the rest of us for making such a big deal out of it."

Elliot took her hands in his. "You know better than that. Hawk's never going to let you see how he really feels. Speaking as a man, I can imagine what's going on in his head. Anger. Shame. Remorse. Over and over again."

"Anger for what?" Kate said. "Laura Lynn's the one who should be angry."

"Honey, Hawk's mad at himself. He knows what he's thrown away. He's angry that he was weak and chose badly. And that he didn't stop it in the beginning. That he lied to Laura Lynn—and to us. He's angry that he ignored his conscience, that he failed—"

"Okay, okay. I get your point." Kate let go of his hands and folded her arms on the table. "Elliot, why did you say that, *speaking as a man*, you can imagine what's going on in his head? Do you think that, because I'm not a man, I can't understand my son?"

"I think you understand Hawk better than anyone," Elliot said. "But you can't fully understand the temptations he faces, because you're not a man."

"Oh really?" Kate arched her eyebrows. "Enlighten me." She was relieved that Elliot didn't react to her sarcasm.

"It's just that men are visual. Sexual temptation for us can start with what we see and escalate rather quickly. We're just wired differently than women. That's why it's so important to keep our guard up. Hawk knew that because he kept his guard up with Laura Lynn."

"Exactly. He knew how to keep his thoughts where they belonged," Kate said.

"Yes, until he saw a gorgeous woman who was flirty and available. His libido might have gone from zero to over the top with that one conversation at the grocery store. After that, his mind got him in trouble—that's where he made his choice—and he couldn't stop thinking about her, and once he gave in, he probably justified his behavior until he couldn't."

"That seems like such a copout, Elliot. Women can be attracted to men without thinking about sex."

"Of course they can. Most women are interested in affection, conversation, and a close relationship. Sex is often optional. Men are the exact opposite."

"So you're saying that men are looking for sex—and that affection, conversation, and a close relationship are optional?"

"If they're operating *in the flesh*, that's exactly what I'm saying. Look at King David. He was a man after God's own heart. And yet he saw Bathsheba bathing and lusted with his eyes and had to have her. Then he wanted her all to himself and had her husband killed in battle. He silenced his conscience until God sent the prophet to convict him. After that, he was devastated over his sin and had great remorse. But the harm had already been done."

Kate looked into Elliot's eyes. "Do you have these temptations?"

"Sometimes. Temptation doesn't ask our permission to put an image or a thought into our mind. But I've gotten really good at recognizing it for what it is and shutting it down immediately. As a Christian husband, I have no desire for any other woman, Kate. And I keep my guard up twenty-four seven. But I'm as vulnerable as any man."

Kate sighed. "I don't understand how a man can be tempted if he really loves his wife."

Elliot leaned his head closer to hers. "Because, as I said, temptation doesn't ask our permission to invade our thoughts. It can happen with a look, a touch, a picture. Honestly, with some of the fashion styles these days, temptation is everywhere we turn. But if our guard is up, we nip it right there."

"But I'm never tempted to be with another man," Kate said. "I can't imagine it."

"Because you're happy in your marriage. A woman who is unhappy in her marriage is probably missing affection and intimacy. She could be tempted to cheat in order to get the affection and intimacy she desires. Or she might read X-rated romance novels or watch steamy movies or TV programs that draw her in vicariously. Without physically cheating, she is able to live out her fantasies through the characters. She's no less aroused than a guy who's entertaining the idea outright. Lust is lust. I don't think God makes a distinction."

Kate nodded. "I can see that."

"All that to say, we shouldn't judge Hawk too harshly. He's already judged himself. He's not the first man to be blinded by lust. King David went on to love and serve God. There were natural consequences to his actions that were very painful. I have every confidence that Hawk has been forgiven and will grow from this, but he can't escape the consequences."

"So you think he's mad at himself, and that's what I'm picking up?"

Elliot stroked her cheek. "I do. And I think a little tenderness from his mother will go a long way right now. He's hurting more than you know."

"You're wise for a man who's lived just three years past the half-century mark." Kate's smile was met with his warm lips, and she relished the moment. "I can't believe how insensitive I've been. Poor Hawk. Here he was, pouring out the whole ugly, humiliating truth. And instead of at least telling him I'm grateful for a son who can't live a lie, I punished him for it."

CHAPTER 6

Hawk pulled into Rocky Springs Park, his eyes open for any sign that he was being followed. It was nearly nine o'clock, and he knew the park wouldn't be crowded this early. He noticed a couple jogging. And a woman filling a gallon jug with spring water. And a line of several young children waiting to ride the same carousel he had ridden as a kid.

As he continued driving on the main roadway through the park, leafy green trees thick on both sides, he spotted a tall magnolia tree on which there was a wood sign painted with a yellow arrow. He slowed and turned at the sign and into a parking lot that was nearly empty. He drove his Jeep under the shade of a huge hardwood tree and cut the motor.

He opened the Walmart plastic bag and took out his cell phone and the battery he'd removed and put them in his glove box. He closed the sack that contained two prepaid cell phones that were activated and ready to go.

He wiped the sweat off his forehead and let his emotions catch up with the realization that Brody had likely been murdered. And whoever killed Brody had kidnapped Kennedy and left Hawk for dead.

They must know that he had survived. Maybe they were trying to find out his name and where he lived so they could make sure he died this time. What did they think Hawk knew that made him a threat?

He slouched in the seat and leaned his head back, hoping Dennis hadn't gotten caught in traffic. How long could he keep all this from Sheriff Granger? The last thing he wanted was for his affair to go public, which would embarrass Laura Lynn and his family, and possibly put them at risk too. And guarantee the return of the media circus that had stalked his family far too often in the past.

Hawk heard a vehicle coming down the road and sat up. He turned just as Dennis's black Chevy Silverado pulled into the parking lot. He waved, and Dennis pulled his truck next to Hawk's Jeep. Hawk got out, grabbed the Walmart sack, and climbed in the front seat of Dennis's truck, a blast of air conditioning cooling his face.

"I'm so sorry about Brody," Hawk said. "I hardly know what to say."

"Me either. Except I want the scum who did this to pay." Dennis's gaze was intensely focused on Hawk. "Okay, I'm here. I took the battery out of my phone. Now tell me what this is about. You know something you haven't told me."

"I know something I haven't told anybody." Hawk breathed in slowly and let it out. "You remember Brody saying that when the guys in the gas masks drove away with the woman, they left the man for dead?"

"Of course I do. I told you."

Hawk cracked his knuckles. "That man was me."

Dennis's eyes were suddenly as big as saucers. "*You?* What the—? Why didn't you say so yesterday?"

"Because I was stunned. Like the wind was knocked out of me. Until you told me what Brody had seen, I didn't know *what* had happened to me. You filled in so many blanks. But there's more to the story than what Brody saw."

"Yeah, like what you were doing with some gorgeous mystery babe. Were you cheating on Laura Lynn?"

Hawk felt his face get hot. He told Dennis about how he had met Kennedy Taylor, how lonely she had been, and how an innocent hug had exploded into more than he could have imagined. He should have run, but he didn't. Instead, he entered into that relationship with his conscience on mute. He told him all he could remember about the day of the sailboat races, and how shocked he was to wake up and find Kennedy's house totally empty.

"All I knew was that I'd been dusted with some kind of chemical and Kennedy had disappeared," Hawk said. "I was blown away. I didn't go to the sheriff because I didn't know if she was a criminal or a victim. I figured her name had to be an alias. I honestly didn't know anything about her background, other than she claimed to be a wealthy heiress. I didn't even know if she was still alive. I was pretty much stuck in the twilight zone until you told me what Brody saw." Hawk turned to Dennis. "You're the only person besides me who knows what went down."

"Which makes me a potential target," Dennis said. "Though I suppose Brody did that. What in the world have we stepped in?"

Hawk shook his head. "My mind's on tilt trying to figure it out. The real estate company has to be in on it. I called them, just to see if they would tell me the same thing they told you. The lady I spoke with said the house had been vacant since October when they got the listing. She told me it was owned by the FAMPRO Corporation out of Little Rock. I read about FAMPRO on their website, but it didn't mean anything to me. I wrote down the name of the contact, the address, and phone number. But I'm thinking if they're looking for the man they left for dead, and don't know my name, I sure don't want to open that door. If they find out I've been snooping around, they're liable to put two and two together. Maybe we should leave things alone. As far as we know, Brody was the only witness to the drone attack and the woman being kidnapped. Maybe they won't pursue it now."

Dennis hit his forehead with his palms. "I can't live like this, man. We need to go to the sheriff and tell him everything."

"I want to. As long as we both go with our eyes wide open."

Dennis sighed. "Meaning what?"

"I doubt the sheriff can protect us," Hawk said. "Or our families. What if we're dealing with a drug cartel? Or organized crime? Or something just as sinister? We'll have to spend hours on end talking to every law enforcement agency you can think of, and then some. Believe me, it's intense. I've been there."

"I know." Dennis took off his cap and wiped the sweat from his forehead. "Look, it is what it is. I'm willing to gamble that we're safer with the sheriff knowing than the two of us out here alone with targets on our backs, scared of our own shadows."

"I agree." Hawk glanced at his watch. "Why don't we head for the courthouse and get it over with?"

"Could we hold off until after Brody's funeral?" Dennis said. "His family's Jewish and it'll probably be done before sundown. I need to be there. And I want my aunt and uncle to have the chance to say good-bye without being hounded by the media and a bunch of strangers who show up just for the drama. It's going to break their hearts to find out Brody was murdered."

"Assuming the sheriff can prove it," Hawk said.

"Well, *we* know."

"We think we know." Hawk heard a crow cawing and shuddered. "Let's hope we aren't opening up a worse can of worms."

Kate sat on the front porch, watching the hummingbirds fight mercilessly for control of the feeder.

"You act like politicians," she said aloud, and then laughed.

She heard the sound of Hawk's Jeep in the distance. It was about time he came home after asking Connor to take his shift because his headache was so bad.

Kate looked out and saw a cloud of dust moving across the far western property line of Angel View.

"I see he's taking the shortcut." Elliot came outside and sat next to Kate.

"Don't worry," she said. "I'm not going to interrogate him. Not today. But I really don't understand why it took him until eleven o'clock to come home. If he were any employee other than my son, he'd have to give me a good reason not to fire him."

Elliot put his arm around her. "Maybe he needed a mental health day."

Kate grinned. "A what?"

"A little grace. Once in a while, we all need a day to reflect and get our act together."

"Well, I hope he's ready to reflect in bed because that's where he needs to be."

Hawk pulled in the driveway, got out of the Jeep, and walked up the steps.

"Did Connor give you my message?" Hawk said.

"He did. About three hours ago." Kate fought to let it go with that. "We've been worried about you."

"I can't seem to shake this headache. I think I'll take some Excedrin and go lie down."

Kate reached up and took his hand. "I realize these past few days have been extremely difficult. I just want you to know how much I love you."

Hawk's eyes glistened. "That means more to me than you know."

"Ta-da!" Jesse stood at the bottom of the steps, holding something furry.

"What've you got there?" Elliot said.

"The first free kitten from Chestnut's litter. Mama said I could have him."

"I said I'd think about it." Kate smiled. "Let's see."

Hawk squeezed her shoulder. "I'm going to go lie down."

"Okay, honey," Kate said. "I'll check on you in a while."

Jesse came up the steps, his fine dark hair windblown, his silver smile reflecting the sun.

"It's a male," Jesse said. "I think." He gently gave the orange-and-white-striped kitten to Kate.

"Oh, he's so darling," Kate said.

Elliot rubbed the kitten's chin. "He's almost as cute as you are." He smiled at Kate. "I'll be back."

"We'll be here," she said, "trying to think of a name."

Hawk washed the Excedrin down with a glass of water and lay back on his bed. He didn't know which was worse, the throbbing headaches or his guilty conscience reminding him that he hadn't told the whole truth. He was going to have to tell his family about the danger he was in and why. If only he had known what Brody knew, he would have reported Kennedy's disappearance right after it happened. He doubted the authorities would have found her without more to go on. But Brody might still be alive.

Hawk sighed. Poor Brody. He must have been so scared. Now Dennis would have to go through the funeral, pretending that his cousin's death was just a terrible accident, all the while knowing that, soon afterward, he would multiply his aunt and uncle's grief by telling them he believed Brody was murdered.

Lord, how do I tell my family? The last thing in the world I wanted to do was embarrass them by having my affair with Kennedy all over the news. Please protect Dennis. And give Brody's parents an extra measure of grace. If Kennedy is still alive, keep her safe and show us how to find her. And please protect me until I can sort this out.

A knock on his door startled him.

"It's Elliot. May I come in?"

"Okay."

Elliot eased into the room and sat on the side of the bed. "I'm sorry you're having such a rough time."

You don't know the half of it. "I'll be okay once the Excedrin kicks in."

"That's not what I meant."

"What *did* you mean?" Hawk said.

"Just that it takes time to work through the pain. Like most of us guys, you're probably trying to rush it. You really can't. Healing has its own timetable."

Hawk didn't say anything.

"The truth will set you free. God said so. You've told the truth. Now you just need to wait on the Lord to keep His promise."

Hawk felt as if he might explode. "But I *haven't* told the truth!" he blurted. "At least not all of it. It's so much worse than anything I've told you. You have no idea." His heart nearly beat out of his chest.

Elliot laced his fingers together, his hands between his knees. "Well, it's never too late to do what's right."

"Don't be so sure."

"It might be too late in *your* timing," Elliot said. "But never in God's."

Two hours later, Hawk sat in the living room with his mother, Elliot, Grandpa Buck, Abby, and Jesse and finished telling everything he knew about Kennedy's mysterious disappearance and Brody's death.

"I'm sorry I didn't tell you sooner"—Hawk looked over at Elliot—"but I was confused and scared. It wasn't until Dennis told me what Brody saw the day of the sailboat races that I realized what had happened to me. Before I'd had time to process that, Dennis called and told me

Brody was dead. I about freaked out. I realized we were in over our heads and had to go to the sheriff. At least now I can fill in some of the blanks for him." Hawk glanced up at Kate. "I'm sorry, Mama. The last thing I wanted was to embarrass Laura Lynn and each of you by having my affair with Kennedy talked about in the news. I guess I can't stop it now."

Kate sat back in her chair and exhaled. "That's the least of our worries. Your safety has to be our first concern. The whole thing scares me to death, but the drone attack is terrifying. You need to see about those headaches, right after you go talk to Virgil. He needs to hear everything you told us."

Hawk nodded. "I know. We'll do it in the morning. Dennis and I agreed to wait until after Brody's funeral. He wanted to spare his aunt and uncle the media intrusion."

"Speaking of the media," Grandpa said, "somebody oughta give Laura Lynn a heads-up before this gets out."

Kate arched her eyebrows. "Virgil isn't going to allow us to discuss any details of what happened to Hawk, Kennedy, or Brody. But she needs to know that Hawk's affair will likely be mentioned in the news. That's about all we can say."

"I'd call her," Hawk said. "But she wouldn't pick up."

"I'll do it. She'll talk to me." Abby sat with her arms folded across her chest. "Is it okay with everyone if I ask Jay to bring Wolf over for the night? I think we'd all feel safer with a German shepherd in the house."

Hawk went to bed early but couldn't sleep. It wasn't just the head-ache that was keeping him awake. After tomorrow his life would be changed forever, not to mention his reputation. What started out as an innocent hug to comfort a lonely woman exploded into a passionate affair with repercussions beyond anything he could have ever imagined. It hurt him to think that Kennedy might be in serious trouble or dead. Or even worse, that his failure to report her strange disappearance might be the reason.

"Hawk, are you awake?" Jesse whispered.

Hawk rolled over on his back. "Wide awake."

"Me too."

Hawk sat up, his back resting on the headboard. "What's up?"

Jesse sat on the side of the bed. "I feel really bad about everything you're going through. I don't exactly know what to say."

"You don't have to say anything. And don't feel sorry for me. It's my own fault."

"The affair part is," Jesse said, "but not the other stuff."

"I think the jury's still out on that. Did Jay bring Wolf over?"

"Yes, but Jay stayed too. He insisted on sleeping on the couch. He said you saved his life once, and the least he could do is help watch out for yours."

Hawk smiled. "He's a great guy. So what happened to the kitten?"

"I'm letting him sleep with Abby tonight," Jesse said, "in case he meows. I don't want him to keep you up."

"That was awfully considerate of you. Did you and Mama decide on a name?"

Jesse shook his head. "We decided we need to get to know him first." Jesse drew circles on the blanket with his index finger. "Can I ask you something?"

"Sure."

"Do you believe the Lord can get you out of this mess?"

Hawk exhaled. "I want to believe it, but I sure don't see how."

"You're not supposed to see how. That's why you have to trust Him. He can do it, Hawk. Look how He helped me. I almost got shot twice, but He brought me home safe."

"Jesse, the sheriff said you had enough faith to make an apostle jealous. I don't."

"All you need is the faith of a mustard seed. I know you have that."

Hawk half smiled. "Yeah, I suppose I do." He reached over with his hand and messed up Jesse's hair. "Are you sure you're not a preacher disguised as a thirteen-year-old?"

"I'm sure." Jesse laughed and pointed to his braces. "Believe me, this hardware is for real." He looked at the clock on Hawk's night-stand. "And so's the time. We'd better get some rest. G'night."

"Good night, Jess." Hawk slid down in the bed and fluffed his pillow.

Lord, I do have the faith of a mustard seed. I need Your help. Your Word says the truth will set us free. And You're the only one who knows the truth of what happened. Help me to find answers. Be with Dennis and me tomorrow when we talk to the sheriff. Help us to be strong. And please protect us from whoever killed Brody.

CHAPTER 7

Hawk was up early on Wednesday morning. He got a cup of coffee and went out on the front porch and sat in the swing and just listened to the sounds of nature that seemed to come alive before sunrise. He hadn't slept much but spent most of the night talking to God. He had laid his heart bare. Now he was ready to talk to the sheriff.

Elliot had called the courthouse yesterday afternoon and arranged for the sheriff to meet with Hawk and Dennis at ten o'clock. Hawk had texted Dennis with that information but hadn't heard back yet. He could just imagine the stress Dennis was under, trying to hold up his aunt and uncle while trying not to collapse under the pressure of being a potential target.

Abby came outside and stood at the railing. "Jay stayed here with Wolf last night, but he left about thirty minutes ago to work on an assignment that's due by four o'clock this afternoon."

"Jesse told me last night that he was staying over, and why. Jay's a great guy, Abby. I'm glad you two are getting married."

"About that," Abby said. "I'm sorry for being hateful the other day. I was shocked and mad that you and Laura Lynn broke up. I acted like a spoiled brat."

"Understandable."

"I did call Laura Lynn," Abby said, "and told her that the affair might be mentioned in the news, but that I couldn't talk about the reason. She's still so numb she didn't react."

"Well, thanks for making the call. I doubt that anything will soften the blow, but at least she won't be caught off guard."

Abby glanced at her watch, then turned around and looked at Hawk. "I've got to go. I open this morning. I just want you to know that I'm praying. I'm really sorry for all you're going through. Despite the affair, you didn't deserve this."

"Thanks, Abby."

She bent down and hugged him. "I love you."

"I love you too." He held her a little longer than he normally would and blinked the stinging from his eyes.

"Bye," Abby said. "I'll see you when I see you."

Hawk smiled. "Not if I see you first."

Abby hurried down the steps, and Hawk noticed that Dennis had answered his text: *Brody's funeral was nice, but sad. The only thing worse was my aunt and uncle's reaction when I told them I thought he'd been murdered and planned to tell the sheriff this morning. I know what you mean about the twilight zone. None of it seems real. I'll meet you at the courthouse at ten.*

Hawk replied: *Ditto. I'll be there.*

Jesse came outside, dressed in khaki shorts and the blue-and-yellow Angel View staff T-shirt he was so proud to wear.

"You going over to Flutter's to entertain the guests?" Hawk said.

"I'm just the voice. The hummingbirds are the entertainers. Did you sleep?"

"So-so," Hawk said. "I did a lot of reflecting and talking to God. I should be a nervous wreck, but I'm not. I got up early, had a cup of coffee, and watched the sunrise."

A smile spread across Jesse's face. "Man, I'm good!" He laughed. "Just kidding."

"I'm *not* kidding," Hawk said. "Thanks for reminding me that I only need mustard seed faith to let God tackle this giant problem."

Jesse put his hand on Hawk's shoulder. "I know you're going to do great today. Just tell the truth. That way you don't have to remember what you said."

"That's kind of profound, Jesse. Did you just make that up?"

"No. Someone I really admire said it to me when I was a kid, and it stuck."

"Who?"

Jesse smiled. "You."

Hawk pulled Jesse into a headlock, evoking laughter that was a full octave lower than in months past, reminding Hawk that his little brother was growing up. "How do you always know just what I need to hear?"

Jesse shrugged and just kept laughing.

"You'd better get going." Hawk turned loose of him and brushed the hair out of his eyes. "The guests await."

"Actually, it's the hummers that await," Jesse said. "I've got eighteen feeders that need to be filled before the guests can enjoy the entertainment."

"Okay, better get crackin'. Love you, buddy."

"Love you too."

Hawk sat quietly humbled, trying to get his heart around Jesse's words. *"Someone I really admire said it to me ..."* Could it be true that his brother hadn't lost respect for him despite his failing? Jesse was old enough to understand what Hawk had done, but he had essentially separated the sin from the sinner. Something Hawk frequently struggled with.

Lord, thanks for letting me receive a touch from You through Jesse. I know You love me more than anyone else can, but he's a great encourager. Be with Dennis and me today as we articulate what we know for Sheriff Granger. Let the truth set us free.

At five minutes to ten, Hawk walked up the steps of the courthouse, Elliot on his heels. When he got to the top, he spotted Dennis, who was wearing khaki pants and a navy polo shirt and leaning against one of the white columns.

Hawk walked over to him. "Hey, man. You ready to roll?"

"Ready as I'll ever be," Dennis said.

Hawk took a step back and introduced Dennis and Elliot, and the two shook hands.

"I'm truly sorry about your cousin," Elliot said.

Dennis nodded. "Thank you, sir. Me too."

"I'm going to leave you two young men to do what you came to do," Elliot said. "I'm just going to hang around the courthouse and do some work on my laptop. I'll be here if you need me. Otherwise, I'll see you when you're done." Elliot looked at Hawk. "I'm proud of you. I know this is tough."

Hawk and Elliot did their elaborate handshake and exchanged a quick hug. "Thanks," Hawk said. "I'll call you when we're done."

Hawk followed Dennis into the courthouse, and the two found Sheriff Virgil Granger standing in the lobby, talking on the phone. Virgil put his cell phone in his pocket and walked over to them. Hawk made the introductions.

"Follow me," Virgil said.

They followed the sheriff through the wood-and-glass door of the Raleigh County Sheriff's Department. Hawk and Dennis passed through the metal detector, and then the three continued walking down a long shiny corridor.

Deputy Hobbs, who had worked the case when Hawk's father and sister were missing, walked up to the sheriff. "Interview rooms one and two are ready, sir."

"Thanks, Jason," Virgil said. "Would you get Mr. Armison and Mr. Cummings situated as we discussed?"

"Certainly." The deputy gave Hawk a nod of acknowledgment and then said, "Gentlemen, come this way, please."

CHAPTER 8

Sheriff Virgil Granger went in his office where Chief Deputy Kevin Mann was waiting for him at the conference table.

"They're here," Virgil said. "My curiosity's on tilt. Kate Cummings called and asked me to hear them out, no matter how farfetched their story may sound. You and I will interview Hawk Cummings. Duncan and Hobbs will interview Dennis Armison. Ready?"

"Chomping at the bit." Kevin ran a comb through his wavy red hair as he rose to his feet. "I'm as curious as you are."

Virgil walked with Kevin down the hall and into the first interview room. The sheriff sat across the table from Hawk Cummings. Kevin took the seat next to Virgil's.

"Hawk, you remember my chief deputy, Kevin Mann."

"Yes, sir," Hawk said. "Good to see you again."

"If you don't mind," Virgil said, "I'd like to record this interview to help us keep the facts straight."

Hawk nodded. "I'm fine with that."

Virgil took the recorder out of his pocket, laid it on the table, and pushed the on button. "This is Sheriff Virgil Granger. It's ten thirteen a.m. on Wednesday, June 7. I'm interviewing Hawk Cummings, who is here to report alleged crimes that occurred on Saturday, June 3. This interview is taking place at the Raleigh County Courthouse in the presence of Chief Deputy Kevin Mann." Virgil looked over at Hawk. "State your full name, age, and address."

"John Hawk Cummings, I'm twenty-four years old. My address is 100 Angel View Road, Foggy Ridge."

"And are you giving this statement of your own free will?"

"Yes, sir."

"You're here to report two crimes. Is that correct?"

"Yes it is."

"And what is the nature of those crimes?"

"Kidnapping and attempted murder."

"Where did these alleged crimes take place?"

"At the home of a twenty-three-year-old woman named Kennedy Taylor. The address is 101 Mountain View Court in Raleigh County. The mailing address is Foggy Ridge."

"And how do you know these alleged crimes took place?"

Hawk leaned forward, his elbows folded on the table. "Because I was there. And I believe someone tried to kill me."

Virgil listened intently as Hawk told his story. He studied Hawk's demeanor. His facial expressions. His eyes. Voice inflection. As far as he could tell, Hawk believed what he was saying. Virgil understood why Kate had called to give him a heads-up. Hawk's story sounded more like a movie than a crime that took place in Foggy Ridge.

"What else can you tell us about Kennedy Taylor," Virgil said, "other than she was gorgeous?"

Hawk shrugged. "I already told you what I know. She obviously lied about inheriting a fortune and buying that house. She said she was twenty-three, but who knows if that's even true? She didn't tell me anything else about herself."

Virgil leaned forward on his elbows. "You want us to believe you were together for six weeks and she never told you anything else about herself? Her favorite color? Her favorite food? Places she's been? Nothing?"

"I can't remember," Hawk said. "We didn't talk that much."

Kevin smirked. "That's right. You found you a hot chick and talking was optional."

"Don't refer to Kennedy that way," Hawk said, his voice an octave higher. "Believe it or not, she was a real lady. She didn't know about Laura Lynn. We didn't intend to get involved—it just happened."

"I'm not judging you," Kevin said. "I'm looking for any clue that might help us figure out who she was."

"I doubt if this is a clue to anything, but she liked love stories and tear-jerker movies on Netflix," Hawk said. "She hated any kind of drama that had violence and wouldn't watch them. She'd always fall asleep." Hawk was quiet for a moment, then he said, "Once when we were just lying there together, she talked about a dream she'd had over and over since she was a little girl, that she grew wings and could fly wherever she wanted and look for her real home. Something like that. I couldn't relate to what she was saying, but I felt her loneliness. Does that help?"

"It might." Virgil looked over at Kevin. "Let's move on."

"Hawk, you never actually saw this hexacopter drone, is that correct?" Kevin said.

"No, sir. I think I did see it, but whatever mind-altering chemical it dusted us with caused me to hallucinate. I saw it as giant black spider that spewed venom. Weird. But I distinctly remember being dusted with some kind of substance that made me cough and choke until I passed out. I thought I was going to die."

"Did you go to the doctor to get checked out?" Virgil said.

"No. I've been having killer headaches, but I didn't want to explain to a doctor why I was having them. They're becoming less frequent now."

"Let's go back to the drone for a minute." Kevin glanced at his notes. "You stated you *think* you saw it. And that Brody Armison, now deceased, claimed to have witnessed the drone attack. But the fact is, there's no supporting evidence that this drone exists, or that it dusted you and Kennedy Taylor with a chemical."

"I have supporting evidence," Hawk said. "I saved the clothes I was wearing and my sunglasses, and put them in a trash bag in case I needed them for proof."

Virgil nodded. "Good thinking. We need to get those from you and have the chemical analyzed."

Kevin stared at Hawk without saying anything—his usual intimidation tactic. Hawk didn't flinch. Didn't seem nervous.

"All right, for the sake of argument," Kevin said, "let's say you were attacked by a drone and dusted with a chemical, and Kennedy Taylor disappeared just as you said. Why did you wait this long to report it?"

Hawk folded his hands on the table. "I guess because my understanding of what happened evolved. At first, I was dazed. I woke up at sunset completely disoriented. Kennedy was gone. Everything in her house was gone. I thought maybe she dumped me. But that didn't make sense. Why would she ask me to spend the day with her if she planned to skip out? Especially since we were getting along so well. So I started to wonder if she was involved in something criminal—or was a victim herself—and I realized how little I knew about her. I wasn't even sure whether Kennedy Taylor was her real name. I didn't know *what* to report. I also worried that if Kennedy was involved in organized crime or drugs or something, I might be guilty by association. I wrestled with it the rest of the weekend. But on Monday, after Dennis told me what Brody told him, a light came on. It finally made sense."

"So this light came on in your head," Kevin said, "and you suddenly knew what had happened to you. Why didn't you tell Dennis right then that you were the man Brody saw?"

"Because I was *stunned*. I could hardly breathe. For the first time, I saw the whole picture. It was mind blowing. I'd been attacked by a spider drone. The spider *I* saw was a hallucination induced by the chemical. I realized that Kennedy had been kidnapped—and all her belongings hauled off—by eight men who had left me for dead. It was a lot to take in."

Virgil cleared his throat. "You said you went to high school with Dennis and his cousin Brody. What can you tell me about Brody?"

"He had some mental issues that made it hard for him to fit in. I don't know exactly what was wrong, but he seemed to be in a world of his own. I never hung out with Brody. No one did. Dennis and I were into sports, and Brody was a computer geek who loved to read. I remember he got bullied a lot, and Dennis and I kept him from getting beat up a few times. We graduated a year ahead of him. That was seven years ago. I could count on one hand the times I've run into Brody since."

Virgil folded his arms on the table. "But he wouldn't forget your face. Didn't it seem odd that Brody was able to describe the drone attack in detail and yet didn't recognize you as the man who was left for dead?"

"Not really," Hawk said. "My hair's a lot shorter now. I have a stubble beard. And I had sunglasses on, even when I passed out. But if Brody was looking at Kennedy through his binoculars, I promise you he wasn't paying attention to me. The woman is drop-dead gorgeous."

"Do you think you could describe her to the sketch artist?" Virgil said.

"Absolutely."

"You seem pretty sure that Brody was forced off the road. Did he tell you he feared for his life?"

"No, I haven't seen or spoken to Brody in ages. Dennis told me Brody was really scared that he was being followed."

"But as you pointed out, Brody also had a history of mental problems," Virgil said. "And yet, without ever talking to him personally about his fear that he was being followed, you believe he was murdered? Hawk, that's a mighty big leap, don't you think?"

Hawk shook his head. "No, sir. Not when you consider all the facts. The drone went right over Brody's head. It most likely photographed him. Whoever controlled the drone had to assume that, at the very least, Brody saw the drone attack and Kennedy being carried off by the two guys in gas masks. It wasn't a stretch for me to believe Brody was being followed. Or that they ran him off the road. They weren't taking any chances that he'd seen too much."

"Which bring us back to your concern," Virgil said, "that whoever allegedly killed Brody is now trying to find you."

"It's not farfetched," Hawk said. "Whoever killed Brody probably kidnapped Kennedy and left me for dead. But they must know I survived. Maybe they're worried that Kennedy told me things in the course of our relationship that could expose them. Of course, she didn't tell me anything, except that she inherited a fortune when her parents died, and she decided to buy that big house and settle in Foggy Ridge. And even that was a lie."

Kevin underlined something in his notes. "How often would you guess the two of you were together over that six-week period?"

Hawk's face and neck turned bright pink, his eyebrows came together. "Is that really relevant?"

"It could be, especially if you were being watched."

Hawk stared at his hands. "Well, for the five weeks prior to Memorial Day, I was seeing Kennedy around nine p.m. on Sunday and all day Tuesday, which was my day off. Now that we're into the tourist season, I only get Sundays off. But this past weekend, I switched days off with my sidekick and I took Saturday off, which happened to be the day of the sailboat races. It was the perfect cover for spending the day at Kennedy's place without anyone questioning my whereabouts."

"So prior to Memorial Day," Kevin said, "you established a five-week pattern of being at Kennedy's house around nine o'clock on Sunday night and again all day on Tuesday. And when did you agree to switch days off with your sidekick?"

"I talked to Connor about it on Friday night."

"Did you discuss it with Kennedy over the phone?"

"Sure," Hawk said, "right after I hung up with Connor. She was excited and invited me to spend all day Saturday with her at the house."

"Did you call her cell phone or a landline?" Kevin said.

"Kennedy didn't like cell phones because of the radiation. She had a landline—an unlisted number."

"When you talked to her on the phone, did you ever hear clicking sounds that you didn't get when talking to other people?"

"Now that you mention it, yes," Hawk said. "I just assumed it was a bad connection, because of where she lived. Is that significant?"

Kevin wrote something in his notes. "The fact that the alleged drone attack occurred when you two were together on a Saturday, which was out of the ordinary and only spoken of over the phone, suggests to me that Kennedy's phone was tapped. My guess is her house was bugged too."

Hawk looked panicked, his face the color of Kevin's hair. "So much for the expectation of privacy. At least they would know that she didn't tell me anything."

"Over the phone, yes," Kevin said. "But most of your conversations took place at her house. Multiple bugs would enable them to clearly hear conversations within range. But pillow talk and the like ... not so much, if you were speaking softly. And if you played loud music or had conversations in the bathroom with the shower on, your voices would probably have been drowned out, which might have made them think you knew they were listening in, and you had something to hide."

Hawk sighed. "That explains why they tried to kill me with the drone."

Virgil glanced over at Kevin, then leaned forward and made eye contact with Hawk. "Son, if a group this organized wanted you dead, they would've made sure you were dead at the scene. It's hard to know what we're dealing with."

"But you have a hunch, right?" Hawk said.

"It's too early to speculate." Virgil turned to Kevin. "Have Hawk tell you where he stashed the clothes he was wearing during the drone attack, and send someone out to the house immediately to collect them. Then get the sketch artist in here. Let's see if we can find out who this woman is."

CHAPTER 9

Kate slid her meatloaf into the oven along with seven foil-wrapped potatoes. She glanced at the clock. It was almost five. The phone rang and she grabbed it.

"Elliot, please tell me you're on your way home," she said. "Kevin Mann sent some officers out here to get the clothes Hawk was wearing the day of the drone attack, but they wouldn't tell me anything. I hate feeling like an outsider."

"I'm sorry, honey. But we're not on our way home. When I talked to you before, Virgil's assistant had just told me that Hawk finished his interview with Virgil and Kevin Mann and had finished working with the sketch artist. I just assumed Hawk was done. But now I've been told that the deputies who interviewed Dennis wanted to question Hawk. And Virgil and Kevin wanted to question Dennis. There's no telling how much longer we're going to be."

"Oh well," Kate said. "I just put a meatloaf in the oven, but dinner can wait."

"I'd rather you didn't make the kids wait. Hawk and I can eat in town. It'll give him time to unwind before he gets home."

"Did Virgil's assistant give you any idea if it's going well?" Kate said.

"Not really. She was just letting me know before she left for the day."

Kate sighed. "Poor Hawk. I'll bet he's wiped out. How are you holding up?"

"I'm fine. I did a little work on my laptop, but I've been praying a lot too. I imagine it's been grueling for Hawk. Not only did he have to revisit in detail everything he knows or thinks he knows related to this whole mess, but I don't imagine it was easy for him to look Virgil in the eye and admit the nature of his relationship with Kennedy Taylor."

"I'm sure it wasn't," Kate said. "Hawk wouldn't want to disappoint Virgil."

"That's all part of stepping up and owning his role in what happened, but I hurt for him."

Kate wiped her hands and sat at the table. "I'm glad you convinced me to let you go with Hawk to the courthouse. He really doesn't need his mother trying to *make it all better*. He relates to you man to man. I can't give him that."

"But you're his mother, Kate. He loves you more than anyone on earth. He just needs something different from each of us, that's all. So how long before dinner's ready?"

"If you don't want me to hold it, it should be on the table around six fifteen."

"I really hate to miss your meatloaf … Do you think there'll there be enough left over for sandwiches?"

"Are you kidding?" she said. "I'm way ahead of you on that one. I even bought an extra loaf of rye."

Elliot chuckled. "Oh me of little faith."

The long stretch of silence that followed changed the mood back to serious.

"Elliot, promise me you'll be careful coming home. I know Hawk did the right thing reporting everything that happened. But now it's on record. Someone's bound to leak it to the press. For all we know, whoever ran Brody off the road is still here."

"Honey, would you be more comfortable if we just came home when we're done and skipped eating out?"

"Truthfully, I would. Abby talked Jay into bringing Wolf back tonight and staying over. I think the kids are scared. I'm trying not to be. They're taking their cues from us."

"All right, Kate. Don't worry. As soon as Hawk is finished here, we'll come straight home."

Virgil sat in his office, his hands folded on his desk, mulling over his and Kevin's interview with Hawk Cummings and their subsequent interview with Dennis Armison. He couldn't believe the trouble that had found these two young men. He hoped it wasn't organized crime. Or a drug cartel. Those situations could get so ugly—and dangerous. He really dreaded the idea of Kate's family being pulled into another violent ordeal.

He was encouraged that Hawk thought the composite sketch looked remarkably like the woman he knew as Kennedy Taylor. Virgil was able to put that composite sketch and all pertinent information on the National Law Enforcement Telecommunications System (NLETS). That was quickest way to find out if she was on anyone else's radar.

A knock on the door broke his concentration, and he looked up at Kevin Mann standing in the doorway.

"You ready for us?" Kevin said.

"Yes, come in and have a seat. Make yourself a cup of coffee, if you like."

Kevin came in followed by Deputy Jason Hobbs. Deputy Billy Gene Duncan went to the back of the room and made a cup of coffee on the Keurig, then took his seat with the others at the conference table.

"Okay," Virgil said. "We've each had a chance to interview both Hawk Cummings and Dennis Armison. Did everybody think their stories were consistent?"

"I did," Kevin said.

Duncan and Hobbs nodded.

"Anything stand out?" Virgil said.

"Armison was shakin' half the time," Billy Gene said. "I figured it was because of dealing with his cousin's death and him havin' to tell his aunt and uncle that he believed his cousin Brody was run off the road. I didn't see none of that with Cummings."

"All that stood out to me with Cummings," Jason said, "was that he seemed embarrassed about his affair with Kennedy Taylor and blushed several times. I'll bet he wishes he'd turned and run from the woman when he had the chance."

"Both young men were obviously nervous," Virgil said, "but we're in agreement that their stories were consistent. Did you find their stories believable?"

"Shoot," Billy Gene said, "they were so far out there, I don't think they *could've* made it up."

"I was impressed by the way their two stories connected," Jason said. "How neither of them knew what was going on until they heard the other half of it. I can't believe I'm saying this, but I found it believable."

"Did anybody else pick up strange vibes from Cummings," Kevin said, "that maybe he was more taken with the woman than he was letting on?"

"Did you?" Virgil folded his arms.

"A couple of times I thought I did," Kevin said. "I mean, I get that he was embarrassed to tell us about the affair. We've known his family a long time, and this was really personal. But to me, it was almost as though he didn't want us to think badly of the woman."

"I got the impression she was more to him than just a good time," Jason said. "But he told us the same things he told you about her. I believe they met by chance. I believe he doesn't know more than he's telling us."

"Which is all that really matters," Virgil said. "So let's assume Hawk got involved with this woman by chance. Whoever kidnapped her could have made sure he was dead at the scene, and didn't. And yet it appears they may have taken out the one eyewitness, Brody Armison. Should we assume they got what they came for, and the threat to Hawk is over?"

"Hawk wasn't an eyewitness to the drone attack or the kidnapping," Jason said. "He really doesn't pose a threat to them."

Billy Gene took a sip of coffee. "Unless they picked up somethin' on the phone tap that led them to believe he was. Then again, they probably didn't because they let him live when they took the woman."

"About all he could do that could pose a threat is identify the woman," Kevin said, "though that would be a moot point if her composite sketch comes back with her ID."

"I'm fairly confident there's no threat to Dennis," Virgil said, "now that Brody is out of the picture. I know I tend to be overprotective of Kate and her family, so I'm asking for your objective input. How good do you feel about sending Hawk home and proceeding with the investigation of Kennedy's disappearance and Brody's accident as if the threat to Hawk is over?"

"I don't see how we can do anything else," Kevin said. "I'd like to see Hawk keep a low profile, but I think it's safe to assume the threat is over."

"I agree," Jason said.

Billy Gene nodded. "Whatever this was about seemed centered around the woman. With her gone and Brody dead, I think the threat to Hawk is over."

"Okay, I'll send Hawk home," Virgil said. "But that's not to say we haven't got a big job on our hands. We need to investigate the disappearance of the woman known as Kennedy Taylor, and investigate the alleged murder of Brody Armison. I've already posted the composite sketch of Kennedy Taylor and supporting information on NLETS. Maybe we'll get a break. We'll get on this first thing in the morning. Thanks for putting in a long day. Go home and enjoy some time with your families." Virgil smiled. "Jill Beth's got curry chicken in the oven, and I can almost smell it now."

⚜

Hawk came out the wood-and-glass door of the sheriff's department and saw Elliot sitting in the lobby, reading a newspaper.

Elliot rose to his feet, met him halfway, and a second later, they were locked in an embrace.

"You okay?" Elliot said.

Hawk nodded. "It's been crazy."

Elliot let go of Hawk and pointed to the bench. "Why don't we sit for a minute? You can give me details on the way home, but tell me what the sheriff said. I assume you're free to go?"

"Yes, Dennis already left. The sheriff thinks the threat to me—and Dennis—is over since Brody's dead. There are no eyewitnesses to what happened."

"So he believes you?"

"Sure looks like it. They plan to start investigating Kennedy's disappearance and Brody's accident and alleged murder right away. Since it's on record, it'll make the news, but mostly because of the investigation into Brody's accident. Of course, we can't talk about this to anyone."

Elliot patted Hawk's knee. "I'm proud of you. It took courage to do what you did. You hungry?"

"Starved."

"Come on. Your mom made me promise to bring you straight home, but she's got leftover meatloaf and a loaf of rye bread with our name on it."

Elliot and Hawk went out the door, past the white columns, and down the courthouse steps. They walked over to the visitor parking lot, and stopped for a moment to remember where Elliot had parked his car.

A man in a dark suit, accompanied by two armed men, crossed the street and walked briskly toward the courthouse.

"I wonder who they are?" Hawk said.

"My best guess is the feds."

"What would the feds be doing at a county courthouse?" Hawk turned and watched as they neared the courthouse steps. "Look, the sheriff's standing in the doorway."

Sheriff Granger came outside, then walked down the courthouse steps. He stood, his face expressionless, as the three men walked up to him. The man in the dark suit started talking.

"The sheriff does *not* look happy," Hawk said.

"He certainly doesn't."

Sheriff Granger exchanged words with the man in the suit, then turned, his eyes shaded with his hand, and seemed to be searching for something. Finally, he motioned with his hand for someone to come.

Elliot glanced over his shoulder. "Hawk, I think he's motioning to us."

"Oh no." Hawk felt sick to his stomach. "What if the feds want to take over the case? If that happens, they won't tell us anything, just like they didn't tell us anything when my dad and Riley were missing. I'll never find out what happened to Kennedy."

"Hawk, it's possible you're better off not knowing," Elliot said.

"I don't see how. It'll haunt me the rest of my life. I know you and Mama think Kennedy was cheap, and you're glad she's gone. But you didn't know her. She wasn't like that. Something about her just drew me in, even before it turned sexual."

"Did you love her?" Elliot said.

"I don't know. I felt something. But it was different than what I felt for Laura Lynn."

Sheriff Granger whistled and called Hawk's name, motioning with his hand for Hawk to come.

"I can't believe this is happening," Hawk said.

Elliot put his hand on Hawk's shoulder. "Let's go see what this is about."

As they began walking toward the sheriff, the man in the dark suit stepped forward. He looked to be around forty. Nice looking, dark hair, and graying sideburns. Smug.

"I'm Special Agent Christopher Romo of the FBI. I'm in charge of this case now. My people will be working closely with the sheriff, but I'm the go-to guy from this point on. Any questions?"

"Yes, about a hundred," Hawk said. "Do you know what happened to Kennedy Taylor?"

"That's what we're here to find out," Romo said.

"But where did you come from?" Hawk said. "I didn't report this to the sheriff until a few hours ago."

"Hawk, we have some things we need to talk about," Romo said. "We're setting up an FBI office in the sheriff's department right now." He turned to Elliot. "Mr. Stafford, I presume?"

Elliot shook his hand. "How do you know our names?"

"I make it a point to learn the names of all persons of interest," Romo said, "*and* their family members."

"So am I person of interest?" Hawk said.

Romo nodded. "Yes, you are. And we need to find out what you know."

Hawk glanced over at Virgil. "But I already told Sheriff Granger everything I know when I gave my statement. I've been answering questions all day."

"Then you won't have any problem telling us," Romo said.

Hawk sighed. "I'm starved. I'm exhausted. Do we have to do this now?"

"We'll make sure you have dinner. And you can rest, if you want. But we'd like you to stay here until we're done."

"How long do you anticipate that will be?" Elliot said. "I'm his ride."

"Mr. Stafford, I suggest you go home and wait for a call from us."

"Is Hawk in trouble?"

Romo held up his hand. "No one is saying that. But he will need to tell us what he knows, for however long that takes."

Elliot's eyebrows came together. "If he's not in trouble, why isn't he free to leave?"

"Hawk can do whatever he wants," Romo said. "But let me assure you, it's in his best interest to cooperate. This is a federal investigation and he's at the center of it. For his safety, and to avoid coming under suspicion, it's in his best interest to cooperate."

Hawk turned to Elliot. "It's okay. I don't have anything to hide."

Elliot looked over at Virgil. "Should I get him a lawyer?"

"Not at this time," Virgil said. "It would be good if Hawk would just answer their questions."

Elliot turned to Hawk and put his hands on his shoulders. "Tell the truth. Trust God to do the rest."

Hawk nodded. "I will."

CHAPTER 10

Kate sat with Elliot, Grandpa Buck, Abby, Jay Rogers, and Jesse in the living room, fighting the urge to call Virgil and give him a piece of her mind.

"So Virgil just stood there and let that FBI agent march in and tell him what to do?" Kate said.

"Honey, he did what any good law enforcement official would do when the feds trump his jurisdiction," Elliot said. "He kept his mouth shut except when asked a question. That doesn't mean that, behind the scenes, he's going to be passive. In fact, Virgil and passive don't even belong in the same sentence. Since he told me I didn't need to get Hawk a lawyer, I'm taking him at his word. If things change, you know he'll tell us."

Abby sighed and linked arms with Jay. "I'm so disappointed. I thought for sure by tonight Hawk would be feeling relieved and the worst would be over."

"Wish Virgil could tell us *somethin'*," Buck said.

Elliot arched his eyebrows. "Actually, if Virgil's following protocol, he can't tell us *anything*."

"How did the FBI even know about the case," Jay said, "if Hawk hadn't told anyone besides Sheriff Granger?"

"That's the question of the hour." Elliot put his arm around Kate. "All I can figure is they were investigating their own case involving Kennedy Taylor, and when it collided with Virgil's, they wanted control."

"So we're just expected to accept that the feds are in charge," Buck said, "and we won't know squat about what's happening in the case?"

"Well, we'll just see about that." Kate picked up her cell phone and keyed in Virgil's private number.

"Honey, what are you doing?" Elliot said. "Don't complicate matters. Wait until we know more before you—"

"Hello, Virgil." Kate put the phone on speaker. "Would you please tell me what's going on? My family's sitting here in knots after Hawk was practically strong-armed by Special Agent Romo to stay and answer the same questions he'd already voluntarily given to you, and then Elliot was told to go home and wait for a call. You, of all people, know that I don't *wait* well!"

"I'm not at liberty to discuss this with you," Virgil said. "Just because I'm close to your family doesn't mean I can do what I want. The FBI is in charge. Any information from now on needs to come from Special Agent Romo."

"You're really going to wash your hands of this—just like that?"

"Kate, I'm not washing my hands of anything. I'll be working very closely with Romo. He's going to need my help. And frankly, I need his. There's a lot to this investigation, and we can't do it justice without the use of each other's resources. That said, I'm not exaggerating when I tell you I could throw away my career by over-stepping on this case. It's not just about your family."

"Okay. I understand." Kate softened her tone. "But the FBI is questioning my son. I think I'm entitled to answers."

"Your *adult* son," Virgil said. "And there's a good chance you're not going to get answers. When the Bureau gets involved in something this complex, you can bet whatever we know is just the tip of the iceberg. They're not going to discuss the details of the case. They're just not. And I won't be able to tell you or Hawk everything that I know. This is the big leagues, Kate."

"But how can I help protect Hawk if I don't know anything?"

"Protecting him isn't your job," Virgil said. "Not on this level."

"What's that supposed to mean?"

"Look, Kate ... whatever Hawk's mixed up in, it's big. It's dangerous. And it's going to take the most qualified people to flesh it out."

Kate's eyes welled and she glanced over at Elliot. "You're scaring me, Virgil. Did Hawk commit a crime?"

"Not as far as I can tell. What he and Dennis told me seemed straightforward and consistent. It's not what they know but what they *don't* know that concerns me. We've got a long way to go in this investigation. You have to trust the Bureau with this. You really don't have a choice. The less your family knows, the safer you'll be."

Kate wiped a tear off her cheek. "Can you tell me when Hawk is coming home?"

"I honestly don't know. He's behind closed doors with Special Agent Romo and several other agents, no doubt telling them everything he knows. It could be hours. Elliot won't need to come after Hawk, though. The FBI will bring him home. The best thing you can do is stay calm. Cooperate. And pray. You've got the best prayer warriors I know right there. I seem to recall that one of them has enough faith to make an apostle jealous."

Jesse grinned as everyone in the family turned and looked at him.

Kate smiled, remembering Jesse's horrible ordeal of last fall and how brave he was.

"Honestly, Kate, you've been through worse," Virgil said. "That may not make you feel any better, but it sure ought to make you know that God's got His hand on your family and He's not letting go."

Kate exhaled. "Thanks for reminding me. You're right."

"Just don't take it personal when I'm not as available as you're used to," Virgil said. "I'm not at liberty to discuss anything the Bureau may choose to share with me. And because it's no secret that I'm a close friend of the family, they may not share anything at all."

Kate sighed. "I'm sorry I raised my voice. Thanks for hearing me out. You know I trust you. I'm just anxious."

"Yeah, I know."

"Good night, Virgil," Elliot said. "We appreciate your candor. I know you'll look out for Hawk the best you can."

"That you can count on."

Kate turned off the phone and yielded herself to Elliot's embrace. "How will we get through this when we don't even know what *this* is?"

"Because God knows," Elliot said. "And His sovereignty trumps FBI jurisdiction."

There was a half minute of silence, and then Abby stood.

"I need an ice cream sundae to clear my head," she said. "Anybody else?"

Jesse's hand shot up. "Me!"

Grandpa Buck raised his hand. "Count me in."

The others nodded.

Jay followed Abby into the kitchen. "I'll scoop. You pour."

Jesse sat on the floor with the orange tabby kitten in his lap and Wolf lying next to him. "Wow, I just realized that every kid in this family has needed the sheriff to get them out of trouble."

"Believe me, I'm well aware," Kate said, holding tightly to Elliot's hand. *Hawk, what have you gotten yourself into?*

Virgil sat at his office computer, reading the short response that had just come in from NLETS concerning the composite drawing of Kennedy Taylor and the supporting information he had posted earlier.

Composite sketch 20180607FFRAR has been positively identified by sources within the Central Intelligence Agency and has been turned over to the Federal Bureau of Investigation for appropriate action. This is an FBI matter and no information regarding this individual will be disseminated.

In other words, it's a dead end. Virgil sighed and took off his computer glasses. What was this young woman into that she was so quickly recognized by sources within the CIA?

A knock on the open door startled him.

"It's me," said Romo. "Is that the response from NLETS I see on your screen?"

"Yes, it just came in," Virgil said. "I'm sure you know all about it."

"You mind if I take a look?" Romo said, not waiting for an answer. He looked over Virgil's shoulder and read the words on the screen. "Short and to the point. I like that."

"It was less than two hours after I posted the woman's composite sketch that you showed up on my doorstep," Virgil said. "Obviously, FBI headquarters in DC relayed it to the Little Rock Field Office, and they relayed it to Fayetteville. Did you even have time to pack a toothbrush before you beat a path to Foggy Ridge?" Virgil hated the sarcasm in his voice.

"Look, Sheriff, I'm really not the enemy. I'm sure it's unsettling having the FBI set up shop in your jurisdiction, but I assure you, I want to work with you and your people to complete this investigation."

Virgil folded his arms across his chest. "You going to tell me what it is we're investigating?"

"I'll make sure you know whatever you need to know, when you need to know it."

"Ah, the good old FBI mantra."

Romo smiled. "Come on, Virgil. This isn't your first rodeo. I don't need to tell you there's nothing *usual* about this case. The woman's ID came from sources within the CIA, which means the Bureau's going to be as closed mouthed as it gets. Who in the Bureau have you worked with before?"

"Sean Meadows. Bing Archer. Boyd Lester. Mitch Carter. Several others," Virgil said. "So are you going to tell me anything?"

Romo was quiet for a moment, and then said, "I did my home-work. You have a long history with the Cummings family. Whatever relationship you have with them cannot enter into your thinking on this case."

"I know that," Virgil said. "It won't."

"You're a good lawman, Sheriff. I believe your intentions are honorable. I want to keep you in the loop to the degree I can. But I have to know you can stay objective."

"The fact that I'm close to the Cummings family is all the more incentive for me to stay objective. I would never do anything to com-promise Hawk's safety."

Romo nodded. "Good."

"That said, I think it's right for me to want to also protect the people who work for me. And blind allegiance to the FBI without any idea of how that might affect their safety is not a reasonable expectation of a sheriff who takes his job seriously."

"Fair enough," Romo said. "Here's what you need to know for now. The woman's real name wasn't Kennedy Taylor, and she will, from this point on, be referred to as Nameless. Nameless is dead, but there is no public record of it. She has a five-million-dollar bounty on her head and is being pursued by a dangerous and wicked man who will do whatever it takes to find her. Our job is to intercept this bounty hunter unharmed and turn him over to the Bureau."

Virgil studied Romo's face. "I assume this bounty hunter knows that Hawk was romantically involved with Nameless?"

"Our sources say yes. Which would make Hawk highly sought after for information he doesn't have, and disposable when Nameless's pursuer is through torturing him."

"So you believe Hawk's telling the truth?" Virgil said.

"I do. But it's a moot point. This bounty hunter is on a mission to find Nameless, and Hawk is in grave danger."

Virgil's mind raced with details that didn't add up. "If this bounty hunter is in pursuit of Nameless, who were the eight men who executed a drone attack and kidnapped her, and I assume killed her, but left Hawk confused and alive—and Brody Armison dead just days later?"

"That's not relevant to my assignment."

"Not yours maybe," Virgil said. "But I have an obligation to pursue Brody's killers."

Romo shook his head. "It's a dead end, Sheriff. These are professionals. They've covered their tracks well. You can forget finding them, and looking would be a huge waste of time and resources. Nameless is dead."

"What am I supposed to say to Brody's parents—that whether or not their son was murdered isn't *relevant*?"

"Of course not," Romo said. "You tell them there's no evidence of foul play. That's the truth. And that Dennis got caught up in Brody's tale, but there's just no evidence to support his allegations."

"And what about Dennis? He's not going to roll over and pretend this never happened."

"You let me handle Dennis. I don't think he'll be a problem."

"Which brings us back to Hawk," Virgil said. "If he's in grave danger, how are we going to keep him safe and this bounty hunter unharmed?"

"I'm working on it."

"So now *I'm* not relevant?" Virgil said.

Romo shook his head. "Not true. I'm still gathering facts. Once I have what I need, we'll meet and discuss the best course of action. That may be yet tonight."

Virgil sat there, his arms folded across his chest. "So this is how it's going to be: you tell me what's relevant and when and what we're going to do about it?"

Romo winced. "Ouch. That's a little harsh. I'm going to go listen in on Hawk's interview. I'll call you when we're through."

CHAPTER 11

Virgil walked up on the wraparound porch of his Victorian home, the scent of honeysuckle taking his mind back to summer nights when he was a kid and slept with the windows open.

Garfield meowed and jumped down from the porch swing and rubbed against his ankles.

Virgil bent down and scratched the cat's chin. "Okay, I admit you're growing on me. But I'm still a dog person." He turned the knob and opened the beveled glass door, and was hit with a blast of cold air, and the pervasive aroma of something delicious.

Drake bounded into the foyer and sat as he'd been taught to do at obedience school, his tail swishing back and forth across the wood floor, his exuberance barely containable.

Virgil rubbed his ears and smiled at his mismatched eyes, one blue and one brown. A German shepherd–Australian sheepdog mix, this rescue dog had turned out to be a lovable companion. "Hey, buddy. Sorry I'm late. I'll bet you're dying to get out and run."

Jill Beth came into the entry hall, wiping her hands with a kitchen towel, wearing a smile that could melt an iceberg. "I hope you're hungry. I made curry chicken—the lowfat version, which means you get seconds."

Virgil took off his hat and put his arms around her, letting his lips melt into hers. "That's the nicest thing that's happened to me today. And I have a feeling that curry chicken is going to run a close second." He hung his hat on the coatrack and followed Jill Beth into the kitchen.

"I thought we could eat in the dining room," she said. "I put candles on the table and some fresh gardenias. I thought it might help take the edge off after the day you've had."

Virgil smiled. "You thought right."

"Oh, and number three son came by after work and took Drake with him when he went out jogging, so you don't have to take him out for a run unless you want to."

"That was awful nice of Reece. To tell you the truth, it does sound good just to sit and enjoy a nice dinner with my sweetheart before I have to go back in later."

"Well, it's just simmering," Jill Beth said, "so I'm ready when you are to get it on the table."

"You won't have to ask me twice." Virgil washed his hands at the kitchen sink, then helped Jill Beth carry the food to the table.

He pulled out a chair and seated her, lit the candles, turned on some soft instrumental music, then stood behind her, his hands on her shoulders, and said grace.

Following the amen, she filled their plates as he took his seat.

"Isn't this nice," he said. "You always know just what I need." He took a bite of curry chicken and savored it. "This is so good, darlin'. I could eat it seven days a week." He couldn't take his eyes off her. Her face glowed in the candlelight, and his mind flashed back to the first dinner they had together as newlyweds.

Jill Beth handed him a roll. "So tell me whatever it was you said could wait until dinner."

"Sorry," Virgil said. "I didn't want to discuss it on the phone. Hawk Cummings is now a person of interest in an FBI investigation."

"You're kidding."

"I wish." Virgil told her the details of Hawk's and Dennis's statements, and about Romo's unnecessarily dramatic arrival at the courthouse steps, announcing he was there to take control of the Kennedy Taylor kidnapping case. Virgil knew he couldn't tell her that Kennedy was dead or that Hawk was at great risk.

Jill Beth put down her fork and looked at Virgil. "Poor Hawk. Do Kate and Elliot know about this?"

Virgil nodded. "Hawk told them the whole story just before he and Dennis came in to give their statements. I talked to Kate earlier about the FBI's involvement."

"They must be disappointed in Hawk," Jill Beth said. "And yet so worried. Hawk must be devastated."

Virgil took a sip of water. "Yes on all counts."

"This Romo sounds like a jerk."

"Oh, maybe not. I get that he's just doing his job, but it would be nice if he didn't make me feel irrelevant."

"Well, he'll find out you're anything but that," Jill Beth said.

"We can only hope."

Jill Beth got quiet for what seemed an eternity. "Virgil, what in the world was the drone thing about? It's frightening. Do you think she was involved in a drug cartel or something?"

"Darlin', I have no idea. But I certainly intend to push Romo for more details before I'm willing to put my people in harm's way."

"Of course, you won't be able to tell me anything."

"Don't worry," Virgil said. "This thing will be over before you know it."

Hawk raked his hands through his hair, his elbows planted on the table that separated him from Special Agent in Charge Christopher Romo and Special Agents Justin Boone and Nick Jefferson.

"I'm not sure what you want me to say." Hawk's gaze moved from Romo to Boone to Jefferson. "I can't think of a single detail I left out."

Jefferson leaned forward, his hands folded on the table. "I find it implausible that Kennedy never talked to you in those, shall we say, afterglow moments. Women always have something to say."

"She *never* talked much," Hawk said. "She might've said something then. She probably did. But she never alluded to being in danger. Both her parents had died, and she inherited a huge fortune. She came to Foggy Ridge to start fresh. That's the extent of her life that she shared with me."

"Didn't she tell you where she was born? Where she grew up?"

Hawk sighed. "No. She didn't. Oh, but she did tell me she hated cell phones because of the radiation."

Romo smiled. "Okay, Hawk, I get that you're tired of being questioned. But Jefferson has a point. We're just trying to jog your memory a little, that's all."

"Sir, my memory doesn't need jogging," Hawk said. "I've told you everything there is to tell."

"Really? What about the dream?" Boone said.

Hawk blew out a breath. "What dream?"

"The one you told the sheriff about." Boone raised his eyebrows. "The dream that Kennedy said she'd had over and over again since she was a little girl."

"You mean the dream where she grew wings and could fly wherever she wanted?"

"Yes," Romo said. "The dream you failed to mention."

"Because it was nothing," Hawk said. "I didn't think to mention it because it was nothing."

Boone pushed his glasses up on his nose. "But you remember it now?"

Hawk shrugged. "Sure. Kennedy mentioned that ever since she was a little girl, she'd had this recurring dream that she grew wings and could fly wherever she wanted and look for her real home."

"And she never once told you what she meant by her *real* home?" Boone said.

Hawk folded his arms across his chest. "It was a dream, for crying out loud. I didn't ask what it meant because I didn't want to spoil the mood. I knew she'd lost both of her parents and figured she was still grieving."

"But she was talking about a dream she'd had since she was a little girl," Jefferson said. "She was clearly talking about something else."

Hawk folded his hands on the table and mused. "Looking back, I suppose you're right. I just remember feeling her loneliness and not wanting to get caught up in it. We had a good thing going. I didn't want the rest of the evening to be a downer."

Boone half smiled. "Fair enough. This is a really important question, Hawk. There's no right or wrong answer. I just need the truth. Did Kennedy ever talk about her country of origin? Her travels? Her father's occupation?"

Hawk thought carefully, his mind trying to separate the carnal from everything else. Finally, he said, "No, but she did have a subtle accent I couldn't place. I asked her about it. She said her father was from the northeast and her mother was from the south, and that some of her words were a blend of both accents."

"But she never hinted at her father's occupation?"

Hawk shook his head. "No, sir. And she never mentioned having traveled. Like I said before, she talked very little about herself or her parents. She shared her heart without words. It's hard to explain, but there was something beautiful about it. In hindsight, if she were holding anything back, I read it as grief."

"Sounds like you were in love with her," Jefferson said.

Hawk felt the heat rush to his face.

"Okay, gentlemen. I'll take it from here." Romo loosened his tie and looked at Hawk. "I know you're anxious to know exactly what we're dealing with. So put on your big boy pants and take a deep breath. Ready?"

Hawk nodded.

"Your lady's name was not Kennedy Taylor. I'm not at liberty to reveal what her real name was, but from this point on, we're going to refer to her as Nameless."

"You said *was*." Hawk's pulse raced as he forced out the words, "Is she ... dead?"

Romo stared at his hands. "She is. I'm sorry. I know you must've wondered about her."

"All the time," Hawk said. "I should've reported her missing right away. If I had, maybe she'd still be alive."

"Don't even go there. Nothing you could've done would've changed the outcome."

Hawk swallowed hard. "I feel bad that I never had the chance to say good-bye. Can you tell me how she died?"

Romo blinked, a flicker of compassion in his eyes. "That's classified. But I assure you, she didn't suffer."

"Can you at least tell me *why* she died?" Hawk said. "I feel like I'm living in the twilight zone. I think I deserve some answers."

"You do." Romo looked at Jefferson and then at Boone. "But it's complicated, Hawk. Let's move on and things will become clearer. You see, Nameless had a five-million-dollar bounty on her head. And there is a highly motivated bounty hunter—an exceedingly bad guy—tracking her down. Our intelligence indicates there's a high probability that he knows she's been involved with you, and he's coming to find you and get you to tell him where she is."

"B-but she's dead," Hawk heard himself say. "I don't know anything."

Romo nodded. "Unfortunately, he won't just take your word for it. If he gets his hands on you, he'll torture you until he's convinced you can't help him, and then he'll kill you."

"You won't let that happen, right?" Hawk could hardly catch his breath and suddenly wished the sheriff was in the room. "Does Sheriff Granger … know this?"

"I told him," Romo said, "just before he went home this evening."

Hawk felt as if his brain were ready to explode.

"This bounty hunter is on a quest to find Nameless and collect his five million bucks," Romo said. "You're his next stop. Count on it."

"Okay, I get the picture!" Hawk said. "You can protect me, right?"

"There is a way, but it will require mutual trust and courage on the part of all concerned."

"Let's hear it," Hawk said.

Romo picked up a pencil and bounced the eraser on the table. "Hawk, we need you to do what might be the bravest thing you'll ever do in your lifetime. We need you to help draw out this bounty hunter so we can capture him and take him into custody."

Hawk stared at Romo, processing his words. "You want *me* to be the bait?"

"My orders are to bring him in unharmed. He's no good to us dead. That said, capturing him is also the only way we can protect you. Otherwise, you'll be looking over your shoulder the rest of your life—and so will your family."

"How serious is the threat to my family?"

"Minimal," Romo said, "as long as the bounty hunter thinks he can get to you. If not, he would likely threaten your family to draw you out. That's why we need your help. I'm not going to lie to you, it's not without risk. But with each member of my team and Sheriff

Granger's team working together to ensure your safety, it's doable. In fact, I think I have a workable plan I'd like to run by the sheriff yet tonight. Before I do that, I need to know if you're on board."

"I guess I'll have to be." Hawk wiped the perspiration off his upper lip. "Does your intelligence know when this bounty hunter is supposed to show up?"

Romo leaned forward on his elbows. "Hawk, I can't get into specifics, but we have to put a plan in place *now*. We have no time to waste."

CHAPTER 12

Kate paced in front of the living room fireplace of the family's log house, then went into the kitchen where Abby had made a big pot of fresh coffee.

"Mama, why don't you sit in the living room and wait for the sheriff and the FBI?" Abby said. "Jay and I will make sure everyone gets something to drink. You need to focus on whatever they have to tell you."

Elliot appeared in the kitchen doorway. "Honey, they're here." He put his arms around Kate. "We prayed long and hard about Hawk and his circumstances. Let's take this meeting as an answer to prayer. Let's just listen to what Special Agent Romo has to say."

Kate didn't want to leave Elliot's arms. Didn't want to deal with Hawk's mess. Or the fact that he was in danger and Virgil wasn't in charge. The doorbell rang. Kate pushed back and looked up at Elliot. "Hold on to me, okay? My knees are like Jell-O."

"I've got you. Come on." Elliot linked arms with her, and just as they stepped out of the kitchen, they nearly collided with Hawk, who threw his arms around them both.

"I'm so sorry," Hawk said. "The consequences just keep getting worse. I no sooner get through one and a worse one pops up."

"God will get us through this." Elliot nodded toward Abby, Jay, Jesse, and Grandpa Buck. "Why don't you go hug your fan club? They'll be so glad to see you."

Hawk walked into the living room while Elliot and Kate greeted the sheriff, and the sheriff introduced Kate to Special Agent Romo.

"Let's go sit in the living room," Elliot said. "All of us are eager to hear whatever you came to tell us."

Elliot introduced Romo to the other members of the family.

"You have a ten-year-old daughter too," Romo said. "Is she going to sit in on this?"

"No," Kate said. "Riley doesn't know anything about this. She's away at camp and won't be back until Sunday afternoon."

"It's probably best." Romo sat next to Virgil on the love seat facing the others.

"I've made a fresh pot of coffee," Abby said. "Any takers?"

"You're reading my mind," Virgil said. "Just black."

Romo nodded. "Same here. Thanks."

"I'll have a cup," Hawk said.

Abby smiled. "Cream and sugar, I know. We'll be right back."

Kate could hear the pendulum clock ticking, her own heart beating, and Grandpa Buck's nasally breathing in the unsettling silence that followed.

Abby and Jay returned with the coffee and took their seats on the floor next to Jesse. Grandpa Buck was in his rocker. Hawk sat with Kate and Elliot on the couch. All eyes were on Sheriff Granger and Special Agent Romo.

"It's late," Virgil said. "But somehow I knew you'd all be right here, waiting to hear the next step. It's my understanding that each of you were up to speed on the statements that Hawk and Dennis gave at the courthouse this morning. So Special Agent Romo is going to update you on where we are now in this investigation. Chris?"

"I'm really glad to see the support you have for Hawk, individually, and as a family," Romo said. "That's going to mean everything in the hours and days to come. Okay, here's what you need to know. Kennedy Taylor did not use her real name. Her real name is classified. From this point on, she will be referred to as Nameless. Our interest in this case stems from the fact that Nameless has a five-million-dollar bounty on her head and is being pursued by a really determined bounty hunter—one evil dude—who will stop at nothing to find her. Our intelligence indicates that this bounty hunter is coming here to find Hawk because Hawk was involved with Nameless and may know where she is. I need to speak freely about some difficult things." Romo looked at Kate and Elliot. "Hawk thinks Jesse is mature enough to handle it, but I did want to give you warning. Are you okay with that?"

Kate looked at Elliot and they both nodded.

"If this bounty hunter catches up with Hawk, he's not going to take Hawk's word for it that he doesn't know where Nameless is. He will do whatever it takes, even torture, to get Hawk to reveal her whereabouts, which, of course, he can't. Once he's convinced that Hawk really doesn't know, he'll kill him."

Kate sucked in a breath, her hand over her mouth.

"Obviously, we can't allow that to happen," Romo said. "I, Virgil, and two of my special agents met earlier to devise a plan to capture this bounty hunter, but it's going to take real courage, intense focus, trusted teamwork, and a little good luck to pull it off."

"So you know what this man looks like?" Elliot said.

Romo glanced at Hawk, then focused his attention on Elliot and Kate. "I wish we did, Mr. Stafford. But we don't. Our intel is one hundred percent sure that the bounty hunter's coming. But, after putting our heads together, my people and Sheriff Granger see only one way to draw this man out in the open. And that's where Hawk comes in. Virgil, maybe you'd like to explain."

Virgil cleared his throat. "We've discussed the situation with Hawk, and he understands that what we're asking is risky. But unless Hawk makes this bounty hunter believe he's accessible, the guy could take one of you at gunpoint and force his way to Hawk. Then one or all of you could be at risk too. There's only one solution: Hawk needs to let us put him out there to draw the bounty hunter from the shadows. Once this guy makes a move, we can close in quickly and take him into custody."

"So, just to clarify," Buck said, "you're plannin' to apprehend the bounty hunter, not take him out?"

"My orders are to bring him in unharmed," Romo said. "I wasn't told why. That's classified. I was told that this bounty hunter is no good to us dead."

"Well, Hawk is no good to us dead either!" Kate said. "You're the FBI. You must have a better plan than using an innocent citizen to do your dirty work."

"I'm anything but innocent," Hawk said. "This bounty hunter is after me because I got involved with a woman I knew nothing about. No one knows where she is, and this person thinks I do. I can't change that. But I trust Sheriff Granger to shoot straight with us. He always has. I'm sure Special Agent Romo wants to do what's best. When this is all over, we'll probably trust him as much as we do the sheriff." Hawk took Kate's hand. "I've got to do this, Mama. To protect me and my future. And to protect the family. If they don't get this guy off the street, we'll be looking over our shoulders for the rest of our lives."

Kate studied her oldest. So bold. So sure of himself. "Hawk, what if something goes wrong, and they can't stop him from getting to you and whisking you away to a place where no one can protect you?"

"Then God will protect me," Hawk said. "Look how He's had his hand on this family through so many dangerous situations. I'm not going to stop trusting Him now."

"I assure you," Romo said, "it won't be necessary to rely on God. My people are the best at what they do. We'll keep Hawk safe."

Kate squeezed Elliot's hand. *Such arrogance*, she thought.

"Maybe the Lord wants us to rely some on both," Buck said. "You said yourself we need trusted teamwork. Can't get much better than that."

Romo's face turned red. "Fair enough. I'm willing to work with God if He's willing to work with me. Okay, here's the plan: You need to keep in mind this is an undercover operation. First, we need to install surveillance cameras and make use of our facial recognition technology. This could help us identify the bounty hunter if he or she is already in the system, which is a real possibility. Do you have surveillance cameras here at Angel View?"

"Yes, we do," Kate said. "Virgil talked me into upgrading them last year."

"Great. I don't see any outside cameras here at your home, though. I'll have a surveillance system installed ASAP and we'll have it linked to our equipment. Again, think undercover. We don't want anything to stand out. This guy's a pro. He'll be looking at his environment with scrutiny. Virgil, tell them how we plan to keep Hawk in our sight."

"We don't think Hawk is safe doing Jeep tours until this thing's over," Virgil said. "In order to get him away from that and sound legit, you need to tell the staff that you have a landscaper coming to draw up plans to beautify the grounds, and that Hawk is temporarily being pulled off his tours to work with the landscaper and to train a new grounds maintenance crew. You'll have to get with the nursery you currently use and tell them you've decided not to outsource lawn maintenance and have hired a crew of your own. Shouldn't be hard for anyone to believe, since Hawk was supervising outdoor maintenance before he started the Jeep tours. This would give us a perfect opportunity to bring in a half-dozen agents posing as the new grounds crew without raising suspicion. We'll get a couple additional agents to pose as the landscapers. Hawk could pretend to work with them too, which would give him a chance to move around and look busy.

"Of course, you'd have to sell this to your staff without raising a hint of suspicion," Virgil said. "If we see we need more agents, we can add some as pest control, housekeeping, maintenance, and the like. What we want is busy, normal activity a person might expect to see at a resort like Angel View."

"And while all this is happening here to keep Hawk moving around the premises," Romo said, "we will have the FBI command center set up behind the empty barn on Pete Jameson's farm, where we can operate in obscurity. I'll be there with other agents and with the sheriff and some of his people, carefully watching Hawk *and* observing who else might be watching Hawk. We'll have agents posing as guests too. And one working at Flutter's as a busboy. We'll be observing people from all angles. We will use drones to monitor the property from the air. We'll have two FBI agents in your home twenty-four seven. Each agent will be awake and in charge for twelve hours and then switch off. That way, there won't be an unfamiliar vehicle parked on your property, and no agents coming and going. That should avoid suspicion and help give you peace of mind while we try to flush out the bounty hunter and take him into custody."

Grandpa Buck wiped his bald head with a kerchief. "I'll say one thing, you folks're sure going to a lot of trouble to get one bounty hunter. Sounds like this operation will cost more than the bounty would've paid him."

Romo smiled. "I doubt that. But the FBI doesn't put a price tag on safety. Before we get out of your way for the night, just understand that the ball is already rolling and things are going to happen at warp speed starting tomorrow morning. It's absolutely imperative that we get our people in place so we can position Hawk where we can observe him all the time. Remember, this bounty hunter isn't going to shoot Hawk. His goal is to get Hawk somewhere alone where he can do whatever it takes to find out where Nameless is. We need to keep Hawk moving around the premises so we can try to pick out the bounty hunter. The facial recognition technology might save us the trouble, in which case we can close in quickly. Otherwise, we'll do it the way we've been doing it for decades. Our surveillance cameras will enable us to study the people who study Hawk. Shouldn't be that hard to pick out the bounty hunter. We're experienced in what to look for."

"What happens," Kate said, "if, despite your best efforts, this bounty hunter isn't on anyone's radar and makes a move you didn't anticipate?"

"Don't worry," Romo said. "I will anticipate every conceivable scenario. That's my job."

CHAPTER 13

Kate and Abby prepared the guest room and bath for FBI Special Agents Natalie Sloan and Clarissa Ortega, who were assigned to stay with the family until the ordeal was over.

Kate put fresh towels in the bathroom, then stepped back into the bedroom just as the special agents were coming through the door with their bags. "I'm really glad you're staying here," Kate said. "I, for one, feel much safer."

"We hope to ease your anxiety," Sloan said. "Don't go to any extra trouble for us. In fact, we'd be glad to help with laundry, cooking, cleaning, whatever you need. Our job is to keep you calm, safe, and informed, but there will be downtime, and we don't mind helping. Also, we play a mean game of gin rummy."

Kate smiled. "Let's play it by ear."

"I have a question." Abby fluffed a pillow on one of the twin beds. "I leave here at five o'clock every morning to open Flutter's Café. Do you think it's safe for me to walk over to the lodge by myself, even if it's still dark outside?"

"We've already got a plan," Sloan said. "We don't want you changing your routine, but there's an easy way to protect you without being seen. I've got the first twelve-hour shift"—Sloan looked at her watch—"from now until noon. At five a.m., I'll slip out the back door thirty seconds before you leave by the front door. You'll start walking toward the lodge shining your flashlight on the path, and I'll be walking just a couple of yards behind you until you make the turn and can't be seen from the road, then we can walk together. I'll walk you over to Flutter's and come right back."

"Okay," Abby said. "That's a good idea."

Ortega sat on the bed. "Special Agent Sloan and I will be staying here in the house round the clock for two reasons. One, we want you to feel at ease, and getting to know us and vice versa will foster that. And two, we don't want to blow our cover by having a shift change every twelve hours."

Abby's eyebrows came together. "It's creepy to think we're being watched."

"The best thing you can do," Ortega said, "is put it out of your mind and just act normal. Remember, our people will be watching too, from the command center. And from numerous places on the property. As long as we make Hawk seem accessible, you won't be in any danger.

Sloan set her bag on the chair in the corner. "Abby, it's possible the bounty hunter could even pose as a customer at Flutter's—someone who seems nosier than your regular guests, especially if he's overly curious about the extra people we've put in place on the grounds. If you're confronted with anyone who seems to be probing for information, stay calm and answer his questions, being sure to mention that Hawk is overseeing the big landscaping project. There will also be special agents posing as customers. A special agent posing as a busboy, and he will have his eyes on you as will Special Agent Romo and Sheriff Granger, who will be watching from the command center, so there's no need to be afraid. All that will be explained to you when you arrive at Flutter's in the morning."

Kate came over and put her arm around Abby. "Let's let these ladies get moved in and go talk with Hawk before he goes to bed." *And before we scare ourselves to death.*

⚜

Hawk sat around the kitchen table with the entire family, who was quickly devouring a double batch of Toll House cookies.

"It's so good having you home," Jesse said. "You weren't even gone a whole day, but it seemed like forever."

"To me too," Hawk said. "I've never answered so many questions in my life. I think for every answer I gave, they thought of five different ways to ask the same question, just to test me." He winked at Jesse. "So I just told the truth. That way I didn't have to remember what I said."

"I have a question for Hawk." Grandpa Buck took a sip of milk. "The feds don't want us changin' our routines. But how're you going to get over to the lodge tomorrow to meet the phony landscapers? It's too risky for you to go by yourself."

Hawk nodded. "They decided to have Connor come get me in his pickup. That would look the most natural, since he's going to be filling in for me on the Jeep tours, and we have to talk shop on some things. He won't know anything about what's going on."

"Did Special Agent Romo or Virgil say how long they thought this ruse would take to play out?" Jay said.

Hawk shook his head. "Not really. Based on their intel, Romo thinks the bounty hunter is on the move now, but he can't tell me anything except that it's imperative that we have a plan in place ASAP."

"Are you scared?" Abby said.

Terrified. Hawk shrugged. "Sure, a little. But I'm even more scared of living the rest of my life afraid. I want this thing over with."

"Well, it can't happen soon enough for me," Kate said. "I'd be more comfortable if Virgil was taking the lead."

Elliot folded his arms on the table. "I'm proud of you for stepping out in faith, Hawk. I know God will honor it."

"I couldn't get over the arrogance of Special Agent Romo saying there was no need to rely on God," Kate said, "that his agents were the best at what they do, and that *they* would protect Hawk."

Elliot smiled. "As long as we know who's protecting Hawk, it doesn't really matter what he thinks."

"No, it doesn't," Hawk said. "Which reminds me, as long as we're all together, would you pray with me before we go to bed? After tomorrow things are going to get crazy, and I don't know when we'll have the opportunity. Don't faint … but I'd like to pray first."

The family joined hands.

"Father," Hawk said, "I confess to You, and to those around this table, that I have sinned. I gave in to temptation and deception and disgraced myself, Laura Lynn, my family, and most of all, You, who I love above all things. It breaks my heart that I have disappointed and hurt those I love. I'm ashamed of my behavior and vow never to put myself in a situation where this could happen again. Lord, I know I am reaping the consequences of what I've sown. And that the consequences may continue to play out for a long time and in many different ways. I can't change what I've done. And that's one of the biggest consequences of all, that I have to live with it. But I also know that You forgive every sin we lay at your Son's feet, and I've done that with sincere remorse and sorrow …" Hawk paused to gather his composure. "So, Father, now I stand before You, cleansed of that sin by the blood of Jesus. I ask for wisdom and protection as I step out in faith and submit this situation to You. Be with Special Agent Romo and his people, and with Sheriff Granger and his deputies, as they seek to capture this vile bounty hunter and keep him from hurting anyone ever again. Protect my family as they suffer through this with me, and be their peace. When we see these things come to pass, we will give You all the glory, in the name of Your Son and our Savior, Jesus Christ. Amen."

Elliot put his arm around Hawk. "Lord, there's absolutely nothing I can add to Hawk's prayer. It seemed to spring up from deep inside him where his faith runs deep. All I ask is that You protect him, that You put a circle of light around him, so that the bounty hunter cannot touch him and the authorities can do their job and get this dangerous person out of commission. In Jesus's name I pray. Amen."

"Amen," Kate said.

The others echoed the amen.

Hawk, unable to contain the weight of emotion that had been building all week, turned to Elliot and wept in his arms. He'd never expected to feel such love at a time when he felt the least lovable.

Kate sat at her vanity table, waiting for her nighttime moisturizer to soak in, and looking in the mirror to see whether those pesky signs of aging around her eyes had been visibly reduced.

Elliot came in the bedroom and shut the door. "Have you got something in your eye?"

"No, I'm trying to see if my night cream has kept its promise to visibly reduce wrinkles, but I can't see well enough without my reading glasses to tell." She smiled without meaning to. "It's funny, when you stop to think about it."

Elliot came up behind her and gently rubbed her shoulders. "You're braver than I am. This is not the week I would choose to take a close look at the signs of aging around *my* eyes."

"Did Hawk finally go to bed?" Kate said.

"Yes, just now." Elliot kissed the back of her neck, then sat on the side of the bed. "He looked spent."

Kate turned and faced Elliot. "I don't think I've seen him cry more than a tear or two since he was a little boy and our sweet yellow Lab got hit by a car. Hawk's really sensitive, but he hides it so well that I sometimes forget."

"I know," Elliot said. "He's unusually skilled at masking his feelings. I think what we witnessed tonight was raw, unfiltered emotion, not something we ever expected to see. Only he knows how God is dealing with him. But I'm sure he's acutely aware of the far-reaching consequences of his affair with the woman he knew as Kennedy Taylor."

"Your prayer was affirming," Kate said. "I think it touched him. He looks up to you and really wants your approval."

"Hawk and I talked for a few minutes before he went to bed. I told him that he's a good man and even good men can make big mistakes. That's what grace is all about. I told Hawk I don't think less of him because he sinned. I think more of him because he repented and took a stand against ever repeating his mistake."

Kate got up and sat in Elliot's lap, her arms around his neck. "I'm so glad you're in our lives, and that I finally had the good sense to marry you." She brushed his lips with hers. "I love you."

"I love you more."

"I love you most."

Elliot smiled and held her close. "Think back on all the nights before we married, when I had to go home, knowing you were lying here alone, scared. Overwhelmed. Having to deal with crisis after crisis by yourself. Never again."

"I'm so glad." She sighed. "Speaking of crises, we're about to be right in the middle of another. We'd better try to get some sleep. Angel View will be under glass when Abby leaves for work, in less than four hours, and I want to be up. The minute she walks out that door, our lives will never be the same."

"Have they ever been?" Elliot said. "Just think of all we've been through. We weren't the same when it was over. We were stronger. We will be this time too."

Kate mused, her mind flashing back over the years. "You're right. I trust God. And I trust us. I just wish I had the same confidence in Special Agent Romo as I do in Virgil."

Elliot smiled. "Don't tell either one of them, but they're merely props. God's in control of this assignment. And if God is for us, who can be against us, right?"

Kate nodded. "I believe that with all my heart. But you might have to remind me. More than once. Well, a lot more than once."

CHAPTER 14

Virgil sat at the conference table in his office with Chief Deputy Kevin Mann. They listened as Special Agent Nick Jefferson finished outlining the plan that would enable Hawk Cummings to draw the bounty hunter out in the open.

"In addition," Jefferson said, "we've had our techs working through the night putting in a surveillance system at Hawk's home, which will be linked into our system within the hour. The surveillance system at Angel View Lodge is already linked in to ours and running with facial recognition capability. Also, the Bureau decided to bring in agents from outside the area to avoid any chance of the actors being recognized by locals."

"By actors," Kevin said, "I assume you're referring to the FBI agents playing roles?"

Jefferson nodded. "That's right. We understand a number of locals eat at Flutter's, so we felt we needed to bring in unfamiliar faces to fill those roles."

"What's the objective regarding Hawk Cummings?" Kevin said.

"To do everything we can to keep him safe."

"Just to be clear," Virgil said, "is that the primary or secondary objective?"

Jefferson loosened his tie. "Sheriff, as you know, Hawk freely chose to help us with this operation. It carries with it a degree of risk."

"That's a given," Virgil said. "What I'm asking you is whether Hawk's safety is primary or secondary."

Jefferson scratched his ear. "Our objective regarding Hawk is to do everything possible to keep him safe. But the primary objective of this operation is to apprehend the bounty hunter and bring him in unharmed."

Virgil held Jefferson's gaze. "And if a situation arose where you could achieve your primary objective but not your secondary, what would you do?"

"We're capable of doing both," Jefferson said.

Virgil folded his arms. "If everything goes perfectly. But what if it doesn't?"

Jefferson dabbed his face with a handkerchief. "Look, Sheriff. We've been after the bounty hunter for a decade. This might be the best chance we'll ever have to get him out of commission. Bringing him in unharmed *is* our number one objective. But again, we're doing everything possible to ensure Hawk's safety."

"I don't doubt that," Virgil said. "But you'd be willing to accept Hawk Cummings's death as collateral damage if that was the only way you could bring in the bounty hunter unharmed."

"That's the job, Sheriff. But we're bending over backwards to protect Hawk. Don't forget that Hawk and his family can never really be safe with this killer on the loose. Given his history, there's nothing the bounty hunter won't do to get to Nameless and claim the five million.

Hawk was under no obligation to put himself in harm's way to help us. He chose it." Jefferson softened his tone. "I realize Hawk means a lot to you, Sheriff. I know you and his family go back years. That's precisely why Special Agent Romo decided not to withhold anything from you. I trust you'll be able to remain objective as we proceed?"

Virgil nodded. "Thanks for your candor."

"Any other questions before I head over to the command center?" Jefferson said, glancing at his watch.

"None here," Kevin said.

Virgil stood and shook hands with Jefferson. "Thanks for taking the time to fill us in. We'll keep this close to the vest. Would you please tell Special Agent Romo that I'll join him at the command center before nine, when Hawk is expected to ride over to the lodge with Connor Richardson?"

"I'll tell him."

Virgil waited until Jefferson left, then turned to Kevin. "I'm not any happier than you are that the feds are running this thing. But it is what it is. I'll be in and out, but I need you to keep the department running. Romo has gone to great lengths to keep this operation undercover. For Hawk's sake, let's make sure it stays that way."

Kevin sat staring at Virgil.

Virgil raised an eyebrow. "What?"

"You're not buying it either," Kevin said. "They have no personal interest in Hawk Cummings. They're using him."

"Hawk volunteered, Kevin. He's a grown man. It's out of my hands."

"Since when are you so compliant when it comes to Kate's family?"

Virgil sighed. "It's not a matter of compliance. I'm not in command. Romo's calling the shots."

"So you're just going to roll over when you know they'll sacrifice Hawk in a heartbeat so some monster who hasn't got a soul can be brought in without a scratch?"

"Who said anything about rolling over? Keep things running here." Virgil patted Kevin on the back. "I'll check in with you later."

Virgil got in his squad car and drove to Rocky Springs Park. He pulled in the main parking lot and turned off the motor. The eastern half of the sky had turned fiery crimson and almost pulsated with streaks of molten pink and golden purple. The White River was covered with a thick blanket of fog, giving him the sensation of being above the clouds.

He sat there for a few moments, spellbound, as Thursday's sun peeked over the horizon, five golden rays fanning out across the expanse, the fog on the White River slowly turning a soft pastel pink.

Virgil finally exhaled and let the glory of the moment fill his soul.

God, You've brought Kate's family through ordeal after ordeal that would've broken most people. They always come out stronger. If I've learned anything from them, it's that You're in control. I don't pretend to understand that, but I trust Your authority more than Romo's. I need Your help.

Virgil mulled over an idea he'd been toying with since he left his office last night. It might mean his career if it backfired. But then, what kind of career was it if he couldn't keep his promise to protect the people of Raleigh County?

He reached under the seat and pulled out a burner phone he had bought at Walmart before he'd gone home last night. He tore open the package and followed the instructions until everything seemed to be working. He reached in his pocket and pulled out a Post-it Note with a phone number written on it. He keyed in the number and heard it ringing. Was he out of his mind? He started to hang up—

"Hello."

"Mitch Carter?"

"Who's calling?"

"Virgil Granger. I hope I didn't wake you up."

"You know better than that. Hey, buddy! How have you been? How's that beautiful wife of yours? And the three musketeers?"

Virgil laughed. "I'm doing well. Jill Beth is beautiful as ever and still the love of my life. As for the three musketeers … our triplets have changed a great deal since you last saw them. They're young entrepreneurs now. They've formed a software company together and are blowin' and goin'. They're all single, so we don't have any grandkids to brag about. How's Sarah?"

"I guess you haven't heard. She passed away last year. Heart attack."

"I'm so sorry," Virgil said. "I hadn't heard. How are you doing?"

"Life's different without Sarah. My son's been living in London for two years. He's a pilot for British Airways. So when the field office in Little Rock asked me to come head up their IT division, I didn't hesitate. That's where I'm working now."

"Information technology," Virgil said. "What a great fit. That's got to be the next best thing to being in the field."

"You know it. So what's on your mind? I'm pretty sure you didn't call just to chitchat."

"No, there's another reason," Virgil said. "I need to tap your brain. But I need us to talk under the radar. I'm calling you on a burner phone. Any chance you could get your hands on one and call me back at this number?"

Mitch laughed. "A burner phone. Really?"

"I'm dead serious."

"Okay, Virgil. You got it. I'll need about thirty minutes. Will that work for you?"

"I'll be waiting. Thanks."

Virgil disconnected the call, his heart pounding. The ball was rolling. It was too late to turn back.

Hawk lay in bed, his hands behind his head, and watched the ceiling fan go round and round. Halo had curled up on his chest, the white ring on the top of her head visible under the glow of the night-light. The steady rhythm of the cat's purring was a welcome comfort.

He couldn't get Kennedy off his mind. He had feared she might be dead long before Romo confirmed it. But the reality of it was harsh and troubling. He wondered if the eight men who had kidnapped her were responsible. Or if they had delivered her to some drug lord or mafia kingpin to pay for the sins of her family. Horrifying images raced through his mind. He knew with his head that there was nothing he could have done that would have prevented her demise. So why did he feel such guilt, sorrow, and loss? Perhaps because he was spared and she wasn't?

Nothing about her led him to believe that she was involved in criminal activity. She had the most beautiful, innocent face. Soft, dark eyes without a hint of guile. And though she talked very little about herself, her way with him spoke volumes about her kind heart.

Who would have placed a five-million-dollar bounty on the head of such a wonderful human being? And what kind of monster would hunt her down by any means necessary? Hawk wanted the FBI to get this guy. Perhaps his helping them do it would be the best thing he could do to honor Kennedy's memory.

It was difficult not being able to talk about her. Romo convinced him it was dangerous to tell anyone she was dead until after they captured the bounty hunter. But even then, who would care to hear about her? His family couldn't see past his sin. And Laura Lynn had been his best friend and confidant. Maybe being alone with his feelings and unanswered questions was part of the consequences.

Hawk heard the bathroom door open and smelled the hot, soapy mist pour into the bedroom.

"Mornin', Jess."

Jesse peeked around the corner of the bathroom door. "I didn't mean to wake you up."

"You didn't. I have fifteen pounds of fur sitting on my chest."

Jesse laughed. He came over to the bed, wearing only his khaki shorts. "You want me to take her?"

"Not really. Her purring is a nice start to a stressful day. You getting ready to go over to the hummingbird garden?"

Jesse nodded. "Special Agent Sloan walked Abby over to Flutter's. It worked fine, so she's going to do the same thing with me. It's kinda cool, but I guess it's really serious stuff. Are you nervous?"

"Sure," Hawk said. "But the sheriff and the FBI will be watching every move I make from the command center, and Angel View will be swarming with agents dressed as workers and guests."

"It's like the movies."

"Totally." Hawk stared at his brother, then reached over and poked Jesse's chest. "Is that what I think it is?"

Jesse looked down and grinned. "Yep. I've got a few hairs on my chest. I'm proud of those puppies. I'm finally starting to look like a teenager."

"Yes, you are. But don't be in such a hurry. I like having a kid brother."

Jesse was quiet for a few moments and then said, "I've been praying you'll be safe. I wish it wasn't so dangerous. But if God let David take out Goliath with a stone and a slingshot, I guess He can help a whole team of FBI guys to capture one bounty hunter—and keep you safe."

Hawk picked up Halo from his chest and moved her to the bed, then sat up facing Jesse. "You always know how to make the Bible apply to the circumstances. How do you do that?"

Jesse shrugged. "I read it a lot. But our youth pastor, Nathan, is really cool. I've learned tons from him."

"Well, I've learned tons from *you*. You're like this wise old guru in a thirteen-year-old body."

Jesse flexed his biceps and flashed a silver smile. "A hairy, manly body."

Hawk laughed and gave him a shove. "Go finish getting ready. I need to shower and get dressed. Connor is picking me up, and I need to go see if Special Agent Sloan needs to update me before I leave."

Hawk sat on the side of the bed, feeling as if he'd swallowed a brick. He'd been trying not to think about the weirdness of this day—or the danger it might hold. He thought again about Kennedy. He vowed to think of her often and remember that he was helping to get the monster who would stop at nothing to find her. If only he'd had the chance to do the same for whoever actually did find her. Since everything relating to Kennedy was classified, he would never know how or why she had died. It was the one consequence that was almost intolerable to bear.

CHAPTER 15

Virgil sat in his squad car, the doors closed and the air conditioner running. Maybe it was the stress, but he couldn't cool down. He glanced at his watch. *Come on, Mitch. I've got to get moving in a few minutes.*

The phone beeped and Virgil looked at the screen. He had a text message. He opened the only name he had programmed into the phone, and read the text: *Call me. I need an excuse to get up and leave the room.*

Virgil keyed in the number and let it ring.

"Thanks," Mitch said, sounding out of breath. "Too many ears in there. Tell me what's going on."

Virgil told Mitch everything he could remember about Hawk's and Dennis's statements, the FBI's almost-spontaneous takeover of the case, and the details of the operation that had been nailed down the night before.

"Christopher Romo is the special agent in charge," Virgil said. "I know he's holding out on me. The case was handed to the Bureau by the CIA. I only know that because of the reply I got to the composite sketch. Everything regarding Kennedy Taylor, now being referred to as Nameless, is classified. Hawk Cummings has agreed to help the FBI draw the bounty hunter out in the open, but protecting him is not their primary objective. I'm afraid they might sacrifice this kid to bring in the bounty hunter. It's out of my hands."

"What can I do to help you?"

"I need a big favor, Mitch. You know you can trust me, but I'll understand if you don't want to get involved."

"Let's hear it."

"I want to know what's been going on under my nose. Who used a drone and kidnapped the woman Hawk knew as Kennedy Taylor? Who is she? Who is this bounty hunter? Or is he even a bounty hunter? What does he look like? Who put a five-million-dollar bounty on the young woman's head? What is the CIA's interest? I'm sure it's all classified."

A long moment of silence made Virgil wonder if he'd made a mistake pursuing this.

Finally, Mitch said, "I have a pretty high clearance level, Virgil, but what do you hope to gain by having the information? I mean, you can't head up the case or change any of Romo's decisions. And you can't share a word of anything you might find out."

"Of course not," Virgil said. "You have my word. I'm not sure if I can verbalize exactly how I feel. But Hawk made a comment that stuck with me. He said he feels like he's living in the twilight zone. Well, so do I. I need to understand what's already gone down and what's about to. This is my town. These are my people. And Kate's family is like my own. Maybe that's not a good enough reason to ask you to take this kind of risk. If either of us gets caught, it'll be the end of our careers. Say the word, and I'll pitch this phone in the lake and forget we ever talked. No hard feelings."

"You're a good man, Virgil. The best sheriff I ever worked with. If you say you need to know this stuff, that's reason enough. Keep your phone handy. If I have something for you, I'll probably text rather than call."

"Are you sure, Mitch?"

"I'm sure. Stay tuned."

Virgil ended the call, put the phone in his pocket, and stared at nothing, his heart racing as if he'd run a marathon. An hour from now, he'd be in the command center and Hawk would be in Connor Richardson's pickup truck, headed for Angel View Lodge. So many details. So many actors. So many things that could go wrong.

❀

Kate sat at the kitchen table, picking at her scrambled eggs.

Elliot bent down, put his lips to her ear, and spoke softly. "Darlin', you need to eat something. It's going to be a long day."

"I'm afraid if I eat, it won't stay down," Kate said.

"How about a glass of milk? It might settle your stomach."

Kate nodded.

Elliot brought her a glass of milk and set it on the table, then sat next to her.

"I'll feel better when Hawk is at the lodge and Virgil has eyes on him," Kate said. "Of course, who knows how long we'll have to wait before the bounty hunter makes a move. If I didn't trust the Lord, I think I'd curl up in a ball and hide."

Elliot smiled. "Aren't you glad you do? I remember a time, not all that long ago, when trusting Him was a terrible struggle."

"It's strange, but this time, it's different. I know God's in control. I know that whatever is going to happen, He's already on the other side of it. He has a plan. We just need to trust Him. It's still hard."

Elliot picked up her hand and kissed it. "You're right."

"I wonder if I should call Ava's mother and see if Riley can stay with them until this thing is over. I really don't want Riley to know anything about it. She's been through enough."

"You might call, just to make sure a plan B is in place," Elliot said. "But Sunday's still three days off. This thing could easily be over by the time Riley gets home from camp."

"Excuse me." Special Agent Sloan stood in the kitchen doorway. "I escorted Jesse to the hummingbird garden. I'm happy to report that Abby was very busy waiting on customers, two of which were our agents. And so was the busboy. Things appear to be operating normally. Is there anyone else we need to talk to before our landscaping actors arrive?"

"I don't think so," Elliot said. "I called Savannah Surette, our general manager, a little while ago and gave her the details you told us to give all the staff people—that we made a decision to go ahead with a major landscaping project that we'd been mulling over because the landscapers had a cancellation. And that we were pulling Hawk off the Jeep tours to oversee it, and Connor will work twelve-hour shifts. I told her I wanted her to know that she would be seeing a lot of workers here for several days. I don't think she was too happy with me for not keeping her informed that this was coming. When it's over, I'll square things with her. I really hated not telling her the truth."

"Thanks for following the script," Sloan said. "It's so important that your own people believe the scenario and things run like they always do. By the way, have you or Hawk talked to Connor about what's going on?"

Elliot shook his head. "Connor just thinks that we're pulling Hawk off the Jeep tours to head up the new landscaping project."

Sloan smiled. "Perfect."

"Have you had breakfast?" Elliot said.

"I had a granola bar and a cup of coffee," Sloan said. "That's plenty when I'm working. I'm more alert when I don't have a lot in my stomach."

Kate glanced up at the clock. "In less than an hour, three of my children will be visible to Virgil and Special Agent Romo from the command center. It's a bit mind blowing, but I'll feel better. I guess we just sit here and twiddle our thumbs."

"I'll have audio," Sloan said. "We should be able to follow what's going on. But just a heads-up, these types of operations can be drawn out and rather tedious. You might want to consider working puzzle books, playing solitaire, knitting, or whatever you enjoy doing to keep your hands busy."

Hawk put on his blue-and-yellow Angel View staff T-shirt and tucked it into his khaki shorts. He placed the matching cap on his head and put his cell phone on his belt clip.

He heard feet on the stairs and turned to the door in time to see his mother, Elliot, and Grandpa Buck peering in at him.

"We want to pray with you before Connor picks you up," Kate said. "Why don't you sit on the bed with me?"

Hawk plopped down on the bed, acting lighthearted, but feeling as if he might lose his breakfast.

His mother sat next to him and linked arms. Elliot and Grandpa stood facing him, each with a hand on his shoulder.

"Lord," Kate said, "we have come before You many times as a family asking for Your protection. But not until now have I truly believed that You will answer our prayers according to Your perfect will, and that You will give me, and all of us, the grace to accept the outcome from Your loving hands. Lord, I put my firstborn in Your care …" Kate's voice failed. She let her head rest on Hawk's shoulder, then continued, "You love him even more than we do, and that's all I really need to know. I ask that You calm Hawk's nerves. Yes, Lord, the queasy stomach he's trying so hard to hide from us. What he's agreed to do for the FBI is unselfish and important. I pray that You would reward his bravery by enabling this operation to succeed in getting the bounty hunter out of commission so that Kennedy Taylor will be safe and can live her life in peace. And that Hawk will come home to us unharmed. We love him so much …"

Elliot started praying, but Hawk didn't hear the words. He was completely stunned that his mother had prayed out loud—and in such a touching manner. And that she referred to Kennedy by her name and not the code word Nameless. That she had put her head on his shoulder when no words would come out. He couldn't remember feeling closer to his mother than he did at this moment.

Hawk was aware of Grandpa Buck praying and hands pressing his shoulders.

"Father, we're so grateful for Your love," Buck said. "And how You've wrapped your arms around this family over and over again. We trust You with Hawk's life and pray that he would handle himself today with honor befitting a child of the King. In Jesus's name we pray. Amen."

Hawk blinked to clear his eyes, aware that the grandfather clock in the downstairs hallway had chimed nine times.

"I guess it's time." Hawk smiled at his mother. "By the way, what's for dinner?"

"Swiss steak, brown potatoes, and asparagus. Strawberry short-cake for dessert. Dinner will be ready at six." Kate put her arms around him. "But we're not going to eat until you come home."

⚜

Virgil leaned against the back wall of the FBI command center, feeling conspicuous in his khaki sheriff's uniform and wide-brimmed hat amid a sea of dark blue shirts with the yellow FBI logo.

The command center was much larger than he had anticipated but was easily concealed behind the barn on the Jameson farm. The mobile unit, the size of an eighteen wheeler, was equipped on both sides with a long, narrow built-in desk unit accommodating six laptops, each placed about two and a half feet apart. But the double row of overhead monitors showing Angel View from nearly every angle was enviable. He could see that Abby was working at Flutter's. Jesse was doing some kind of demonstration with hummingbirds. Hawk was outside down by the gazebo, talking with two special agents dressed as landscapers. Other monitors showed detailed images of the inside of the café, the front desk, and the big cedar deck on the backside of Angel View. It was really quite impressive.

He hated that he felt like an outsider—which he clearly was, despite Romo's pretense of inclusion. At least most agents made eye contact and didn't pass him by as if he didn't exist.

"Hey, Sheriff." Romo put his cell phone in his suit pocket and walked over to him. "What do you think of our new mobile command center?"

Virgil smiled. "Not too shabby."

"It was designed to provide a state-of-the-art communications platform—telephone, Wi-Fi, satellite, and video teleconferencing capabilities as well as a fully integrated VoIP redundant radio system—which gives us full duplex communications interoperability for the fire department, city, county, and state police departments."

Virgil arched his eyebrows. "Uncle Sam obviously didn't skimp on quality."

"The surveillance system allows us to monitor high-traffic areas of the lodge, indoors and out. Right now, we've got eyes on all three Cummings siblings and whoever they come in contact with. That's where our facial recognition feature is invaluable. And in case you were wondering, that monitor up on the top right is showing the Angel View grounds from the drone."

Virgil tried not to react to Romo's patronizing tone. "Looks like you've thought of everything."

"Of course we have." Romo slapped him on the back. "That's what the FBI does, Sheriff."

Virgil looked up, his neck burning under his collar, and wished he could slap the arrogant smile off Romo's face. "Speaking of what the FBI *does*. Just to be clear, is it your policy to mislead the people who stick their necks out to help you?"

"Pardon me?"

"I'm just wondering why you didn't tell Hawk that bringing in the bounty hunter unharmed was your primary objective," Virgil said, "and that keeping him safe was optional."

"Whoa, Sheriff. That's a little harsh, don't you think?"

"Is it? Was Hawk informed that his death would be considered acceptable collateral damage?"

Romo made a sweeping motion with this hand. "Take a look at all this top-notch equipment. We're utilizing every means we possibly can to keep Hawk safe."

"I don't dispute that," Virgil said. "But that kid agreed to help you, believing that his safety was your *utmost* concern."

"I told Hawk we will do everything in our power to keep him safe, and that's the truth."

Virgil chewed his lip. "And you don't think you were being disingenuous by letting Hawk believe the two of you were on the same page?"

"Are you judging me? Need I remind you, Sheriff, that it's not your call? I've been given a job to do. I'm doing it the best way I know how."

"Then you should be ashamed."

Romo came a step closer, his red face a striking contrast to his black suit. "I suggest you watch your mouth. You're a guest in my command center. I welcome your support. But if you try and interfere with this operation, there will be severe consequences coming from powerful people way above my pay grade."

CHAPTER 16

Virgil drove back to town, mad at himself for letting Romo push his buttons, but not a bit sorry for shaming him for misleading Hawk. The kid deserved to understand the extent of the risk he was taking before he made the choice. And Romo knew a lot more than he was letting on.

Virgil's burner phone beeped. He pulled into a medical plaza and parked in the back row under a shade tree.

He read the text message: *Four attachments.*

Virgil clicked on a photo and tapped the screen to enlarge it. It was a picture of a forty-something man and a young girl, perhaps fifteen or sixteen years old. The man was nice looking. Reminded him of the Ivy League type. Dark hair, just a tad long, dark suit, and glasses. The young girl was beautiful. Her dark hair covered her shoulders, her eyes were soft and innocent.

He clicked on the document and made it larger. It was something from Tehran, dated August 16, 2011. Probably written in Farsi. He scrolled to the bottom and saw the English translation. Some of the words had been redacted. Virgil scanned the document until he found something that made sense and didn't have any text blacked out. It appeared to be taken from a news article.

Renowned nuclear physicist Dr. Dalir Parviz Kermani (46) and daughter Abrisham Kermani (16) were special guests at a banquet held Saturday night at Tehran's elegant Parsian Esteghlal Hotel, honoring Kermani's twenty years of service to the Iranian government and his recent promotion to a top-level position in the nuclear program.

Dr. Kermani has a master's degree from Massachusetts Institute of Technology in Cambridge, Massachusetts, USA, and a PhD in nuclear physics from the University of Manchester, Manchester, UK. His vast knowledge of nuclear physics has made him a leader in the research and development of nuclear power plants in Iran.

Carolyn Morrison Kermani, Dr. Kermani's late wife, was killed tragically in an automobile accident in February of this year while visiting relatives in Cambridge, Massachusetts, USA.

Dr. Kermani's new position will require traveling extensively for the Iranian government as part of his involvement in advancing the use of nuclear power in Iran. His daughter Abrisham will continue her education at the Baumar International Girls School in Cambridge, Massachusetts, USA.

Virgil looked at the picture again. If this was supposed to be Dr. Kermani, he didn't look Middle Eastern.

Virgil googled "images of Iranian men," and a screen came up showing dozens of images. None of their features resembled Dr. Kermani. Virgil remembered that Iranians are primarily of Persian descent. He googled "images of Persian men." Some of them were fair skinned.

Some had lighter hair. Many could be mistaken for Westerners. Dr. Kermani easily could. Virgil looked at the daughter. She was stunning. But he didn't see any distinguishing ethnic feature. She could easily pass for a Westerner too. Then again, her mother was American.

So who were they? He tried to put seven years on the man, but no one came to mind. He put seven years on the daughter, but all he got was a twenty-three-year-old beauty. Ah, the age Kennedy Taylor claimed to be! Hawk had talked about how gorgeous she was. Could this be her?

He clicked on the third attachment. It appeared to be a bounty posting of some kind. The wording was French. He scrolled to the bottom for the translation. It was a classified document of the United States government, posted March 2017. Parts of it had been redacted. From what he could tell, someone was offering a $500,000 bounty for the arrest and/or return of Herbod Abbas Jalili, age thirty-nine, citizen of Iran and hired assassin working for the government of Iran and possibly others. Last known residence, Paris, France. Believed responsible for the assassinations of at least thirty government officials and family members across Europe and the Middle East. The contact name and information had been redacted.

He clicked on the fourth attachment, another photograph. A man about forty, dark hair, dark eyes, looked Middle Eastern. So was this guy Herbod Abbas Jalili the bounty hunter Romo told them about? The post referred to him as an assassin. With a bounty on his own head.

Virgil keyed in Mitch's number and let it ring. Maybe a little explanation from Mitch would clear things up.

"Hey. Where are you?" Mitch said, his voice barely above a whisper.

"In my squad car. I was coming back from the FBI command center when I heard your text come in. I'm sitting here in a medical plaza parking lot, looking at the four attachments you sent, not sure if I'm right about who these people are. Can you talk?"

"For a couple minutes," Mitch said. "Tell me what you're thinking."

"I'm thinking the first picture is of Dr. Kermani and his daughter Abrisham—goes with the article. Am I close?"

"Spot on."

"I'm still trying to make sense of the bounty document and the second photograph. Romo said the Bureau is after the bounty hunter who is tracking Nameless, aka Kennedy Taylor, now positively identified as Abrisham Kermani."

"That's right."

"But this document puts a bounty on an Iranian assassin," Virgil said. "What am I missing?"

"Just that Romo's reference to him as the bounty hunter sounds better than calling him an assassin, which would probably make Hawk think twice about getting involved. Look, I couldn't send you everything I saw, but our intel from the CIA confirms this Jalili is on a mission for the Iranian government, who offered him five million dollars to take out someone."

"Abrisham?"

"That's my guess," Mitch said.

"Why would they want to kill her? Man, this thing's making my head spin."

"Okay, here's my two cents. I'm going to give it to you straight, and after this you're on your own. It's too risky for me to dig any further."

"Okay, go," Virgil said.

"This is only my theory. All right, say Dr. Kermani meets Carolyn Morrison, an American woman, while he's going to school at MIT, and eventually marries her. They leave Cambridge and move to Tehran, and he works for the government's nuclear power plant program. In 1994, they have a daughter, Abrisham. He continues working in research and development of nuclear power plants. But did you notice when Carolyn Morrison had her tragic accident? In February of 2011. In August of 2011, Dr. Kermani was honored for his twenty years of service to the Iranian government and his new *top-level* position in their nuclear program."

"Are you saying they killed his wife to force him to get more deeply involved in the nuclear program?"

"Makes sense."

"But why are they after his daughter?" Virgil said. "If he's doing what they want?"

"Maybe he isn't. If I were Dr. Kermani," Mitch said, "and hated the Iranian government for killing my wife and forcing me to build a nuclear bomb, especially if I found it to be morally repugnant, I would turn in a heartbeat—and work with the US to stop Iran. He's in a perfect position to work as a double agent. What better way for him to get back at the Iranian government. My guess is that Dr. Kermani got caught giving the US classified information on Iran's nuclear program and went into hiding. He would've contacted the CIA and told them he'd been compromised and feared for his daughter's life. They would have enlisted the FBI's help to pick up the daughter and keep her under the radar."

"Pick up the daughter?" Virgil said. "You're suggesting the *FBI* might have used a drone to knock her out, and then whisked her away without a trace?"

"It's not out of the realm of possibility."

"So, is she under the radar," Virgil said, "or is she dead, as Romo claims?"

"I can't answer that. But if she is dead, they would definitely want to keep it under wraps because our intel indicates the assassin Jalili, whose picture is the fourth attachment, is actively tracking her down, and on his way to find Hawk. This guy's wanted all over Europe and the Middle East. They're not going to let him slip through their fingers."

"No matter who they use to get him," Virgil said.

Mitch sighed. "Sorry, buddy. I know that's a lot to set on your shoulders when you don't have the authority to do anything about it. But at least now you know."

"Thanks, Mitch. I really had no right to ask you to divulge classified information."

"What classified information?"

Virgil smiled. "Yeah. Right."

"Don't be a stranger."

"I won't. Take care."

Virgil blew out a breath and rubbed his eyes. This was even more complicated than he'd imagined. No wonder Romo wanted him to back off. Hard to say what kind of pressure was being put on him to get this assassin. Still, it was wrong to lead Hawk to believe his safety was their utmost concern when actually it was their least.

CHAPTER 17

Hawk pulled off his cap and wiped the sweat from his forehead. The sun was directly above him, and his stomach was making gurgling sounds. He put his cap back on and looked down at Special Agent Gary Barron, who was down on his hands and knees, measuring a section of ground.

"You're really into this playacting," Hawk said.

Barron smiled. "I wanted to be a landscaper before I wanted to join the FBI. I love this stuff. I'm not exactly playacting. I'm really going to design a new landscaping project, just for the fun of it. How's that for playing the part?"

"If the FBI gave Oscars, I'd nominate you right now." Hawk noticed Abby motioning him from the door to Flutter's. "My sister's trying to get my attention. I'll be right back."

"Not so fast," Special Agent Ryan Ziegler said. "We don't want you that far from at least one of us until we have eyes on the bounty hunter. I'll come with you."

Hawk jogged over to Abby, Ziegler on his heels. "What's up?"

"Benson made lunch. You want to eat up here under the umbrella. Or out on the lawn?"

Hawk looked at Ziegler. "What do you think?"

"A landscaper would probably grab a bite and eat on the ground, under a shade tree."

Hawk looked at Abby. "That's what we'll do."

"Okay, I'll be right back," she said.

"Your sister's pretty," Ziegler said. "I've always loved auburn hair."

Hawk smiled. "Down boy. She's engaged."

"Of course she is." Ziegler rolled his eyes. "The good ones always are."

"So what do you do when you're not working?" Hawk said.

"I don't know. I'm never not working. I love this job."

Hawk laughed. "I hope you do because no woman is going to go for that setup."

"I know," Ziegler said. "Don't remind me."

"So what were you looking at while you were talking to me?" Hawk said.

"Nothing really. It's just a habit to observe my surroundings."

"Like what?" Hawk said.

"Oh, I noticed that guy sitting by himself at the umbrella table in the back of the deck. He wasn't having lunch, just something to drink."

"Maybe he was waiting on his order," Hawk said.

Ziegler grinned. "Then y'all better work on your customer service, because he's been there for fifty minutes. Don't worry, I notified the command center fifteen minutes go. They've got eyes on him. See that big oak tree straight ahead? I noticed a drone flying just a few feet above it while we were talking. No worries, it was ours. And see that boy in the red shorts standing on the pier? When the other kid was reeling in his fish, the kid in the red shorts stole something out of his back pocket and threw it in the water."

"Whoa, you're good. I would never have noticed any of that stuff," Hawk said.

"It's just something you learn."

Abby opened the door and came outside.

Hawk introduced her to Ziegler, and she handed them four sacks, three with lunches, the fourth with drinks.

"Benson said to enjoy." Abby lowered her voice. "Nice to meet you, Special Agent Ziegler."

Ziegler watched her turn and walk inside. He shook his head. "Yeah, the good ones are always spoken for."

Hawk turned around and started walking back to where Barron was happily working on Angel View's phony landscaping project. "I wonder how long we have to keep up this ruse before we identify the bounty hunter?"

"No way to know. Our intel says he's either headed this way or already here. Now it's just a waiting game."

Kate watered the flowers that lined the front porch, then went up the steps and collapsed on the porch swing. She took off her straw hat and fanned herself with it, which seemed to excite the four ruby-throated hummingbirds that were battling over control of the feeder Elliot had hung.

Elliot came outside with a big glass of lemonade. "I've got two straws. Want to share?"

"Oh, I'd love some."

He sat holding the glass, and Kate drank down her half in a few gulps.

"Well, look at you," Elliot said. "And here I thought we would have a romantic moment of sipping lemonade together."

Kate laughed. "I'd almost forgotten how hot the summer sun can be."

Elliot took a sip and handed Kate the glass. "Here. You need it more than I do. I can always go and get a refill."

Kate drank and drank, then looked up at him, feeling sheepish. "I did leave a few sips for you."

He smiled. "I see that." He slipped his arm around her. "There. Now I think we look natural enough, in case we're being watched."

"I really appreciated Clarissa and Natalie insisting we call them by their first names," Kate said. "Makes them feel like part of us— well, sort of. You know what I mean."

Elliot nodded. "I also appreciated being able to listen to the interaction between special agents at the command center and those working in the field. Though I must admit it does all sound the same after a while when all you get is audio."

Kate looked up at him. "It was thoughtful of Abby to call and tell us that Hawk and the two FBI actors look very authentic working outdoors. And that they've been laughing and talking and really looking the part."

"I'm surprised they let her call us," Elliot said. "Someone could've overheard the conversation."

"Didn't you hear her say she was locked in the bathroom and talking barely above a whisper?"

"I missed that part. I couldn't hear her." Elliot laughed. "You know, a very natural thing for *us* to do would be to walk over to the lodge and see what the landscapers are doing."

"You're right. It would look very unnatural if we didn't at least make an appearance."

"Why don't I go find Clarissa and see what she thinks about it?" Elliot said.

"Thinks about what?" Clarissa's voice came from the doorway.

"Honestly," Kate said. "I think you could hear a fly crawl up a wall."

"That's why I get the big bucks." Clarissa stood in the doorway behind the screen door. "Talk fast, your air conditioning is pouring outside."

"We were just thinking that, in keeping with acting relaxed and natural," Elliot said, "that we should walk over to the lodge and see what our landscapers are doing and take a few minutes to mingle with the guests. Is that allowed?"

"Sure," Clarissa said. "Since it's light outside and the two of you will stay together, there's no need for me to leave the house and walk you over. I'll call the command center and let them know. They'll have you in their sights. Just remember what to say if you're asked about the landscaping project. You'll need to seem natural while telling a fib for the greater good."

Kate chuckled. "I don't remember anyone ever insisting that I fib."

"Well, just remember, girlfriend," Clarissa said. "That little Pinocchio you tell could be important to the success of this mission. All the details need to fit. Our bounty hunter isn't going to show himself until he feels sure that things are normal and no one here suspects anything."

"How sure are you that the FBI will get him?" Elliot said. "Seems like such a long shot."

"Oh, we'll get him. Failure is not an option."

Kate and Elliot walked into the office at Angel View Lodge, and Savannah Surette lifted her eyes and smiled.

"Well, there you are," Savannah said. "I saw you outside talking with the landscapers. When are you going to let me see the plans on this new landscaping project you've been keeping a secret?"

"We haven't seen any plans yet," Kate said. "But this isn't a secret. We just hadn't planned to do this for a while, and then the landscapers had a cancellation. Sorry we didn't tell you, but we thought we had plenty of time."

"Aw, that's okay," Savannah said. "It's not as though you two haven't had lots to think about since you tied the knot."

You have no idea, Kate thought.

"I suppose we have been preoccupied with each other at times." Elliot pulled Kate closer and smiled. "But it's time we set our sights on Angel View and make some improvements that have been needed for a while. We're as eager to see what our landscapers come up with as you are."

"I *was* surprised you pulled Hawk off the Jeep tours," Savannah said. "We get so many signed up now that we can hardly keep up with it."

"Connor can handle it," Elliot said. "He actually offered to work double shifts to make extra money. And, if we need to, we can hire someone to help him. But Hawk knows these grounds better than anyone, and he's the best choice to oversee the project, which includes a whole new grounds crew, don't forget. They'll need to be trained."

Kate hoped Elliot wasn't overdoing his acting role.

"Yes, I can see your point," Savannah said.

Kate squeezed Elliot's hand. "Well, don't let us keep you. We just walked over to see how things were going."

"Glad you did. From my perspective, things are going just fine. All our rooms are filled. All the boats are out. There's a crowd down fishing off the dock. Another crowd swimming at the pool. And most everyone I meet has a big smile on their face."

"I love hearing that," Kate said. "You're doing a terrific job of running things."

"Then you'll be glad to know that, just today alone, we sold a dozen sets of your cookbook and pasta sauce. You're going to need to can some more sauce before the summer's over or we won't have any for the Christmas season."

Kate held up her palm. "I hear you. I promise to get with it as soon as I can get fresh tomatoes. It'll be fun turning my kitchen into a canning factory for a weekend. Abby said she'd love to help."

"And just so you know," Savannah said, "Jesse was a huge hit showing the guests how to let the hummingbirds light on their fingers. We sold out of feeders, and I won't let that happen again. I'm getting another shipment brought up here from Murchison's in the morning. We're also selling so many hummingbird wind chimes and stained glass I'll need to reorder those too. I'm telling you, that gift shop is hopping, and it's only June 8. At this rate, it's going to be a banner summer."

Virgil sat in his office, his feet on his desk, his hands clasped behind his head, his mind toggling between the information Mitch had gotten for him and his distasteful confrontation with Romo.

There was a knock at the door.

"Come in," Virgil said.

Kevin Mann came in and sat in the chair next to Virgil's desk. "Dare I ask if you're feeling any better after your uncomfortable encounter with our arrogant special agent in charge?"

"Can't say that I am," Virgil said. "Usually I can blow off this kind of thing, but not when it's the principle of it that sticks in my craw. Romo intentionally led Hawk to believe the FBI will protect him, no matter what. We both know that's not true. The FBI's primary objective is to bring in the bounty hunter unharmed. Hawk has the right to understand that their objective will come before his safety, if they have to choose between the two. Romo isn't telling him that, and I can't say a word."

"It is what it is, Sheriff. As maddening as it may be, your hands are tied."

Are they? Virgil mused. "It's Romo's case, and I need to stay out of his way. But that sure doesn't mean I have to play dead."

Kevin leaned forward on his elbows, his hands clasped together. "What are you saying?"

"Oh, nothing. I'm just frustrated at being out of control. I'm sure Romo's not telling me everything either."

"Have you ever worked with a fed who did?"

"Not in a long time," Virgil said. "But I've always found a way to deal with it. Romo just rubs me the wrong way. I'll find a way to work around it." *Thanks to Mitch.*

CHAPTER 18

Special Agent Christopher Romo sat on a bale of hay outside the FBI mobile command center, using his iPhone to FaceTime with his five-year-old son.

"I painted you a picture at my school today," Timothy said, his bright blue eyes the size of nickels. "It was a big, *big* fire twuck with a loud siren and four firefighters holding on the sides. It was going really fast. And the childwen were all waving."

"Be sure to save it for me so I can look at it when I get home," Romo said. "We can frame it for your special picture wall in my study."

"I will. Oh, I get to go fishing in Mister Tyler's pond. Mama said I could if I cweaned my room by myself. And I did. Yay!" Timothy clapped.

"I'm proud of you for helping your mother," Romo said.

"When are you coming home, Daddy? I like it better when you're not gone."

"I miss you too. I just need a couple more days to finish here. Then I'll be home."

Timothy's eyes narrowed. "How much is a couple more?"

Romo held up two fingers. "Listen, buddy, Daddy's got to go. Remember to leave the porch light on so the angels can see to come watch over you and Mommy."

"Okay. Luff you, Daddy."

"I love you too, Son."

Romo disconnected. Anytime he interacted with Timothy, the world seemed so simple, so full of adventure and promise. Out here, he had to put on a different mind-set—one that sometimes conflicted with his own values and made it hard to sleep at night.

The sheriff's words still burned on his conscience: *"And you don't think you were being disingenuous by letting Hawk believe the two of you were on the same page?"*

Romo stood. He didn't have to answer that question. The important thing was he did what was necessary.

His phone rang. It was his boss in Little Rock.

"Hello, Marcus."

"I see you're fully operational," Marcus said.

"Yes, we're set up on a vacant farm, just a few miles from Foggy Ridge. It's ideal."

"And how do you like the features of the new command center?"

"What's not to like?" Romo said. "All I can say is, above and beyond. We've got eyes on all the common areas of the lodge, indoors and out. The facial recognition feature is ready and waiting."

"Is the Cummings family on board?"

"They are, sir. Everything's going like clockwork. Our actors are in place, and everything's copacetic."

"Great to hear. Now *get* Jalili without harming a hair on his head."

"We will."

"Christopher, I don't have to tell you how important this assignment is. The CIA is breathing down the deputy director's neck, and his office is all over me. We've been told we can't fail on this one. Do you understand what I'm saying?"

"Of course I do. Don't worry. Jalili has to get to Hawk Cummings if he hopes to find Nameless. And Cummings is totally on board to help us draw him out in the open. If Jalili shows up, we've got him. We won't fail."

"And once Jalili is in custody, are you ready to make the video?"

"Everything's set. Special Agent Nadia Vaughn from the Milwaukee Field Office was selected. She's being briefed as we speak."

❧

Virgil sat in his office, the frustrations of the day making him not want to go home yet, lest he spoil Jill Beth's mood. She'd sounded so cheery on the phone and was so eager to serve him the pot roast she had slow cooked all afternoon with carrots, celery, onions, and potatoes. His mouth watered just thinking about it. But he needed to claw his way out of this irritable mood first.

For the past eight years—since Micah and Riley Cummings disappeared without a trace—Virgil had been in a position to help and to comfort the Cummings family through tragedies and near tragedies. When Micah's body was found in a shallow grave, after five years of hoping he'd be found alive. When Abby spotted a girl that looked like Riley and, against all odds, convinced Jay to help her find the child—and they were nearly killed freeing Riley from her kidnapper. When Jesse was the sole eyewitness in a drowning and the murderer tried to silence him. Virgil had grown close to Kate and her kids. Having his hands tied now was not only maddening but humiliating. And deeply personal.

A knock at the door broke his concentration. He looked up and saw Deputy Duncan at his door. "Come in, Billy Gene. What's on your mind?"

Billy Gene came in and sat in one of the chairs next to Virgil's desk.

"I've got plans for some vacation time," Billy Gene said, "but now I'm not sure about it."

"Did you talk with Kevin?"

"He did." Kevin breezed through the door, pulled up a chair, and sat next to Billy Gene. "And I told him we should talk to you."

Virgil sat back, his arms folded across his chest. "I'm listening."

"Well, you see," Billy Gene said, "I've got a reservation to stay up at Angel View for three days and do some fishin'. I'm supposed to check in this evening."

Virgil raised an eyebrow. "Oh? I wasn't aware."

"My fault," Kevin said. "I failed to add his name to the vacation roster, but I've corrected that now."

Virgil felt the corners of his mouth twitching. "I see."

"I don't think Billy Gene should postpone this vacation," Kevin said. "He's been putting in long hours and still finding the time to go to the shooting range."

"I always strive to keep my skill level up to par." Billy Gene grinned, exposing a gold tooth. "I still hold the record for the most bull's-eyes."

"The nice part about Billy Gene getting away like this," Kevin said, "is that he doesn't eat at Flutter's, so other than the Cummings family, it's unlikely anyone will know him. It's the perfect place for him to relax without spending time and money on traveling out of town."

"I agree it's a well-earned vacation," Virgil said, tongue in cheek. "What are you going to fish for?"

Billy Gene's grin got wider. "Never can tell what might be bitin'. I plan to keep my eye on the line at all times."

"And you'll let me know how the fishing is going?" Virgil said.

"You bet I will, sir. You'll be the first to hear."

"Well, then," Virgil said, rising to his feet, "I guess it's settled." He shook hands with Billy Gene and winked. "Use your time wisely, Deputy. A vacation's a terrible thing to waste."

"Yes, sir."

Billy Gene left, and Virgil and Kevin couldn't contain their smiles.

"You're shameless," Virgil said.

"Just thinking of you, Sheriff. It's not right what Romo's doing."

"This could come back to bite all three of us. I assume Billy Gene knows that?"

"He does," Kevin said. "We talked it over. And we seriously doubt the FBI would want the public to know how they misled a good kid like Hawk Cummings into helping them."

"And you didn't do this because he's Kate's kid?" Virgil said.

"No, sir. What they're doing is wrong, no matter whose kid it is. But that made it easy for Billy Gene and I to put our necks on the block with yours."

Virgil swallowed the lump in his throat and patted Kevin on the back. "Thanks. That means a lot."

❧

Hawk turned around at the back steps of the family's log home and waved to Special Agents Ziegler and Barron, who stood at the end of the path where they could remain hidden while keeping an eye on him. He walked up the steps to the cedar deck and opened the back door to the living room.

"Hey, Hawk!" Elliot put down the newspaper. "Welcome home."

Kate came out of the kitchen, drying her hands with a towel. She put her arms around him, her eyes sparkling. "Oh my! You made it for dinner."

Jesse darted out of the kitchen, Abby, Jay, and Grandpa Buck right behind him.

Hawk couldn't remember the last time he'd been covered with so many hugs and kisses. "Good heavens. If I didn't know Mama was making Swiss steak, I'd think we were having the fatted calf. It's just me, people. In serious need of a shower, as I'm sure you've all just discovered."

"We're just glad you're home, boy." Grandpa patted Hawk's soggy shoulder.

"We listened to the FBI chatter on Natalie's phone," Elliot said. "It helped to pass the time, but we're sure glad you're home safe and sound."

"I wanted to rush over and give you a hug when we came by and pretended to meet the landscapers," Kate said, "but I was afraid that wouldn't seem natural."

"Do you think?" Hawk laughed. "Ziegler and Barron would've never let me live it down."

Elliot winked. "Not to mention all those guys watching from the command center."

"It's worth mentioning here," Kate said, "that not only did Hawk pull it off, but Abby and Jesse did a superior job of acting natural so that this seemed like any other day at Angel View. Well done, one and all."

Jesse took a bow, then grabbed Hawk by the arm. "Come on, big brother. You smell as bad as I do. We need to get cleaned up for dinner or they'll mistake us for the hogs and throw us scraps."

Natalie Sloan shook her head. "You are one fun, kooky family, that's all I've got to say."

Kate laughed. "Stay tuned. It can get worse."

"Are Natalie and Clarissa going to join us for dinner?" Jesse said.

"The command center has surveillance of the exterior of the house," Natalie said. "I'm sure we can safely sit down and enjoy dinner together."

"Natalie, do you want Wolf in or out?" Jay said, his German shepherd sitting at his side. "I'll be sleeping on the couch."

"Does he bark at every rabbit and mouse?" Natalie said.

"No, ma'am. He's used to all that. If he barks, it'd be a good idea to pay attention."

Natalie laughed. "Welcome aboard, Wolf. Looks like you'll be sleeping in tonight."

After dinner, while the others were out in the kitchen playing gin rummy, Kate and Elliot pulled Hawk into their room and closed the door. Hawk sat on the side of the bed.

"Virgil called before you got home tonight and wanted us to tell you something," Kate said. "This is just for us to know, not Natalie or Clarissa, or anyone else."

Hawk looked surprised. "Okay. What did he say?"

"That Romo is really running the show," Elliot said. "Virgil feels like a bystander. Romo's not using any of Virgil's deputies to assist in the operation."

"I thought Romo and Sheriff Granger were working together."

"So did Virgil," Elliot said. "But it's not working out that way. Romo's authority trumps Virgil's, and he wants his own people to be the actors, and I guess everything else too. What Virgil wants us to know is that Deputy Billy Gene Duncan is taking a few days of his vacation up here. And even though he's a guest, he will be observing what's going on."

"Why the secrecy?"

"Well," Elliot said, "except for our family, no one in the FBI or on the guest roster will recognize him. He just doesn't want you to blow his cover. He's not going to do anything but keep Virgil apprised of things. But he can't be having you, Abby, Jay, Jesse, or Buck speaking to him and addressing him as Deputy Duncan. I guess you could say that since he wasn't invited up here by the FBI, he's here undercover."

"Oh," Hawk said, "I get it. So I should just ignore him?"

Elliot arched his eyebrows. "I think you have to. Otherwise, Romo will be curious who it is you're talking to or waving at and have the surveillance cameras zero in on him. He just wants to blend in like any other guest at Angel View. Virgil said it would be a favor to him and make him feel a whole lot better, just knowing Billy Gene was up here keeping an eye on things. You know we're family to Virgil. Being shut out of this case is really tough."

Kate nodded. "Virgil has been there for us through everything in the past eight years. Sitting this one out is torture for him."

"Yeah, I'm sure it is," Hawk said. "Okay, I can pretend I don't see Deputy Duncan as long as he knows I'm not being rude by ignoring him."

"Believe me, he knows," Elliot said. "That's exactly what he wants."

"What about Abby, Jay, Jesse, and Grandpa?"

Elliot looked at Kate. "We told them Deputy Duncan was there on vacation and did not want to be pulled into the case, so should they see him, to just ignore him and not talk to him. They all agreed. You're the only one we told about Virgil's conversation."

"No worries," Hawk said. "I won't say anything. And if I see Deputy Duncan, I'll pretend I don't. But there's a part of me that's uncomfortable with the sheriff being at odds with Romo. Part of the reason I trusted Romo was because the sheriff seemed to."

Elliot patted Hawk's knee. "Virgil never said he didn't trust Romo—just that Romo likes to be in control. Probably if we let him, he'll do a fine job, and this will be over soon. Just go back out there and do what you did today. If the bounty hunter is at Angel View, Romo's team ought to be able to spot him in the crowd before long."

"I'm nervous about the guy making a move," Hawk said, "especially when I don't really know what that will look like."

Elliot smiled. "That's why you're surrounded by FBI actors, Hawk. But remember, you've got God with you. He'll work *His* plan. And that's the one that counts."

"You're right. No point in worrying."

"Did Special Agents Ziegler and Barron say anything about putting a mike in your ear tomorrow?" Elliot said. "I thought I heard someone at the command center talking about it on the radio."

Hawk nodded. "They did, actually. I guess that's the plan. When the time comes, I hope I can do what they're counting on me to do. And not freeze."

Elliot pulled Hawk to his feet. "I have every confidence you will. Not in your own strength, but in His. We'd better get back out there or Natalie and Clarissa will come looking for us."

Hawk sat in the kitchen by himself after everyone in the family had gone to bed. Everyone except Abby and Jay. Hawk pretended to be reading the newspaper but stole a few well-spaced glances at the two lovebirds sitting together on the couch. Even their kisses seemed so innocent. He thought of Laura Lynn and what he had thrown away. He hoped that Jay would make smarter choices than he had, and that Abby and Jay would be true to their commitment to save themselves for marriage.

So why couldn't he stop thinking about Kennedy? He wished he'd had a chance to say good-bye. He wished he could ask her forgiveness for not telling her that he was in a serious relationship. They had never talked about God. What they believed. Whether they thought what they were doing was right or wrong. Their relationship had begun in a sweeping flood of passion. They just allowed themselves to be carried downstream, never stopping to assess the damage. And then she was taken and he was left behind with scores of unanswered questions he would take to his grave. He felt a wave of sadness come over him, and he willed it away. He couldn't allow himself to grieve right now or he would never be able to help the FBI catch the man who would have killed Kennedy, had he gotten to her first. Hawk just wished he knew who had.

Lord, what's wrong with me? I know my relationship with her was all wrong. What we shared, You ordained for marriage, not something to be enjoyed lightly and without a lasting commitment. But is it wrong that I should grieve her passing? She was a lovely person and I miss her. I've never felt closer to anyone in my life. I wish I understood why. I guess not understanding is another consequence.

He watched as Jay and Abby kissed good night, and then as Abby got up and slowly, reluctantly, let go of Jay's hand. She walked down the hall to her bedroom, and Jay curled up on the couch and spread an afghan over himself.

Nicely done, Hawk thought.

"I didn't know you were still up," Clarissa said in a hushed voice. "I was just going to brew a pot of coffee and make some notes on my laptop. The kitchen table is about the only place I can do it while everyone's asleep."

"No worries," Hawk said. "I'm finished reading. I'm headed for bed."

"You okay? You look concerned."

"I'm fine," Hawk said. "I was just thinking about Kennedy Tay— Nameless. I'm sad she's dead. I never had the chance to say good-bye."

"I'm sorry. You've been through a lot. The Bureau owes you a debt of gratitude for helping us to get the bounty hunter. It'll be over soon, and you can get back to real life."

Whatever that is. I'm not even sure anymore. "I hope you're right. Good night, Clarissa."

"Good night."

CHAPTER 19

Deputy Billy Gene Duncan stood staring at himself in the bathroom mirror in his room at the Angel View Lodge. He decided he might look more like he was on vacation if he skipped shaving this morning. He took his razor and trimmed his stubble until it looked more like a five o'clock shadow. He smiled. Not exactly Tom Cruise, but cool looking nonetheless.

He put on a pair of denim cargo shorts and a white T-shirt. Then he took a tiny Bluetooth earpiece out of its case and pushed it all the way into his ear. After putting on the neck loop transmitter and syncing it to his cell phone, Billy Gene threw on a short-sleeve plaid shirt and buttoned it, completely hiding the transmitter.

He put the SOS button in his right shoe and laced his white Nikes. He added a red-and-gray Razorbacks cap. A pair of shades. *Black Hawk Down* in paperback—and voilà! Instant tourist. He laughed. He never read novels, but he'd seen the movie a dozen times and could easily talk about it, if asked what he was reading.

When he heard a knock at his door, he checked his watch. Seven o'clock straight up. "Who is it?"

"Room service."

Billy Gene took off his sunglasses and cap, looked through the peephole, then let the young man into the room. He set the tray on the desk.

Billy Gene signed the ticket and included the tip. "Thank you kindly. When y'all said thirty minutes, you were right on the money."

"We try. Thank you, sir."

The young man left, and Billy Gene sat down and instantly began to devour three eggs over easy, three strips of bacon, grits, hash browns, an English muffin, orange juice, and black coffee. He had just stuffed the last bite of the English muffin into his mouth when his cell phone rang. He took a gulp of coffee, then answered the call.

"Hey, boss. I'm synced and ready. You should be in."

"Yes, I hear you loud and clear," Virgil said. "Can you hear me through your earpiece?"

"Yes, sir. Like you were standin' right here."

"Would you try your silent SOS button and see if it's working?"

Billy Gene pushed the foot device two times, signaling a yes.

"Perfect," Virgil said. "So how's it going so far?"

"I haven't been out in the light yet, but just now finished a he-man's breakfast in my room, and was going to go outside and look around. I know this property pretty well, but I'll be lookin' with different eyes."

"Good plan," Virgil said. "Just remember that the command center has surveillance on almost every inch of the common areas outside, as well as the gift shop and Flutter's. I'm going to bite the bullet and go apologize to Romo, and pretend to be a part of things. Tell me what you're wearing so I'll be able to spot you on the surveillance cameras."

Billy Gene described his attire. "Oh, and I'm sporting one of those Tom Cruise five o'clock shadows. Makes me look cool. The feds aren't the only ones with actors."

Virgil chuckled. "Okay, Mr. Cool. Keep your earpiece in and your eyes on Hawk Cummings. I'll be in touch."

"Will do."

⚜

Virgil pulled up to the barn on Pete Jameson's farm and turned off the motor. He would make himself apologize because he had taken an oath to protect the people of Raleigh County, and that's what he planned to do, whatever it took. Once he cleared the air with Romo, no one would think twice about him standing around watching the FBI's surveillance cameras. Thanks to Mitch, and despite Romo, he now knew what the bounty hunter looked like. Though Virgil's burner phone was in the back of a trash truck on the way to the landfill, Jalili's face was clear in his mind. If he could spot him before Romo's people did, maybe he could think of a way to use Billy Gene instead of Hawk to draw him out in the open.

Virgil got out of the car and went up the steps to the front door of the command center and stepped inside. Special agents were walking all directions, but he instantly spotted Romo sitting at one of the computers.

Moving over to the side where he wouldn't be in anyone's way, Virgil looked up at the surveillance monitors. On the top-left screen, he saw Abby in Flutter's carrying a tray with breakfast orders. The next screen showed Savannah's car parked outside the lodge office, the "open" sign lit in the office window. The monitor on the upper right showed the drone moving slowly above one side of Kate's log house. Another on the bottom left had a view of the gazebo and the back lawn of the lodge. The next screen showed two couples with children come out of the back exit of the lodge and walk into Flutter's. On the bottom-right monitor, Virgil saw Jesse entering the hummingbird garden, pulling a red wagon loaded with tall bottles—probably nectar to refill the feeders. Looked like the beginning of a typical day at Angel View.

Virgil glanced over at Romo, who was on his feet, walking in Virgil's direction.

Here goes. Virgil set his phone so Billy Gene could hear and put it in his shirt pocket.

"Well, hello, Sheriff," Romo said. "I'm surprised to see you."

"I owe you an apology," Virgil said, trying to look sheepish. "I had no right to judge you. You're the one in charge of this operation, and I'd really like to lend my support. Can we start over? I promise to keep my two cents to myself."

Romo held out his hand and shook Virgil's. "Of course we can start over. Yesterday's history."

"Anything new I should know about?" Virgil said.

"Our intel is ninety-nine percent sure the bounty hunter is already here. Before Hawk arrives this morning, one of our agents staying at the house will have fitted him with an invisible earpiece and wire so we can hear everything he's saying. We will be watching facial expressions and movements of all the men we see on the surveillance monitors, and especially the men who are in closest proximity to Hawk."

"Too bad you don't know what this bounty hunter looks like," Virgil said, knowing full well that Romo did know.

"Yes, but don't forget we have the facial recognition turned on, and if he's in the system, we've got him."

"Unless he's disguised himself," Virgil said.

Romo's face looked blank. "I doubt that. He has no reason to think anyone here knows he's coming."

"You're probably right," Virgil said. "I tend to play it safe and plan for the worst."

Romo pointed to the surveillance screens. "Connor Richardson just pulled up with Hawk."

Virgil pretended his phone vibrated. "Excuse me, I need to take this."

He walked away from Romo, his phone to his ear. "Are you hearing all this?" Virgil said to Billy Gene.

"Oh, yes, sir. Most of it, anyway."

"Where are you now?"

"I'm down at the pier, lookin' up the hill at Flutter's. I see Richardson's burgundy truck. Looks like Hawk just got out and is walkin' over to the landscapers."

"Right. And both landscapers are FBI actors," Virgil said.

"Copy that."

"If you go into Flutter's, two male customers are FBI actors. And so is the busboy."

"Good to know," Billy Gene said.

"And all of the grounds crew are FBI actors as well."

"They've got a bunch of folks out here," Billy Gene said. "Guess I just better act like a tourist and don't pay them any mind."

"That's the plan. They've got Hawk fitted with a setup much like yours so they can hear what's going on around him."

"Did I hear Romo correctly, that the bounty hunter is here?" Billy Gene said.

"Yes. And I think they know what he looks like but aren't telling me."

"Why would they do that?"

"I wish I knew," Virgil said. "But it's pretty obvious they're shutting us out of this operation … Billy Gene, you do know if they figure out what we're doing, it'll be our careers, right?"

"Yes, sir. But they won't. I'm going to sniff out the bounty hunter and lead him right under their uppity FBI noses. Hawk will never be in danger."

"I like your attitude," Virgil said. "Let's hope you're right."

Hawk walked over to where Ziegler and Barron were standing.

"Good morning, Hawk," Ziegler said. "I understand you're feeling wired this morning."

Hawk laughed. "You could say that."

"That's it, smile. You're live," Barron said. "Why don't we head down to the gazebo to start out? Special Agent Romo wants you to move around the grounds today and pretend to work with the grounds crew. There are special agents that will move with you, but without being conspicuous. If the bounty hunter is here, and our intel says he is, he might decide to make his move. That's what we want."

"Okay," Hawk said. "Can you explain what you anticipate *his move* might look like?"

Barron nodded. "If you're by yourself where he has some breathing room, we expect he'll start to slowly close in. The special agents in the command center will have him spotted on surveillance monitors and tell you where he is and what he's doing, and any moves you need to make. You'll hear everything. You need to trust us without questioning. You may have just seconds to respond. Understand?"

Hawk nodded, his stomach feeling as if a small army were marching across it in spiked shoes.

Ziegler put his hand on Hawk's shoulder. "In other words, if command says to walk ten feet and stop, you do it. If they say turn left and walk over to Flutter's, do it. As long as they're in control of what you do, they can protect you. Don't surprise them."

"All right," Hawk said. "I'm a robot."

"Hawk, this is Special Agent Romo in the command center. You're coming in loud and clear, and we've got you on visual. I don't want you to worry about a thing. Remember, the bounty hunter's not going to harm you while you're out in public. His goal is to get you alone where he can question you. We're not going to let that happen. That's why it's so important that you trust and obey our commands. And look natural."

"I understand, sir." Hawk shuddered. This whole thing was downright creepy. His eyes scanned the back lawn at Angel View. He saw a few guests jogging. A man and woman and two kids heading for the pier. And an elderly couple walking their West Highland terrier.

"You ready to get to work?" Barron said.

Hawk nodded. "Sure. So what am I doing?"

"You're going to train your grounds crew," Ziegler said. "Do what you'd normally do if we weren't here. Just keep communicating with the command center so we're all on the same page."

Billy Gene stopped and made small talk with some of the guests, hoping that if the powers that be in the command center were watching, he'd look like a tourist.

"Billy Gene, are you there?"

"I am, Sheriff. Doesn't sound like there's much going on."

"No. Not yet," Virgil said. "I've seen you on the surveillance camera a couple times. No one here recognized you. Seen anybody out there worth a second look?"

"No, sir. Not really."

"Seen any men of Middle Eastern persuasion?"

"Hmm … now that you mention it, I just passed a guy standin' outside Flutter's talkin' on the phone who looked like he could've been a distant cousin to Saddam Hussein. Is that important?"

"I don't know," Virgil said. "Maybe."

"What're you thinkin', Sheriff?"

"Just that nobody here's telling me anything. So I'm looking for anyone that doesn't seem like a typical guest."

"This is a tourist place, Sheriff. How do we define typical? I've seen whites, blacks, Hispanics. Foreigners. Old folks. Little kids. And every age in between."

"All right," Virgil said. "I get your point. I'm just curious … did you happen to notice if the fella who was on the phone outside Flutter's was speaking English?"

"No, he definitely wasn't, but I'm sure it wasn't Arabic. It sounded more like French—you know, kinda nasally soundin'?"

Jalili's last known address was Paris! Virgil's pulse raced, but he kept his voice calm and steady. "Billy Gene, I need you to go see if the guy is still there. I'll stay on the line."

"Okay, I'm strollin' back to Flutter's like I'm in no hurry. I see him still on the phone."

"Good. Take a picture or two of something on the grounds. Be obvious about it, like you're a tourist. And then pass him by."

"I'm holdin' up my phone and taking a picture of the gazebo," Billy Gene said. "Now a picture of the lake. Very nice. Okay, I've turned around and am walkin' in his direction. I'm only about thirty feet away. Well shoot, if that don't beat all."

"What happened?"

"He smiled so I smiled back. I'll just keep walkin' past him and turn left so I'm out of his line of vision. Okay, he can't see me. Now what?"

"Keep him in your sights," Virgil said. "Be as invisible as you can, and don't let him make you. Let's see if he's watching Hawk."

"You got it, boss."

"I need to go. I'll leave this on so you can hear what's being said here."

"Copy that."

CHAPTER 20

Hawk gathered the FBI actors who were posing as grounds crew and showed them the flower beds that needed to be weeded and fed. All the places along the back lawn that needed to be trimmed and edged. And he showed them the toolshed where they kept the bags of lawn fertilizer and insect control.

Special Agent Barron peeked his head in the door. "Why don't we break for lunch? It's twelve straight up, and Abby said the chef made us Mexican food and would have it brought to us. We can sit in the shade and eat out here." Barron turned to Hawk. "Special Agent Romo wants you to start putting a little more space between you and us. You could start by going to check with your sister and letting her know we're ready when they are."

Hawk smiled. "I'll be right back." He didn't allow himself to think about being more vulnerable. He jogged up the back lawn to Flutter's and went inside.

Abby hurried over to him. "Is everything okay?"

"Fine," Hawk said. "I came to tell you that we're ready for lunch when you are."

"I'll go tell Benson. We'll bring it out to you."

Hawk nodded. "Thanks."

Abby turned around and walked toward the kitchen.

"Command center, are you there?" Hawk said.

"This is Special Agent Romo, Hawk. What do you need?"

"I'm inside Flutter's. I'm just wondering if it's okay to jog back to where the guys are."

"Actually, I'd like to see you *walk* back to where the guys are. Nice and deliberate, but not too fast. That way we can get our surveillance to show us the faces of the men in close proximity to see if anyone is watching you. Don't worry. You're not in danger. Just act normally."

Easy for you to say, Hawk thought. "Okay, sir. I'm on the move."

Hawk pushed open the door and waited until a couple with their three children squeezed past him, then went outside and walked toward the eight men sitting in the shade.

"Hawk stop *now*," Romo said, "and start looking through the grass like you dropped something. We just want to see what the people around you do."

Hawk did what he was told. He bent down and ran his hands through the grass, pretending to look for something. "Do you want me to pretend I found it too?"

"Sure, but keep searching for another minute or so," Romo said. "This is just an exercise to draw the bounty hunter out of the shadows and closer to you."

"Have you spotted him?" Hawk said.

"Not yet. But we will. Just keep doing what we say. It might take several times of doing things like this before he is comfortable enough to show himself."

Hawk kept looking through the grass for another half minute, and then snatched a rock and clutched it in his closed fist, adding a smile to go with his pretend victory. He got up and continued walking toward the guys. "Hey, I found my key," he shouted.

"Well done," Romo said. "Now go sit with them and enjoy your lunch."

Hawk dropped down in the grass, wondering if he looked as phony as he felt. "I don't think I'm going to win an Oscar for that performance."

"I'm not so sure," Barron said, giving him a hearty slap on the back. "You did great."

The others smiled and acted happy for him. He wasn't sure if they were showing their pretend gladness that he'd found his pretend lost key, or whether they were signaling their approval of his performance. It didn't really matter. All this pretending was giving him a headache.

Kate sat in the living room, knitting a pink-and-white afghan for a friend's baby shower, praying off and on for Hawk's safety and for the successful capture of the bounty hunter. Elliot and Buck had gone into town to get groceries. Abby and Jesse were still working at the lodge.

She listened to the *tick tock, tick tock* of the grandfather clock in the hallway. The house was eerie quiet—something she had rarely experienced as a mother of four very active children.

Natalie's shift had ended at noon, and she had gone to bed. Clarissa had insisted on doing laundry so Kate could have some time to herself.

But as she sat there alone in the quiet, Kate longed for the happy chaos of family gatherings. The good times when all four of her kids were seated around the dinner table, Abby with Jay, and Hawk with Laura Lynn. And her two youngest, Riley and Jesse, ever amusing— so innocent, yet wise beyond their years. The children's Grandpa Buck with his quiet wit and warm heart. And Elliot, the stabilizer. The other half of her heart.

Lord, thank You for all You've given me, and even for all You've taken. So many times in recent years, I wondered if I could ever move past the pain. Ever learn to trust You with those I hold so dear. And look how You've restored and healed this entire family. I trust You with Hawk's life. I pray You will protect him and bring him home safely again tonight. I praise You and thank You in Jesus's holy and precious name.

Kate looked up, startled by Clarissa's sudden presence.

"Don't make a sound," Clarissa whispered, her finger to her lips. She held her gun in her other hand and tiptoed ever so quietly over to the back door and slowly slid the bolt lock, then moved away from the glass door.

Kate sat still as stone but couldn't silence the pounding of her heart. And then she heard it—the sound of footsteps outside on the deck. The drapes were drawn to keep out the afternoon sun, but she could clearly see the silhouette of a man.

He tried opening the door. Then again. And again.

Natalie emerged from the hallway holding a Taser gun. What was going on?

Kate couldn't have moved if she'd wanted to. If this was the bounty hunter, she hoped they could stop him because they had orders not to harm him.

❦

Virgil stood behind the FBI special agents and watched the monitor as a man—short, medium build, a ski mask covering his face—stood on the back deck of Kate's house.

"Special Agent Sloan," Romo said, "get Mrs. Stafford out of there. Have her lock herself in the bathroom."

Sloan went over to Kate, pulled her to her feet, and quickly ushered her out of the room.

"Sheriff, are you there?" Billy Gene said.

Virgil turned and bent down to tie his shoe. "I can't talk now," he whispered. "There's a situation at Kate's."

"Sir, I think this guy is moving on Hawk. What do you want me to do?"

"Are you sure?"

"Sure as I *can* be."

"Then the man at Kate's must be a decoy. Stop him, Billy Gene. Don't hurt him. And don't blow your cover. Go!"

"Copy that."

Virgil stood and looked up at the monitor and saw Hawk, his arms folded across his chest, watching the FBI actors weeding the flower beds.

"Hawk!" Billy Gene shouted, waving his Razorbacks cap in the air. He walked over to Hawk, a big smile on his face. "Hey, buddy. Long time no see."

Virgil couldn't take his eyes off the monitors. Romo's people made no effort to stop Billy Gene. Then again, why would they blow their cover when they could clearly see he wasn't the bounty hunter?

"I'm *really* surprised to see you." Hawk's facial expression matched his dismay. "How have you been?"

"Good. Me and my bride moved up to Springfield, Missouri. I got a good job workin' for Bass Pro."

"Is that right?" Hawk said.

Special Agent Barron jogged over to where Hawk was standing. "Excuse me for interrupting, Hawk. I need your direction on how to proceed."

Billy Gene held out his hand. "I'm Kirby Stanfield, an old friend of Hawk's. I used to live in Foggy Ridge."

"Gary Barron. I'm doing a landscaping project for Angel View. Nice to meet you."

The two shook hands.

"I'll let you get back to work," Billy Gene said. "Hawk, next time you're in Springfield, call me. I'm in the book. Heather and I will have you over for dinner."

"I'd like that," Hawk said.

"Good to see you, man." Billy Gene slapped Hawk on the back and then walked up the back lawn toward Flutter's.

Virgil exhaled. *Amazing job, Billy Gene.* Virgil moved closer to the monitor where all the agents had gathered. One of the female agents was stealthily walking around the south side of Kate's house, a Taser gun in her hand.

The other female agent, gun drawn, moved down the north of the house.

"Sloan," Romo said, "he's gone down the deck steps and is headed toward the south side of the house. He's armed. Don't miss."

The agent inched her way to the end of the house and waited, her Taser gun pointed and ready.

Virgil's heart nearly pounded out of his chest. Maybe the guy Billy Gene was tailing was just a guest after all. None of this made sense.

All at once, Sloan bent her arm and buried her face, muffling a loud sneeze.

The intruder, a ski mask covering his face, stopped—then turned and took off running full bore toward the woods.

"Stand down. Do not pursue. Repeat: stand down!" Romo spit out an obscenity. "We were that close!"

"I'm sorry, sir," Sloan said. "I really tried to muffle the sneeze."

"Just get back in the house. He never saw you. At least your cover wasn't blown."

Virgil moved away from the monitors and agents all talking among themselves. "Did you hear all that?" he said softly.

"Most of it," Billy Gene said. "I'm confused. Why didn't the feds grab the guy I've been following when they had the chance? If I could tell he was closing in on Hawk, couldn't they?"

"I can't answer that. Hold on." Virgil stepped outside and pretended to be texting. He spoke under his breath. "About the only thing I'm sure of right now is the man you've been following isn't the bounty hunter or they'd have been all over him. Send a picture of him to my phone. Let me see what I can find out."

"So we're back to square one?"

"Looks like it," Virgil said. "I'll say one thing, what you did was ingenious. You stopped the guy. You protected Hawk. And you didn't blow your cover. You really know how to think on your feet."

"Glad you approve, Sheriff. Only he wasn't the bounty hunter. What now?"

"Keep your eyes open, Billy Gene. He's out there."

Kate heard Natalie say it was safe to open the bathroom door. She unlocked it and came out. Natalie seemed really upset.

"What's wrong? What happened?" Kate said.

Kate heard a door shut, and then Clarissa came and stood next to Natalie, looking equally upset.

"Will someone please talk to me," Kate said. "Is Hawk all right?"

"Hawk's fine," Natalie finally said. "Let's go sit in the living room."

The agents sat on the couch facing Kate.

"What was that all about?" Kate said. "You scared me half to death."

"We think the man on the deck who tried to get in may have been the bounty hunter," Natalie said. "If he was watching the house, he would have seen Elliot and Buck leave. Maybe he planned to hide in Hawk's room and surprise him later. We just don't know."

"So he got away?" Kate said.

Natalie sighed. "It was my fault. I had to sneeze and tried hard to muffle it. He heard me and took off running toward the woods."

"Did you chase him?" Kate said.

Clarissa shook her head. "Special Agent Romo told us to stand down. The man hadn't seen us, so our cover wasn't blown. Right now, that's more important than risking an unsuccessful foot chase and him realizing we were waiting for him. He would disappear and we'd never get him.

"As it is," Natalie said, "for all he knew, the sneeze could have come from you or someone else in the family who was outside."

Kate laid her head back on the couch and blew the bangs off her forehead. "This thing is making me crazy."

CHAPTER 21

Hawk finished his lunch, trying not to show how thoroughly confused he was by the stunt Deputy Duncan had pulled pretending to be Kirby Stanfield, an old friend from Foggy Ridge. Something was up. Hawk knew it. But he couldn't even ask about it as long as he was being listened to at the command center.

"You okay?" Special Agent Ziegler said.

"Sure. Why?"

"You're awfully quiet."

Hawk smiled. "Don't want to talk with my mouth full while I'm live at command central."

"Seriously, you okay?"

Hawk shrugged. "I guess so. I'm still uneasy about the guy trying to break in at the house."

"Your mom is safe with Sloan and Ortega," Ziegler said. "And if it *was* the bounty hunter, he never knew our agents were there, so we're still good to go."

"Yeah, I know. I suppose I am a little edgy." *I wish someone would explain Deputy Duncan's behavior.*

Ziegler patted his knee. "You're doing great. Hang in there. This will all be over soon."

Hawk nodded. "I'm ready for that."

"Hawk, this is Special Agent Romo. How are you holding up?"

"All right, sir. I'd feel better if I could talk with my mother. Make sure she's okay."

"I can arrange that. Hold on …"

Hawk looked out across the back lawn at Angel View. Guests were laughing and joking around, having so much fun, completely oblivious to the FBI's presence or the operation in progress. He spotted Deputy Duncan sitting at an umbrella table on the back deck, having a soft drink and reading what appeared to be a novel.

"Hawk, can you hear me? It's your mother."

"Hey, Mama. I hear you had a bit of a scare."

"It's never dull," Kate said. "Elliot and Dad had gone into Foggy Ridge to get groceries, and I was enjoying some quiet time. All of a sudden, Clarissa came into the room, her gun drawn, and locked the sliding glass door. I could hear footsteps outside, and then I saw the silhouette of a man on the deck. I froze. Then Natalie came in with a Taser gun and told me to lock myself in the bathroom. Which I gladly did. Honestly, it was all over in ten minutes. Whoever was out there ran away. He never saw the agents, so their cover wasn't blown. Goodness, Elliot and Dad are back now. I feel a lot better. I'll say one thing, Natalie and Clarissa had things under control. I was never really afraid."

"That's so good to hear," Hawk said. "I was worried."

"Don't be. How are things going there?"

"Okay, I guess. It's slow. Would you believe I ran into an old friend who used to live here? He came right up to me in the middle of a covert operation and started a conversation. I had to talk with him and not let on, but I stayed cool and he had no idea anything was going on." Hawk laughed. "Crazy, huh? Would you call Virgil and tell him I ran into Kirby Stanfield and kept my cool? He'll get a big kick out of that."

"I don't recall the name," Kate said. "Does Virgil know him?"

"Definitely. I'd better go. It was nice of Special Agent Romo to let me talk to you. I feel better now, knowing you're okay."

"You take care of you," Kate said. "We'll wait to have dinner until you're home."

"Okay. Don't forget to call Virgil. Love you."

"Love you too."

⚜

Kate took the phone off speaker and disconnected the call. She looked over at Elliot, who was lying next to her on the bed, resting his eyes. "Did you find that odd?"

"What?"

"Hawk asking me to call *Virgil*. He actually called him by name twice during the conversation. He's never done that. Never. He always calls him Sheriff Granger or the sheriff."

"Maybe they have a more personal relationship now. They've been through a great deal together in the past couple days."

"Well, I wonder what's so important about this Kirby Stanfield that Hawk would ask me to call Virgil and mention he ran into him."

"I don't know. Are you sure you're not reading into it?"

Kate sighed. "No, I'm not sure. But my maternal instinct is telling me that Hawk is saying more than the obvious, and I should do what he asked and call Virgil."

Elliot turned on his side. "Trust your instinct. Call Virgil. If you're wrong, you're just passing on an interesting tidbit from your son. But if you're right, there's a reason Hawk wants Virgil to know."

Kate kissed his cheek. "Thanks." She keyed in Virgil's cell phone number. "I hope I'm not reading into it. Virgil is so busy that I hate to—"

"Hello, Kate. I'm sorry about what happened. You okay?"

"Yes, I'm fine. Elliot's here and I've got you on speaker. I wouldn't bother you right now, but Romo let me talk with Hawk a few minutes ago. Hawk wanted me to call and tell you that he ran into Kirby Stanfield today in the middle of a covert operation and managed to keep his cool. He thought you would get a kick out of it. Does that make sense?"

"Yes, I happened to be at the command center when it happened and watched it myself. Hawk carried on a conversation with him and never missed a beat. It was great. I'm sure Romo was impressed. I know I was."

"Hmm ... I was so sure Hawk was saying more than the obvious."

"I don't know about that. Since Hawk and I can't communicate right now, he probably just wanted to be sure I knew about his Oscar-worthy performance."

"So much for maternal instinct. How are things going there?"

"I've been watching everything from the command center," Virgil said. "It's been intense at times, especially the incident at your place, but they're still waiting for the bounty hunter to make himself obvious enough to pick out of a crowd. I know the time must grate on you. But we have to wait it out."

"How's Deputy Duncan's *vacation* going?" Elliot said.

"Fine. His eyes and ears are wide open. I'm very glad he was able to take off."

"I'm glad he's at Angel View where he can help you keep an eye on things. Virgil, you be careful," Kate said. "And make sure Romo and his people are watching out for Hawk."

"I will."

Kate disconnected the call and laid her head back on the pillow. "Virgil's not telling us everything."

"Sweetheart"—Elliot took her hand—"he tells us what we need to know, when we need to know it."

Kate smiled. "You're right. We've been doing this so long, you'd think I'd know that by now."

Billy Gene continued to follow the man he suspected had his eye on Hawk. Without being too obvious, he tried to get a facial shot of the guy. He finally managed to get one decent shot and sent it to the sheriff.

If the man was on vacation, he sure didn't know how to have fun. All he'd done all day was stroll around the grounds and talk on the phone. And change his clothes—twice. Because he was hot and sweaty? Maybe. Or was it because he didn't want to stand out if the area was under surveillance?

Billy Gene was uncomfortable that the FBI had him on video as Kirby Stanfield. If his true identity were ever found out, it would point back to Sheriff Granger. If Romo wanted to be nasty about it, he could charge them both with interfering with an FBI operation and make sure neither of them ever worked in law enforcement again.

Although Billy Gene did what he had to do under the circumstances, he was anything but under the radar now. And if they questioned Hawk about this fictitious friend, would he be able to do as good a job of covering it up as he'd done earlier?

"Billy Gene, can you hear me?" Virgil said.

"Loud and clear, Sheriff."

"Kate just called. She said Hawk insisted that she call and tell me he ran into his old friend Kirby Stanfield in the middle of today's covert operation—and kept his cool. Hawk thought I'd get a kick out of it. Kate thought it was odd, but I told her I watched it live, and he did great. And then we dropped it. I think it's a nonissue."

"Well, that's good. It's all I could think to do at the time. I just hope it doesn't come back to bite us both."

"I don't think it will," Virgil said. "Romo lost interest once Hawk acted like he knew you. Everyone at the command center turned their attention to the incident at Kate's. To me, it still seems just a little too coincidental that the man showed up at Kate's just as you thought the guy you're tailing was closing in on Hawk. Then again, what was your guy going to do with Hawk while he was surrounded by the landscapers and grounds crew? It doesn't make a lot of sense."

"I can't figure that one either, Sheriff. Maybe it was a bad call. Did you take a look at the picture I sent you?"

"I did," Virgil said. "That is the guy whose face has shown up on the surveillance cameras off and on all day, and no one here flinched."

"So he's obviously not the guy. You want me to stop following him?"

"You were sure when you called me," Virgil said, "that this guy was going to move on Hawk."

"Yes, sir, I was. Guess I was wrong."

"Billy Gene, I've known you a long time. I'd be a fool to blow off your hunches. I think there's more going on here. I just can't put my finger on it yet. Stay on this guy until Hawk goes home, and then see what he does. I'd sure like to know his room number."

"Oh, I already know he's in 215. I followed him there earlier when he went back to his room to change clothes. For the second time."

Virgil chuckled. "Did you? And …?"

"I got his license number when he went out to his car to get his briefcase. He's driving a rental car—a red Nissan Sentra. Arkansas plate: XTL0926."

"Excellent work," Virgil said. "Once Hawk goes home for the day, treat yourself to a nice steak dinner on me. Then get a good night's sleep before we start this all over again tomorrow. Meanwhile, I'm going to do a little detective work of my own."

CHAPTER 22

Virgil was itching to get home to Jill Beth's Swedish meatballs, but he wasn't quite ready to end his day. He stared at the picture Billy Gene had sent to his phone. That was definitely not the bounty hunter, aka Herbod Jalili. This man was a few years older. His eyes were steely cold like Jalili's, but his features were more refined.

He keyed in Kate's number.

"Hello, Virgil."

"I didn't interrupt your dinner, did I?"

"No, not at all. Hawk just got home safe and sound, and he's taking a shower before dinner. What's on your mind?"

"Two things. One, I wanted to check up on you and see how you're feeling after today's scare."

"Not too bad. Elliot is checking every lock and feeling very protective, but Natalie and Clarissa were wonderful. I'm really fine. What was the second reason you called?"

"Promise you won't laugh?" Virgil said. "Billy Gene left his expensive new sunglasses and his wallet out on one of the umbrella tables, and a real nice guy in 215 turned them in. Billy Gene couldn't believe every nickel and his credit cards were still in his wallet. He wants to go thank him and invite him to dinner, but he forgot the guy's name. Could you check your computer and get that for me? Billy Gene didn't feel comfortable bothering you with it, with all you've got on your mind. Of course, I'll bother you anytime."

Kate laughed. "You know I don't mind. Let me get to my computer, and I can pull that right up. Let's see … guest roster. Second floor. Room 215. Mr. Javed Saman. First name is spelled J-a-v-e-d. Last name: S-a-m-a-n. Says here he's a New Yorker."

"Thanks," Virgil said. "I'll call Billy Gene and give him the guy's name so he can thank him personally and offer to buy him a steak. Did Hawk feel good about today?"

"He did. He's so proud of himself for keeping a poker face when his friend came up to him today—and in front of all those agents present and at the command center."

"He handled himself like a pro, Kate. Never missed a beat. Be sure to tell him I said so. I'm going to scoot. Jill Beth's got Swedish meatballs with my name on them."

"Enjoy," Kate said. "Give her my love."

Virgil chuckled. "Will do. Thanks again."

Virgil disconnected and then keyed in the number for Deputy Kevin Mann.

"Hey, Virgil. How're things going at the command center?"

"So-so. I guess it depends on whether you enjoy spending time in Fed City with most everything classified. Romo is definitely running the show. I trust you have the department running smoothly?"

"Yes, it's been quieter than usual. Nothing we couldn't handle. How's Billy Gene's *vacation* going?"

Virgil told Kevin everything that had happened that day, including the attempted break-in at Kate's and Hawk's amazing response to Billy Gene's brilliant performance as Kirby Stanfield. "I'm telling you, Kevin. It was something to see. I thought for sure Hawk would blow it, but he never missed a beat. The feds bought it hook, line, and sinker."

"I'm confused," Kevin said. "Which one is the bounty hunter?"

"It can't be the guy Billy Gene was following because the feds didn't react to his face on camera. They won't admit it to me, but they know what the bounty hunter looks like."

"So it's the man who tried to break in at Kate's?" Kevin said.

"We can't be sure since he had his face covered."

"Don't you hate it when you get a smart one?" Kevin said. "So what now?"

"The agents out at the house will need to be vigilant because the guy could come back. He never saw the agents when the sneeze scared him off, so he might try it again. My guess is that tomorrow Romo will have Hawk take a greater risk and move away from the actors posing as landscapers and grounds crew. He's going to want to draw the bounty hunter out where they can ID him and then move in to apprehend him."

"What about the guy Billy Gene was following? Have you eliminated him?"

"Well, here's the thing. Billy Gene and I both feel there's something more going on here. The guy is definitely not the bounty hunter, or they would've been all over him. But he was definitely watching Hawk. I want to know why. Which is where you come in."

"How can I help?" Kevin said.

"Grab a pencil and something to write on. I want you to get me everything you can on the guy Billy Gene is following."

Virgil told Kevin everything he'd obtained on Javed Saman and what he'd done to get it.

Kevin laughed. "Good for you. Okay, it's my turn. Let me see what I can find out. If this guy is using his real name, I shouldn't have too much trouble running down some information on him. I'll do my best."

"Thanks, Kevin. I know you will. Let me know the minute you have something."

"Definitely. And, boss … I take back what I said about you rolling over. I should've known you wouldn't let Romo shut you out."

"I took an oath to protect the people of Raleigh County, Kevin. He didn't. And I intend to do my job."

"If I start right now," Kevin said, "I may have something for you by morning."

❦

Hawk got out of the shower and dried off, then wrapped a towel around his waist and stood at the bathroom sink. His eyes looked tired. He could hardly believe he was working with the FBI on such an important operation. It was a little scary, but he was doing it for Kennedy. To honor her memory. He could hardly wait until they captured the man who sought to murder her in cold blood for the five million dollars. But would he ever know who had actually done it? Or why? It was one day short of a week since Kennedy disappeared, but it felt like a lifetime ago. He was a changed man on many levels.

At this time last Friday night, he was on the phone with Kennedy, excited about spending all day Saturday with her. Lies. So many lies he told to protect his time with her. He deceived Laura Lynn. His parents. Himself. Even Kennedy. He'd confessed it all, sincerely sorry for the way he handled it, for all he had thrown away. So why was he dredging it up? Perhaps because tomorrow would mark one week since Kennedy disappeared from his life.

So much to handle in a week's time. So much pain. And sorrow. Death. And regret. Regret not only for his wrongdoing, but for all he had lost. And not just Laura Lynn. He did love her and always would. But he was finally able to see that his relationship with Kennedy was more than physical. It was still confusing. But he was beginning to understand that the inexplicable emptiness he now felt was the consequence of his having partaken of the pleasure God intended for marriage, completely unprepared for how the oneness of that intimate union would impact his soul and spirit.

"Mama said dinner is almost ready." Jesse stood outside the bathroom door, holding the orange-and-white-striped kitten that was still without a name.

"Good grief, Jesse. Don't sneak up on me like that," Hawk said. "Next time whistle or something so I know you're coming."

"Sorry. Dinner's almost ready."

"Remind me what we're having," Hawk said.

"Chicken parmigiana, those little brown potatoes, asparagus, salad, and sourdough rolls. Chocolate pudding for dessert. Yum."

"Guess I'd better get dressed and get down there."

"You look worried," Jesse said.

"I suppose I am. I'm letting the FBI use me for bait to catch a vicious killer. It's not exactly a safe place to be."

"Home isn't all that safe either." Jesse put the kitten down and let him play with the shoelace on Hawk's Nikes.

"Yeah, I'm really sorry about what happened today. At least Natalie and Clarissa were on top of it."

"Elliot tightened the locks on all the windows," Jesse said, "and bought a special lock for the sliding glass door. He insisted that we have the alarm system turned back on, and he's going to give us the new code at dinner."

Hawk sighed. "More consequences. None of this would be happening if I hadn't gotten involved with Kennedy."

"Probably not." Jesse picked up Hawk's clean clothes and tossed them to him, then flopped on the bed. "But don't forget what Romans 8:28 says, 'And we know that in all things God works for the good of those who love him, who have been called according to his purpose.' I'm pretty sure that *in all things* means even when we mess up."

"I can't imagine what good could possibly come of this."

"Well, even if it's just a lesson that changes you and makes you more like Him, it's pretty cool."

Hawk smiled as he pulled his shirt on. "You have an answer for everything. I don't know how you do it."

"My youth pastor gave me the formula," Jesse said. "One, read the manual. And two, follow the instructions."

"In other words, read the Bible and do what it says."

Jesse grinned. "Yep. It's simple. But not always easy."

Hawk swung his wet towel like a lasso and threw it at Jesse, evoking a deep, husky laugh befitting an almost-eighth grader. "Come on, Saint Einstein. Let's go pig out on chicken parmigiana."

⚜

Kate sat around the dinner table, glad to see her family together. She had almost come to grips with the fact that Laura Lynn was never going to be her daughter-in-law. But it was still painful to see Hawk without her. And watching Abby and Jay's relationship blossom was comforting in the midst of all the pain and disappointment.

She smiled watching Jesse. He seemed comfortable in his own skin, whether he was teaching guests interesting facts about hummingbirds or conversing with his grandpa Buck about the Korean War.

The one empty chair at the table belonged to Riley. Kate was more than ready for her baby girl to come home and share every detail, but knew that if the bounty hunter wasn't caught by tomorrow night, they would have to let her stay with Ava's family until this awful ordeal was over.

Elliot put his hand on hers. "I hope you're not missing the joy of the moment by worrying."

"Not really," Kate said. "There's nothing I enjoy more than when we're all gathered around the table. I just wish we were done with the bounty hunter. Riley will be bursting with excitement when the bus pulls into the church parking lot on Sunday night. If she goes to Ava's first, it might be anticlimactic for her and for us by the time we see her. I want to hear all about her favorite things at camp and the new friends she made—while she's still bubbling over."

"Have you ever known Riley not to be bubbling over?" Elliot said.

Kate laughed. "You have a point."

"Let's just take it a step at a time. Worrying won't change the outcome, but it will definitely keep you in knots."

"You're right."

"So when do we get the alarm code?" Jesse said.

The room got quiet and all eyes were on Elliot.

"I'm going to let Natalie address that," Elliot said.

Natalie came around and stood behind Elliot. "The alarm system will be turned back on, just until the bounty hunter is locked up in FBI custody. Kate has made it clear how much she hates it, and I respect that. But after what happened this afternoon, I think it will give you peace of mind. Remember, the FBI surveillance cameras monitor the entire exterior of the house, so should our intruder come back, the agents in the command center will see him, just like they did today, and notify Clarissa and me, and we will immediately act. The alarm is just an extra security measure for *your* peace of mind."

"The reason I hate it," Kate said, "is because the last time we used it, I was a nervous wreck from the alarm going off by mistake because someone didn't properly set it or failed to enter the code in time. Of course, that defeated the whole purpose, like crying wolf too many times."

"To help with that," Natalie said, "since Abby and Jesse are working at the lodge, I can disarm and reset the alarm when I walk them over. I can do the same when Hawk leaves to ride over with Connor. Or when any of you leaves. Also we'll keep it engaged when everyone is home in the evening. I think the easiest way to be sure it isn't accidentally set off would be for Clarissa and I to be the only ones to set and disarm it. One of us will always be available, so it shouldn't be a problem. And your mother will feel better knowing there will be no false alarms, right, Kate?"

"Absolutely."

"Does anyone have questions?" Natalie said.

Jesse raised his hand. "I do. What if we forget and open the door and you're not close by? How will we key in the code before the alarm goes on?"

Natalie nodded. "First of all, we're going to post a reminder on the exit doors so you won't forget. Anytime you need to go out, you tell Clarissa or me and we'll go with you."

"So you're not going to give us the code?" Jesse said.

"Your mom and I asked her *not* to give us the code," Elliot said. "It's only going to be for a short time. It'll be safer and less nerve racking if they monitor the alarm."

"Are we all on the same page?" Natalie said.

Everyone nodded.

"Okay, I'm going to set it now for the night."

CHAPTER 23

Virgil lay staring at the ceiling fan, Jill Beth sleeping peacefully in his arms. What was he missing? Billy Gene was too sharp to have misjudged the movements of Javed Saman—or whatever the guy's real name was. He was sure enough that Saman was making a move on Hawk Cummings to have risked blowing his own cover, which would ultimately have pointed to Virgil—not something he would do lightly.

"Hey, Sheriff, I hear your wheels turning," Jill Beth said, barely above a whisper.

"Go back to sleep, darlin'," Virgil said, stroking her hair. "My mind's working overtime. I'll nod off here in a minute."

"Okay." She nuzzled closer.

Virgil wished he could tell Jill Beth exactly what was going on, but they had both learned years ago when to draw the line. She never asked questions when he stopped talking about a case. But because they were best friends, it was often difficult to keep a professional distance. In this case, he would not have wanted her worrying about Hawk. And he couldn't tell her—or anyone—that he had contacted

Mitch and gotten classified information. He would take that secret to the grave.

He had disposed of the burner phone and made sure it was on the way to the landfill. But he had done his best to memorize the information Mitch had attached, including the image of the bounty hunter, Herbod Abbas Jalili. Hard to say what the guy looked like now or what disguise he wore. One thing Virgil was sure of, the man using the name Javed Saman was not the bounty hunter. But who was he? What interest did he have in Hawk Cummings?

Virgil moved his arm and gently set Jill Beth's head on her pillow, then ever so quietly slipped out of bed and walked down the hall to the kitchen. He took a decaf K-Cup, put it in the Keurig, and turned it on. He waited a minute for his coffee to brew, then picked up his cup and sat at the table.

He turned on the TV and started watching cable news, then turned it off. He couldn't concentrate. What he wanted was answers, not world problems to clog his mind. Was Jalili the would-be intruder at Kate's? Hawk had been easily accessible numerous times at Angel View Lodge where Jalili could have said hello and started up a conversation like any other tourist passing through. Why hadn't he? Unless he suspected the FBI was there.

Virgil bounced his pencil eraser on the table. He didn't see how Jalili could have known the FBI was there. Romo had done a good job of keeping his people out of sight and his actors in place. They seemed authentic enough. If Jalili had suspected an FBI presence, would he have attempted to break into Kate's house in broad daylight? Surely he knew—or at least suspected—that Hawk would be working during the day. And he was a professional assassin. How hard could it be for him to have found out that Hawk was heading up the landscaping project?

Virgil took a sip of coffee and heard his phone beep with Kevin's tone. He picked it up and read the text: *I attached the background check on Javed Saman. Also, there's no record of him living in New York City or anywhere in the state of New York. Currently living in Paris. He's not wanted by the FBI and not on record at NCIC. Not on Interpol's radar. His financial record is squeaky clean. Going to bed. Will talk with you in the morning. KM.*

Virgil opened the attachment.

Javed Saman, born March 14, 1970, in Ahvaz, Iran. Parents were schoolteachers. 1980 – family moved to Paris where his father took a job as professor of Persian Cultural Studies at Université Paris Diderot.

1988–1992 – Javed attended École Polytechnique (Paris Tech) in Paris, France. Graduated with a bachelor's degree in computer science. 1993–1997 – Served in the French Foreign Legion. February 1, 1998 – married Marie Adrienne DuBois in a civil ceremony in Paris. 1998–2005 – Lived in Paris working as IT specialist for the Gendarmerie Nationale (French national army). January 28, 2006 – Divorced from Marie Adrienne Saman, no children. 2006–2017 – Lived in Tehran, Iran, working as IT administrator for Law Enforcement Force of the Islamic Republic of Iran (police force). Current address: Paris, France. Employment: Baker at La Boulangerie Délicieux. Passport current, two trips to New York City in 2017 (tourist), and one in 2018 (tourist).

Virgil reread the attachment. This guy was no stranger to the military and law enforcement. He didn't appear to be on anyone's radar. Everything looked clean and in order. Could Billy Gene have been wrong? It was possible this man was nothing more than a tourist. Virgil's gut told him differently. And he trusted Billy Gene's instincts almost as much as he trusted his own.

The mantel clock struck two. Virgil got up and headed for the bedroom, thinking maybe he could sleep now. At least he wasn't operating in the dark. Javed Saman was no longer a stranger. Whether he was friend or foe had yet to be determined.

⸙

Hawk's eyes flew open, his heart pounding. He suddenly remembered a selfie Kennedy had taken with a background of fall foliage. He saw it on her dresser mirror and admired it, and she insisted he keep it. That was weeks ago. Where was it? He remembered putting it in a place where it wouldn't be discovered by anyone in the family.

As Hawk sat up on the side of the bed, he looked at the clock: 5:20 a.m. Jesse was sleeping peacefully on the other side of the large upstairs room they shared and wouldn't be up for another forty minutes. Halo lay curled up on the dirty clothes Jesse should have put in the hamper, the orange-and-white tabby kitten nestled next to her. Hawk heard water running and figured Abby was taking a shower. She had to be at Flutter's just before six.

Hawk sat thinking, his elbows planted on his thighs, his hands locked between his knees. Where did he put that photo of Kennedy?

Why did it even matter? Whatever it was they had was over. It was wrong. It hurt people. He had confessed the sin and put it behind him. So why couldn't he just let her go? It confused him that he still had feelings for her. Then again, *she* was not the sin. She was sweet and intelligent, beautiful and expressive. It was the relationship they fell into and willfully continued that was sinful. That he *had* rejected. That he deeply regretted. But he didn't regret knowing Kennedy, even though he ached deep inside as he struggled in silence to make sense of her disappearance and death. There was so much he wished he had said to her. Things he wished he had asked.

The cigar box in the closet! That's where he had put the photo. He sprang from the bed and went over to the closet, took the box from the top shelf, and brought it down. He flipped the switch to turn on the closet light, sat on the bed, and opened the box. There on the top, right where he had put it, was the photo of Kennedy. Looking at it now, the emptiness he'd been feeling ached all the more. He picked up the photo and let the light reveal her beautiful face. He traced her facial features with his finger, remembering the times he had done that when they were together. Her soft brown eyes spoke volumes, as if she were longing for something she could never have. He saw her pain. Why hadn't he asked her what she was thinking and feeling? He knew why. Because he was content to enjoy her pleasures without an ounce of commitment.

Hawk blinked to clear his eyes and wiped a runaway tear from his cheek. How could he have been so shallow? Not only had he betrayed Laura Lynn, he had also robbed Kennedy, not just by ignoring her pain but also by withholding from her his feelings, his thoughts, anything truly authentic about himself. He had become the guy he had always criticized, the one who uses a woman only for pleasure, letting her think she was building a relationship.

It hurt to acknowledge this about himself. If anyone besides the Holy Spirit had revealed it to him, he felt sure he would have died of shame. As it was, he knew he'd been forgiven, and his sins removed as far as the east is from the west. Still, he wished he'd had the chance to ask Kennedy's forgiveness as he had Laura Lynn's. He had wronged them both. But Kennedy died without ever knowing how sorry he was. Another consequence he would have to live with.

He stared at her picture for a minute longer. He would never forget her. He pressed his lips to the photograph and put it back in the cigar box, then set the box back on the closet shelf.

He had meant for his relationship with Kennedy to remain strictly physical and uncomplicated. But he had learned the hard way that sins of the flesh are never uncomplicated.

Kate lay in Elliot's arms, enjoying the peace she knew would be hard to hold on to once they were immersed in another high-tension and seemingly endless day of waiting while Hawk was used to bait the bounty hunter.

Lord, I am so ready for this to be over with. Please put a circle of Your light around Hawk and keep him safe. Help the FBI to get this monster into custody so we can get on with our lives.

"You're awake," Elliot whispered.

"How'd you know?"

"I always know." Elliot kissed her forehead. "Good morning, Mrs. Stafford."

Kate smiled. "I love being Mrs. Stafford."

Kate didn't feel the need to say anything else. She enjoyed these quiet moments of comfortable silence with Elliot. A long time passed. Finally she said, "This is Saturday. The bounty hunter has to be caught today or we won't get to see Riley tomorrow."

"That's true," he said. "But we can't force him out, so we'll just have to wait him out."

"I think the word *wait* should be declared an unacceptable four-letter word and treated with the same disdain as the others."

Elliot laughed. "Did you really just say that?"

"I did. When I think of all the waiting I've done in the past eight years, it borders on unbelievable."

Elliot stroked her hair. "I admit you've done more than your share. But you wouldn't have seen God work if His answers had come right away."

Kate sighed. "I know. I just wish He'd step it up a bit. Waiting has never been my strong suit."

"Which is probably why He keeps letting you experience it. Practice makes perfect."

Kate sat up and leaned her back against the headboard. "At least this time I have tried to stay cool and trust that God has Hawk's back."

"You have been amazing," Elliot said.

"The scare last fall with Jesse and Liam Berne and that whole saga finally broke me." Kate slipped her hand into his. "I am tired of waiting, but I've learned not to tell God how to keep His promises. I know He will. And whatever the outcome, I know it will be right.

That doesn't mean I'm not afraid, but that's just the flesh trying to rattle my faith."

Elliot looked up at her. "Spoken like a true believer."

"Which I definitely am."

"How do blueberry pancakes sound for breakfast?"

"With bacon?"

"Sure."

"Are you cooking or am I?" Kate said, the corners of her mouth twitching.

"Please … *I* am the breakfast chef. Besides, this is Saturday, and you know what that means."

"Spaghetti night," Kate said. "I wonder how long I've been making spaghetti on Saturdays."

"As long as I've known you. And you still make the best."

Kate nudged him in the ribs. "Let's go have those pancakes. Maybe the aroma of my spaghetti sauce simmering on the stove will make things feel normal around here."

CHAPTER 24

Virgil sat in his office on the first floor of the Raleigh County Courthouse, looking at the magnificent swirls of golden pink and purple that lit up the morning's sky. He took a sip of coffee and focused his attention across the courthouse lawn. The traffic on Main Street was light at this hour. Old Melvin Mayfield sat on a wrought-iron bench, feeding the birds and one very persistent squirrel.

On the corner, Miguel Perez had set up his rolling cart, and there was already a line of people waiting to buy breakfast tacos.

A knock at the door caused Virgil to turn. "Hey, Kevin. Come on in. Thanks for coming in so early. Make yourself a cup of coffee. I'm going to move over to the conference table."

"Thanks. I'll be right there." Kevin went to the back of the room where the Keurig was set up. A minute later, he carried a fresh cup of coffee, placed it on the table, and sat across from Virgil. He handed him an envelope. "The forensics report came in on the substance used in the drone attack."

"Already?" Virgil quickly opened the envelope and read the short paragraph aloud.

Chemical analysis of sample 2094-RalCtySherDept-06012018 has shown the substance to be nonlethal and negative for long-term side effects. The name of the substance, its origin, and chemical combination have been labeled CLASSIFIED by the Federal Bureau of Investigation.

"I guess I should be grateful that Romo threw us another bone," Virgil said. "At least Hawk is out of the woods. That's one less worry."

"No kidding," Kevin said. "So what'd you think of Javed Saman?"

"First of all, thanks for your hard work. I really appreciate it." Virgil took a sip of coffee. "Actually, I'd like to hear your thoughts on Saman."

"He's never been convicted of a crime," Kevin said, "or even charged, as far as I could tell. He favors law enforcement and the military, even when choosing employers. I'm impressed he served in the French Foreign Legion. He hasn't left a trail of suspicious dealings, though usually any connection with Iran is suspect in my mind. However, the guy was Iranian and his father was a professor of Persian culture. His father's pride probably rubbed off on Saman, and he wanted to go back to his home country and discover his heritage. He lived more of his life in France, so nothing about his going back there seemed suspicious."

"I don't disagree with any of that." Virgil traced the rim of his cup with his index finger.

"But …?"

Virgil smiled and lifted his gaze. "But what in the world is he doing working at a French bakery? I could understand if he was ready for a career change or a way to pay the rent while he's looking for a job in his field. But I'm wondering how a baker gets time off for three vacation trips to the United States in twelve months. Plus, that much travel seems excessive on a baker's salary."

"He could have saved a lot of money from his other jobs," Kevin said. "He didn't have a family to raise."

"Even if he did have the money, he's not a bakery *chef*. He's a baker. Why would the bakery be willing to let a baker take off that kind of time, especially when he just started?"

Kevin rubbed his chin. "I see your point. What are you thinking?"

"I could be all wet," Virgil said, "but I'm thinking Javed Saman isn't working at the bakery at all, that he's using it to cover up what he's really doing."

"Which is?"

Virgil pursed his lips. "I don't know yet. But I doubt seriously he's been making éclairs. I want to know what he's doing in Foggy Ridge."

Kevin flashed a crooked smile. "Translated, that means, 'Kevin, clear your calendar. I've got more work for you to do.'"

"And that kind of perception," Virgil said, smiling wryly, "is why you're my chief deputy."

Virgil keyed in Kate's cell phone number and glanced out the window. The line for Miguel Perez's breakfast tacos was moving quickly.

"Hello, Virgil."

"Good morning, Kate. I assume you've been informed that the report came back from forensics on the chemical used in the drone attack?"

"Yes, Natalie—Special Agent Sloan—just told us! We're over-the-top excited! Virgil, what chemical was it? She didn't have that information."

Neither do I. "Since Romo's in charge of the case, you'll need to direct your questions to him. But truthfully, the only thing that matters is that Hawk is going to be fine."

"I know. You should've seen his face. Such a relief."

"How are you holding up?" Virgil said.

"Better than I should be. As long as I remember the Lord's in control."

"Don't tell Romo." Virgil chuckled.

"Did you pick up on his arrogance the other night," Kate said, "when he assured us that it won't be necessary to rely on God because his people are the best at what they do?"

"I heard him. I think he embarrassed himself when he said he was willing to work with God, if God was willing to work with him."

"Elliot reminded me that as long as we know who's protecting Hawk, it doesn't really matter what Romo thinks. Speaking of Romo—does he feel they're making progress?"

"Not that he's expressed to me, but I wouldn't expect him to speculate. If you'll remember, Romo did say he anticipated that the bounty hunter would take a little time before he felt comfortable enough to approach Hawk. Each day, they've let Hawk move a few yards farther away from the FBI actors, hoping the bounty hunter will show himself. They're watching Hawk closely." *And so are we.*

"This whole thing with Hawk is dizzying." Kate sighed. "He's putting on a brave face, but I don't think the reality of it has hit him yet. He's hardly had time to breathe. And whether or not I like it, he must have some feelings for Kennedy Taylor. It was hard enough on him waking up in a stupor with her gone and the house completely cleaned out as if she'd never lived there. But then hearing Dennis retell Brody's account of the drone attack and kidnapping was positively terrifying. Hawk needs closure. Yet I wonder if he's ever going to know what happened to her. Or if she's dead or alive."

He knows. "Hawk's strong," Virgil said. "I have confidence in him to get on with his life after this. I'm just sorry for the way it ended."

"Me too, but I'm glad it's over," Kate said. "You and I haven't really talked about it, but you know me well enough to know that I would never approve of what Hawk was doing. But I see his pain. And as a mother, I do feel bad for him."

"We all do. And I respect him for stepping up when he's still in a world of hurt. He's been a hundred percent cooperative with my department and with Romo's people. He's a good man, Kate."

"That I know," she said. "He made a mistake. But he's not the mistake. Hopefully he's a little wiser now."

"I couldn't have said it better. I guess I should get off and get over to the command center. Hang in there. This really will be over soon."

Virgil finished telling Billy Gene everything Kevin had found on Javed Saman.

"There you have it," Virgil said. "Any questions?"

"Just the ones you don't have answers to," Billy Gene said. "What brought Saman to Foggy Ridge is right up there. Shoot, we're barely on the map."

"Unless he chose Arkansas as his vacation spot. Foggy Ridge would be in most every northwest Arkansas vacation brochure."

"A guy in France decides to take a third trip to the States in a year, and out of all the places he could visit, he picks Arkansas?"

"It's possible," Virgil said. "We are the *Natural State*. There's a lot to see and do here."

"Except Saman hasn't left Angel View to see or do anything," Billy Gene said.

"Good point. But what are the odds Saman's arrival in Foggy Ridge is tied up with the bounty hunter?"

"Sheriff, I admit the odds are slim, but I saw him with my own eyes. He's got his eye on Hawk and came awful close to movin' in on him. Any chance there's more than one guy after the five million?"

"Romo never alluded to it," Virgil said. *Like Romo never told me the bounty hunter was really an assassin working for the Iranian government.* "He just said an exceedingly bad man was tracking down Kennedy Taylor and was on his way here to get Hawk to tell him where she is. Let me try to find out more details. Of course, I'd have to do it in such a way that Romo doesn't get suspicious that we're keeping an eye on Hawk ourselves."

"Sheriff, we have to know what we're dealin' with," Billy Gene said. "Especially since we're determined to keep Hawk safe, and Romo's determined to capture this bounty hunter unharmed.

Saman could be a threat to either or both. There's only one of me out here. I've got to know how Saman fits into the scenario."

"I know," Virgil said. "I agree with you. But if Romo gets even a hint that we might be operating outside his command, we could both be selling magazines for a living."

"I understand the risk," Billy Gene said. "I made my choice."

"Okay. I'm headed over to the command center. Let me see if I can't pull something out of Romo. I'll get back to you. Keep your ears on and Saman in your sights."

"Copy that."

Virgil walked into the FBI command center and got the usual lukewarm reception. No one paid much attention to him. This was his county, and he was not going to be intimidated by the feds. He spotted Romo talking to a couple of men in FBI T-shirts.

Virgil stood looking up at the surveillance monitors. It appeared to be a typical day at Angel View. Abby was taking orders at Flutter's. Jesse was outside in the hummingbird garden, filling the feeders. Savannah's car was parked outside the office and the "open" light was on. The FBI actors were already positioned on the back lawn and looked believably busy. Hawk should be arriving in about four minutes.

"Hello, Sheriff." Romo walked up to Virgil and slapped him on the back. "Ready for round three?"

"Bring it on," Virgil said. "Chris, I've been meaning to ask you something. How can you be sure there's just one bounty hunter? I mean, if this guy knows about the bounty on Nameless, wouldn't others know too?"

Romo's eyebrows came together. "No. Each bounty hunter is hired by the bondsman that provided bail for the fugitive. That's the only person who can collect the bounty. You should know that."

"I know that's how it is in the US, but you never specified where the bounty originated," Virgil said.

"I didn't think I had to."

"Okay," Virgil said. "So Nameless is a fugitive with a five-million-dollar bounty on her head. Bounty hunters typically get ten to twenty percent of the bail money. That would mean bail was set between fifty and a hundred million dollars. That's a whopping sum. We must be talking drug cartel. Organized crime. Something huge."

"Nice try, Sheriff. That's classified." Romo shot him a condescending look. "All you need to know is there's one bounty hunter, and we have one job: to bring him in unharmed. Why are you just now bringing this up?"

"Just the way I'm wired," Virgil said. "When I don't know all the facts, my mind goes into overtime. I've had a lot of time to think about this. Most bounty hunters in Arkansas make between fifty-eight and seventy-two thousand dollars in an entire year. This must be some bounty hunter for a bondsman to be willing to pay him more than five times what he'd normally make in a lifetime. An assassin, I could understand. But a bounty hunter? Especially one wanted by the FBI? I'm just trying to get my mind around it." Virgil watched to see if Romo reacted.

"I've said all I'm going to say about this, Sheriff. It's classified. Live with it."

Romo walked away. He was definitely rattled.

Virgil was caught between a rock and a hard place. He couldn't let Romo know that he knew this so-called bounty hunter was a hired assassin working for the government of Iran. But he couldn't tell Billy Gene either. Virgil sighed. And he still didn't know who Javed Saman was.

Virgil went outside and walked a short distance away from the mobile command center, putting it behind him. He arched his low back and stretched. "Billy Gene, did you hear that?"

"Yes, sir. I didn't know that much about bounty hunters and what they make. But you did make me think twice about why a bondsman would be willing to pay a guy more than five times of what he'd make in a lifetime. Come to think of it, bounty hunters aren't usually the bad dudes either. Do you think Romo could be lyin' about who this guy is?"

Of course he's lying. Virgil sighed. "I'm not sure of anything, Billy Gene, except that I didn't find out any information that would tell us who Saman might be."

"Maybe it'll become clear," Billy Gene said. "But until I know differently, I guess I'll have to consider Saman an enemy."

CHAPTER 25

Virgil walked around the command center all morning, observing the overhead screens and feeling almost invisible. The special agents were all busy and tending to their various areas of expertise. It was almost noon and they had not spotted the bounty hunter.

Virgil saw Romo coming his way.

"I'm going to have a hot dog, Sheriff. Would you like one?"

"I would, thanks," Virgil said. "I had an early breakfast and it's long worn off."

Romo handed him a nice warm hot dog, and Virgil unwrapped it and took a bite, surprised at how plump and juicy it was. "Mmm. This tastes like Polish sausage."

"Actually, I did hear someone say that. Sorry I don't have condiments, but I can offer you a Coke."

"Thanks."

Romo walked over against one wall and took a can of Coke out of the cooler, popped it open, and handed it to Virgil. Then took one for himself.

"This tastes mighty good about now," Virgil said.

"No kidding. I'd hate to guess how many of these I've eaten in my career."

Virgil smiled. "Me too. I promise you it's more than my wife would approve of. She thinks I don't eat right when I choose for myself."

Romo chuckled. "She must be related to my Annie. Always worrying about me eating too much fat. Too much cholesterol. Too much sugar. Too much starch. But that's what makes it taste so good."

Virgil nodded. "Exactly. Have you got kids?"

Romo's face was suddenly radiant. "A five-year-old son, Timothy. I talk to him online every night I'm away from home. I'll tell you, Virgil, no matter how bad it gets out here or how much evil I encounter, ten minutes with my little guy and I'm a new man."

Virgil smiled. "Jill Beth and I raised triplet boys—Rob, Rick, and Reece. They're twenty-eight now, but I remember feeling the same way. Kids change you."

"They really do," Romo said. "We're expecting another in October—a little girl. Annie's already got the room painted pink and is adding all the girly things. I get a big kick out of seeing her so happy. It can't be easy being married to a fed. In fact, I think the spouses of law enforcement officers deserve a lot of credit. We do what we love, and they worry about us. And keep the home fires burning so we can hardly wait to get back to them."

Is this the same arrogant Romo? "Have you and Annie picked out a name for your daughter?"

There was that radiant look again. "Yes, Lacy Sophia Romo. Sophia was my mother's name. And we both love the name Lacy."

"Sounds pretty," Virgil said. "Jill Beth and I always hoped we'd have a little girl someday. But the triplets were a handful and then some. The older they got, we decided just to be blessed with three busy boys. I promise you, it was never boring at our house."

Romo chuckled. "I'll bet not. Timothy can be a handful at times, but he's such a joy, you know?"

"I do know." Virgil popped the last of his hot dog into his mouth and washed it down with a gulp of Coke.

Romo was quiet for a moment and then said, "Virgil, when your boys were at home, did you ever worry that the mental time you spent on cases would take away from your family?"

"Sure I did. But Jill Beth is amazing. She had just the right personality and skill set to keep up with the boys and their activities and make it so I could come home and step right into whatever they were doing, without hardly missing a beat. Sometimes I'd show up in the ninth inning of their ball games, but she'd give me a quick rundown, and when it was over, I could discuss the game with them. They were inseparable in grade school and middle school. Their high school teachers insisted they needed to find themselves and made sure all their classes were different." Virgil laughed. "But you know what? After they graduated from college, the three started a software company together, and they're practically inseparable again. We think we may end up with a triple wedding one of these days."

"I can tell you love your sons," Romo said. "Guess it takes one to know one."

Virgil smiled. "Well, I suppose—"

"We've got facial recognition on the bounty hunter!" someone shouted.

Virgil felt the same rush he always got when a case kicked into high gear.

Romo guzzled the last of his Coke and tossed the can in the recycle bin. "Come on, Sheriff. This is what we've been waiting for."

Romo hurried over to the surveillance monitors, and a number of agents gathered around him, while others ran to the computers.

Virgil fixed his phone so Billy Gene could hear and said just above a whisper, "I'm back."

"There you are, Sheriff. I'm trackin' Saman. He's been on the phone a lot, but he's definitely got his eyes on Hawk. I'm sure of it."

"I can't talk. They've spotted the bounty hunter."

"Really! Where?"

"Not sure yet. Listen ..."

⚜

"We've got facial recognition on the bounty hunter!"

Kate heard Clarissa's voice and came rushing out of the living room and into the kitchen. Elliot and Buck were right behind her.

Clarissa sat at the head of the table. "Please, everyone, sit. I'll put it on speaker. You sure you want to listen live? It can be nerve racking."

"I'm sure," Kate said, reaching for Elliot's hand.

"Me too." Buck sat at the table across from Kate and Elliot.

"Goodness, it's really happening." Kate put her hand on her heart. "Lord, watch over my son."

"Keep him safe, Lord," Buck said. "Help him do as he's instructed."

"Father, we put Hawk in Your very capable hands," Elliot said. "Give wisdom to the FBI special agents and let them bring this man into custody unharmed. In Jesus's name, I ask it. Amen."

"Amen," Kate, Buck, and Clarissa said at the same time.

Natalie came into the kitchen and sat next to Buck.

⚜

"Where's the bounty hunter? Bring him in closer," Romo said.

"Sir, I'm pulling up his face on number six."

"There he is," Romo said. "Oh yeah, that's him. That's definitely him. Where is he?"

"Sir, he's on the path leading back up to the lodge from the pier. Let me back it up. Right there. That's him in the khaki shorts and white golf shirt."

Romo nodded. "Yes, I see him."

Virgil's heart nearly pounded out of his chest. He recognized Jalili from his picture. His hair was much shorter, and his beard merely stubble now, but that was him. He was walking amid a steady stream of people. His eyes were all over the map, taking it all in. Virgil stood behind a dozen agents, squinting to make out all the details on the monitor. He dropped his handkerchief on the floor and bent down to get it. "Billy Gene, let me know when you've spotted the bounty hunter, but don't lose sight of Saman."

"Copy that."

Virgil stood up straight. At six feet four inches tall, he had an unobstructed view of the monitor.

"Okay, people," Romo said, "this is what we've been waiting for. Actors, look natural and just keep doing what you're doing. Hawk, stay where you are and try not to look intense. That's it. Perfect. For now, just be the guy heading up the landscaping project. I'll let you know where the bounty hunter is. And if and when you need to do anything else. We've got your back."

Virgil kept his eyes on the screens. The bounty hunter—the deadly assassin wanted all over Europe and the Middle East—was now walking *his* turf. Jalili looked out across the back lawn, just like he knew exactly what he was looking for.

"I think he may have spotted Hawk," someone at the computers said.

The bounty hunter squinted and kept looking in Hawk's direction.

A chill crawled up Virgil's spine. This was the real deal. It was so hard not being the one in command.

"Sheriff, I've spotted the bounty hunter," Billy Gene said. "He's comin' up the path from the pier. I'm just yards from Saman. He's standing in the shade, talking on the phone, Flutter's about fifteen yards directly behind him."

Virgil put his hand to his mouth. "You're on one of the monitors now, Billy Gene. Look relaxed, like you're on vacation ..."

Billy Gene said something to two little boys, then picked up a Frisbee that had landed next to them and tossed it back to the sender, a big grin on his face.

"That's it," Virgil said. "Blend in."

"Hawk," Romo said, "the bounty hunter has spotted you. He's playing it safe. Still walking with people all around him. We need to draw him out of that crowd after he makes the turn and comes this way. I need you to move over to where Special Agent Barron is. Pretend to be talking to him about something."

Virgil's heart raced, adrenaline coursing through his veins. Barron was less than a foot from the paved path the bounty hunter was on. Hawk was walking over to him, as instructed.

Virgil held his hand to his mouth. "Billy Gene, how close are you to Hawk?"

"Ten yards. Saman is to my right, about fifteen yards from Hawk. He hasn't stopped lookin' at him. But he's not movin' in."

"Can you see the bounty hunter?"

"Yes, but it's hard to keep him in my line of vision with all the people around him. They're probably all-day boat renters comin' up from the pier to have lunch."

"You'll be able to see him better after he makes the turn. Let's listen …"

"The bounty hunter is testing the waters," Romo said. "He's not going to get drawn out until he feels safe. He's looking for anything or anyone that seems out of place. So stay cool, people. Everybody, do your job."

Hawk stood next to Special Agent Gary Barron. He pointed at the ground and then folded his arms across his chest. "The bounty hunter's getting closer. My knees feel like Jell-O, man."

"Yes, but you're surrounded with FBI," Gary said. "We'll cover you. All you need to do is be Hawk Cummings, head of the landscaping project."

"Yeah, right. That's me." *Am I really doing this?*

"Hawk, it's Romo. I want Gary to get down on this knees and act like he's measuring. You just stay where you are and talk to him, nice and relaxed, so the bounty hunter will see your lips moving. Maybe an occasional smile."

"Okay," Hawk said. "I can do that." *This is for you, Kennedy.* "So, Gary. Are you as hungry as I am?"

"Starved."

"I think once we get the bounty hunter into custody, we should order the biggest, juiciest, totally loaded pan pizza we can think of."

"You really know how to hurt a guy. We may not be eating for a while, you know."

Hawk laughed nervously. "Just making conversation, friend. Just doing as instructed."

"Hawk, it's Romo again. The bounty hunter has made the turn and is about twenty-five yards straight in front of you. Don't look over at the sidewalk. I don't want him making eye contact. I want you to walk about ten yards to your left, away from the sidewalk, and squat down, facing Gary. Take out your tape measure and pretend to be measuring."

Hawk did as he was told. His heart was pounding like it would explode. He wanted to look up at the sidewalk, but he resisted the temptation. If he had known when he met Kennedy that the relationship was going to result in this moment, he would have run as fast as he could. *Lord, help the FBI to get this guy. I just want it over with.*

Virgil pretended to blow his nose. "Are you there?"

"Yes, sir," Billy Gene said. "I've got eyes on the bounty hunter and on Saman. They're both takin' some measured glances at Hawk. Sure looks to me like they know who he is."

"Since everyone's watching the bounty hunter, keep your eyes on Saman. Keep listening."

"Copy that."

"Hawk, it's Romo. The bounty hunter is on the far side of the sidewalk and seems to be keeping his distance. You're not in any danger. I want you to stand up and stretch, and wipe your face with the red kerchief in your right back pocket. That's it. Great. Now fold your arms and hold that pose. Gary, call his name, like you're trying to get his attention. Perfect. The bounty hunter should be there any second. Hawk, don't react. Stay cool. He's just going to do a walk-by ... Easy ... easy ... He should be visible any second ... Where'd he go?" Romo said. "I don't see the bounty hunter. Number six, let me see a headshot. He's not there! Anybody? Has anybody got eyes on the bounty hunter? Come on, where are you ...? We've lost him!" Romo spit out an expletive, then yanked out his earpiece and stormed over to the computers, his voice raised. "He didn't disappear into thin air! Find him. Get him back on camera."

Virgil heard loud voices arguing over technical issues, but he didn't understand what they were saying. He kept his eyes on the guests coming up the sidewalk. The bounty hunter was nowhere in sight. "Billy Gene, do you have eyes on the bounty hunter?"

"I did till he closed in behind that tall man in the Rangers ball cap a few yards back. I've lost him. Saman hasn't moved. He's watchin' every move Hawk makes and then looking out at the folks walking on the sidewalk. I'm tellin' you, Sheriff, there's something cookin'.'"

"Okay, keep watching Saman," Virgil said. "I don't think there's any way the bounty hunter made us. He's out there. He's just testing."

❦

Kate threw up her arms and sat back in her chair. "How could they lose him?"

"I know it's unsettling," Clarissa said, "but this is pretty standard. The guy's a pro. He is going to test and retest before he breaks away from a crowd to speak to Hawk."

Natalie leaned on her elbows. "Clarissa's right, Kate. People are his cover, his safety. If our actors are consistent, he won't suspect a thing. He has no real reason to think we're waiting for him anyway."

"Then I sure don't understand all his *testing*," Buck said. "What reason does he have to act so paranoid?"

"Just the nature of his profession," Natalie said.

Elliot's eyes narrowed. "Why? What has he got to be paranoid about? Isn't the bounty hunter hired by a bail bondsman to go after a person who jumped bail? He would be the only one who could collect the bounty, providing he brought the fugitive in, right? So Buck's got a point. What is there to be so paranoid about? Why all this testing?"

Natalie glanced over at Clarissa. "It's just the way it's done."

"Is this guy really a bounty hunter?" Elliot said. "Or is that a code name?"

"That's classified," Clarissa said.

Elliot arched an eyebrow. "So it could just be a code name?"

"What we know for sure is the guy is coming to get Hawk to tell him where Nameless is. He's dangerous. And we need to get him into custody without hurting him."

"Why such pains to keep from hurtin' the fella?" Buck said. "If he's that evil, like y'all say he is, couldn't you just shoot him in the leg and stop him?"

"Again, Buck, we aren't told everything. Our job is to take him in unharmed."

"I sure hope you have the same regard for Hawk," Kate said.

Natalie smiled. "We do. We're going to protect him with everything we've got."

"So you think this bounty hunter will come back?" Kate said.

"Honey, he's just testin' the waters. He'll be back. You can count on it."

CHAPTER 26

Hawk looked at his watch. It had been over two hours since the bounty hunter had evaded them. It was getting hotter, and harder to look busy. One of the FBI actors brought Gary a cart of petunias to plant.

Hawk picked up one of the plastic crates and set it on the ground where Gary was working. "I don't know how you can get into this with the bounty hunter out there somewhere, maybe even watching us."

"Believe it or not, it helps to keep me focused," Gary said. "You feeling antsy?"

"More like stressed." Hawk sighed. "Man, I hope we don't have to do this for days. I feel like I could lose my lunch."

"You're doing great, Hawk. Really. I'm not just saying that."

"Thanks. I really want to help. But how long can we keep up this ruse of the landscaping project?"

"Until we run out of flowers." Gary smiled and looked up at Hawk. "The bounty hunter had a successful walk-by or disappearing act—whatever it was. He's probably feeling safe now. That's a good thing."

"Safe to do what, though?" Hawk said. "He can't approach me this way, with all of you close by. Obviously, I'm going to have to man up and move away from you where he might actually feel comfortable making a move."

"Are you eager to do that?"

Hawk rolled his eyes. "What do you think? But I can't stand around with this mounting stress, wondering where he is. I'd rather just get it over with. I'm willing to be the bait because I know you've got my back. But let's get on with it."

"Stay put," Gary said. "I'll talk to Special Agent Romo and see what the plan is."

Gary walked away, his phone to his ear.

Hawk got down on his knees and dug a small hole. Gently, he placed one of the petunias into it and scooped dirt around the flower. As he patted down the dirt, he had a flashback of Kennedy's soft hands pulling the dead leaves off a green plant she had in the kitchen. He still couldn't believe she was dead. *I can do this for you. I know I can.*

"How're you holding up?"

Hawk looked up into the face of Special Agent Ryan Ziegler. "Not as well as I'd like. I was telling Gary I need to move away from you guys if we want the bounty hunter to approach me. He's never going to do that as long as I'm this close to anyone."

Ryan squatted down next to Hawk. "We know that. We just want him to get far enough away from the guests that we can grab him. He's smart. He's doing exactly what we expected him to do. Once he gets brave enough to do a walk-by without a bunch of people around him, we'll make our move."

"What if he sees you or reacts faster than you do?" Hawk said. "You've already said you can't hurt him. What if he's got a gun?"

"You let us worry about the bounty hunter. You just keep doing what you're—"

"We've got eyes on the bounty hunter!" Romo's voice came through loud and clear. "Actors, get into your positions. Hawk, I need you to stand up and let Gary plant the flowers. Number six, zoom in on the bounty hunter's face. Oh yeah, there you are, Mr. Houdini. What's his twenty?"

"Sir, he's sitting by the playground. There's at least two dozen children and almost that many parents. He's got sunglasses on, so he could be watching the actors."

"Hear that, people?" Romo said. "Look believable. Hawk, walk around to each actor and pretend to be giving instructions. Point at the ground while you're talking. Look positive and not too intense."

"Okay, here we go," Hawk mumbled to himself. He started with Gary and then walked over to Ryan. "They really pay you guys to do this?" Hawk flashed a crooked smile. He pointed to the ground and then moved on to another actor, who was about ten yards away.

"That's it," Romo said. "Great. The bounty hunter is over there watching. Keep it real, people."

❦

Virgil stood behind the two rows of agents crowded around the surveillance monitors. "You there?"

"Copy that," Billy Gene said. "I've got eyes on the bounty hunter. I'm sitting in the shade, my back leaned against the shade tree, about forty yards directly in front of the playground. I'm pretending to read *Black Hawk Down*."

Virgil put his handkerchief to his nose. "What about Saman?"

"Oh, I've got eyes on him too. He's watchin' every move Hawk makes. I just can't figure him out. Do you think he could be workin' with the bounty hunter?"

"Don't think so," Virgil said. "No one here is paying any attention to him."

"Well, I sure am."

"Good. Keep me posted," Virgil said.

"Will do."

❖

"Special Agent Romo, this is Hawk."

"I'm here. What's up?"

"Sir, I feel like I should be doing something to draw the bounty hunter out in the open. With all this waiting around, we could lose him. You can see him right now. And I'm not in danger. Why not let me get out there away from all the actors and see what he does?"

"You sure you're up for it?"

"Truthfully," Hawk said, "it couldn't be any more stressful than just waiting out here with a big target on my back."

"Fair enough. Actors, you can't react to whatever happens unless I tell you to. Hawk, you have to do exactly as I say."

"I will."

"Okay, pick up a shovel and walk across the back lawn toward the playground. Go to the big oak tree with the hummingbird feeder hanging on it and stop."

Hawk, butterflies in his stomach, left his safe haven and walked across the lawn, stopping at the big oak tree.

"Now lean on the shovel, and look like you're thinking about building a circular flower bed around the base of the tree. Look as natural as you can. I want to see what the bounty hunter does when you're there by yourself."

"He's getting up," Romo said. "The bounty hunter is on the move! Heads up, people. Everybody, stay cool. Assume your roles. Number five, give me a head shot. Number six, bring him in a little closer. That's it. Hawk, you okay?"

"I'm shaking on the inside and my knees are ready to give out, but I'm okay. What do I do if he talks to me?"

"Answer him," Romo said. "We've got your back. Just stay calm and don't blow this. I think we'd all like to get this guy and go home."

"You've got that right. Where is he?"

"He's on the phone, walking in your direction. Remember, he's not going to shoot. He wants to talk. He may ask a question about the lodge. About anything. This is an icebreaker. Just be natural."

Hawk exhaled a nervous laugh. "Right. How close is he?"

"About twenty yards. He's got his phone to his ear. But he's coming to you. That's what we want. You're a hero, Hawk. We all respect you for what you're doing."

"You sure you've got my back?" Hawk noticed his hands were shaking a little.

"You are surrounded with FBI. Relax. This is your moment."

⚜

Kate tapped her fingers on the kitchen table and shifted in her chair. "This is making me crazy. Hawk, be careful. Lord, protect him. Put a circle of angels around him and don't let anything evil touch him."

Elliot whispered, "Amen."

Buck put his hand on hers. "Baby girl, God's got this. Just like He always does."

Kate nodded. "I know, Dad. I really do. But my wits aren't cooperating."

Elliot chuckled. "Now that's a good one. Sounded like something Riley would say."

"I guess we're not going to meet the camp bus tomorrow afternoon," Kate said. "I miss that little munchkin."

"Clarissa, why are they lettin' the bounty hunter walk over to Hawk?" Buck said. "Couldn't they just shoot him with a rubber bullet?"

"Special Agent Romo knows what he's doing. And you heard Hawk. He wants to get this done."

"Poor guy is probably exhausted," Elliot said. "Look at what's happened to him in a week's time. First he's knocked out with a chemical, and when he wakes up, Kennedy is gone and her house totally empty. He owns his affair and tells Laura Lynn, and they break up. Then he faces the humiliation of telling the family about the affair. Then Dennis tells him what Brody saw, and he realizes Brody was talking about Kennedy and him, and the drone attack. He's told that Kennedy was kidnapped by eight men. Brody thinks he's being followed, then is killed when his car goes off the road and down an embankment. Hawk and Dennis get up the nerve to report everything to the sheriff. Then he's detained by the FBI, questioned for hours, and enlisted for this unnerving assignment. Romo said Hawk was a hero. I think so too."

Kate wiped a tear off her cheek and linked arms with Elliot.

"He's done everything he can to make things right," Buck said. "But that's a whole lot of hurtin' inside of a week."

Clarissa held up her palm to quiet them. "The bounty hunter stopped. He's writing something on what appears to be a business card. He's just waiting to see if Hawk reacts to his presence."

"I hope not," Kate said. "But I sure am."

⚜

Virgil's heart pounded as if it would explode. Everything was about to play out. He put his hand to his mouth. "Where are you?"

"I'm standing," Billy Gene said, "leaning against the same tree, pretending to text. The bounty hunter stopped walking and wrote something down. I think he's testing Hawk to see if he acts nervous with him standing there. So far, Hawk's been amazing."

"Where's Saman ...? Billy Gene ...?"

"Sheriff, I've gotta go—*now!*"

Virgil stared at the monitors. Hawk was leaning on the shovel, looking pensive. The bounty hunter, the vile *assassin* wanted in Europe and the Middle East, was no more than ten yards from him, talking on the phone.

"Hawk," Romo said, "the bounty hunter is easing his way toward you. He's about thirty feet behind you, talking on his phone again. I'm going to ask you to do something difficult and brave. I need you to be even more of an actor."

"And do what?"

"I want you to turn around slowly," Romo said, "and make eye contact with the bounty hunter. Smile or somehow acknowledge him."

Hawk exhaled and whispered. "I can do this. I need to do this. Lord, help me do this. Okay. Here goes."

Every agent in the room was fixated on Hawk. Virgil's heart pounded so hard he was sure they could hear it. *Come on, Hawk. This is the moment of truth.*

Hawk turned slowly, still looking at the ground around the tree. Finally, he lifted his gaze and looked at the bounty hunter and smiled. "Hey, man. You doin' all right?"

"Yes. I am fine. Thank you."

"It's getting hot out here," Hawk said. "Be careful not to get overheated. That'll put a damper on your vacation big time."

The bounty hunter nodded. "Yes. Big time."

Virgil scanned all the monitors, hoping to spot Billy Gene, but the cameras were focused on the main event. Something was going on. Virgil could feel it. He resented that his hands were tied and his authority trumped by Romo. Why did Billy Gene have to get off the phone so abruptly?

"Sheriff, are you still there?" Billy Gene sounded out of breath.

Virgil turned around, his back to the agents. "Yes, what's happening?"

"Saman has a gun. In his hand. What do you want me to do?"

"Where is he?"

"Behind the bounty hunter."

"Where are you?"

"I'm behind Saman."

"I trust your instincts, Billy Gene. The success of this operation depends on the bounty hunter being taken in unharmed. But do what you need to do to protect Hawk, whatever it takes. Go."

Virgil could hardly breathe. He spun around and stared at the monitors, listening to what was being said in the room—and on the other end of the phone.

"Number six, zoom in on that man standing behind the bounty hunter," Romo said. "We saw him on camera earlier. Do we know who he is? He seems to be inching closer. I'd sure like to know why."

"I don't recognize him," someone said. "But isn't that Hawk's friend, Kirby something-or-other behind him?"

"Hawk, isn't that your friend, a few yards behind the bounty hunter?" Romo said.

Hawk made eye contact with Billy Gene and sensed something was wrong. His pulse surged, and he was hot all over. He wanted to run, but he had to see this through. "Yes, that's him. Do you want me to say something?"

"Actually, I'd like him to leave," Romo said. "But I don't know how to get that done without blowing everything."

Hawk kept getting bad vibes from Billy Gene but couldn't figure out why. Then he saw it—the man standing directly behind the bounty hunter had a gun pointed at his back!

Billy Gene charged the guy like an angry bull and knocked the gun out of his hand just as it discharged.

People screamed and were running in all directions. It was utter chaos.

The bounty hunter looked alarmed, and turned to run. Billy Gene stuck his leg out and tripped him, sending him falling facedown on the ground.

Without thinking, Hawk jumped on the bounty hunter's back and straddled him, fighting to hold him down.

The man who fired the gun had the wind knocked out of him. Billy Gene slapped handcuffs on him.

Hawk rolled off the bounty hunter so Billy Gene could subdue him. In a matter of seconds, Billy Gene pulled the bounty hunter's arms behind him, put on the handcuffs, and pulled him to his feet. "Surprise, sweetheart. You've got a blind date with the feds."

Hawk got up and was immediately surrounded by at least a dozen FBI agents.

"You okay?" Gary said.

Hawk nodded. "I'm fine. What just happened?"

Special Agent Ziegler poked Billy Gene in the chest. "Who *are* you?"

"I'm Deputy Billy Gene Duncan of the Raleigh County Sheriff's Department. I'm off duty. Up here to enjoy a relaxing weekend."

"You told us you were an old friend of Hawk's," Gary said.

"Sorry about that. It's never good to tell people you're a deputy when you're trying to get some R and R."

"Well, Deputy, you've got some explaining to do. You just interfered with an FBI operation in progress." Ziegler smiled. "And I, for one, am grateful to you." He shook Billy Gene's hand. "We're going to need to talk to you. It may not turn out to be the relaxing weekend you'd hoped for."

"Oh, don't worry about that." Billy Gene winked at Hawk. "Dealin' with the feds will be a nice change of pace."

Romo glared at Virgil. "You want to tell me what that was all about?"

"It appears that one of my off-duty deputies just saved your heinie," Virgil said, trying not to smile.

"Don't get smug," Romo said. "I made it clear that this was *my* operation."

"And by all accounts, it was successful. Congratulations. I'm sure the higher-ups in the Bureau will recognize you for capturing the bounty hunter."

"You were working behind my back."

"How do you figure that?" Virgil said. "I've been standing here all this time. But I'll tell you something. This is my county, my turf, my people. I took an oath to protect them."

"I didn't need your help," Romo said. "The operation was right on track."

"Except you didn't know that your bounty hunter was being hunted. A good deputy taking a few days of vacation saw the gun and acted accordingly."

Romo's eyes narrowed. "Vacation, huh? Then tell me why he knew to tackle the bounty hunter."

"Actually Hawk tackled him quite handily. Deputy Duncan subdued him in order to get the cuffs on. As for Hawk, he really is a hero."

"Just so you know," Romo said. "I wouldn't have put him at risk."

"I believe you did all you could to protect him. But we both know that if he had been hurt or killed, you would have considered it acceptable collateral damage." Virgil shook his head. "I'm sorry, but anyone who agrees to help me and my deputies, after being told we've got their back, is not—nor ever will be—acceptable collateral damage. We leave no man behind."

"We live in different worlds, Virgil. Sometimes I have to make decisions that keep me up at night. Decisions I hope Timothy and Lacy will never know about."

"Being a fed is tough. I'm not sure I could do it. But I'm glad there are good people who do." Virgil put his hand on Romo's shoulder. "But don't think you're the only one who's had to make decisions that haunt you for a long time. I think it's the nature of law enforcement. The biggest difference between your job and mine is that mine is subjective. I love this community. These people. I grew up here and know many of them by name. I feel it when any of them is in peril. My biggest challenge is putting my feelings aside and being objective. On the other hand, you don't know the victims or the perpetrators, so staying objective is easy. Your biggest challenge is knowing when to give yourself permission to feel. Either way, it's a balancing act."

"What an interesting perspective. I never thought of it quite that way." Romo seemed lost in thought. Finally, he said, "I like you, Sheriff. You're a good man. I'm not going to ask what part you played in this. The truth is, Deputy Duncan saved the day. A gunshot wound at close range would likely have killed the bounty hunter or critically injured him. As it turned out, we got him into custody unharmed and successfully completed the operation, which will make some powerful people very happy."

"Did I hear *we*?" Virgil said.

"You did. I intend to put in my report that our success was largely due to the cooperative efforts of the Raleigh County Sheriff's Department. Oh, I'll get razzed unmercifully, but it's a small price to pay. I really am grateful."

"The CIA will be too." Virgil winked. "You might even get a promotion."

Romo laughed. "Stranger things have happened."

A comfortable silence settled over them for half a minute.

Finally, Romo said, "Seriously, Virgil, thanks for your help. I'm ashamed that I misjudged you and didn't think you would be an asset to the operation. Nothing could be further from the truth."

"I appreciate you saying that. If you hadn't offered me a hot dog today, I might never have gotten a glimpse of the man behind the badge. Not only are you a good lawman, you're a heck of a dad. And just for the record, you were outstanding with Hawk. You never put him in harm's way beyond the obvious risk he understood going in. In fact, I was impressed with the way you organized and ran the entire operation. But I tend to be disagreeable when I'm shut out of a case that involves the people I swore to protect."

Romo held out his hand. "I guess we both learned something."

Virgil shook his hand. "We did. So does this mean you're going to tell me who the shooter was?"

"Nice try, Sheriff. And yes, it's classified."

Virgil laughed. "You're still using your office in the courthouse, aren't you?"

"Yes, but not for long. I promised Timothy I'd be home on Sunday and take him to the pool. I'm happy to say that I have no trouble giving myself permission to *feel* when it comes to that." Romo winked.

CHAPTER 27

Kate, Elliot, Buck, Natalie, and Clarissa cheered at the news that Hawk was safe and the bounty hunter was unharmed and in FBI custody.

Kate wiped the tears off her face and sat back in her chair and whispered a prayer of thanksgiving.

"I'll tell you what," Buck said, "that grandson of mine is a hero in my book. And that Deputy Duncan—wasn't he somethin'?"

"Oh, did you folks know him?" Natalie said.

Kate jumped in before her dad could say anything else. "We've known him for years. He worked the case when my late husband and daughter were missing."

"Well, that was good thinking and quick action on the deputy's part," Clarissa said. "If the shooter had hit the bounty hunter at close range, he would probably have died right there. Another split second, and we'd be looking at an entirely different outcome."

"Who was the shooter?" Kate said. "Where did he come from? Why wasn't the FBI prepared?"

Natalie and Clarissa looked at each other and shrugged.

"Whoever he was, he wasn't on the FBI's radar." Natalie walked over and disarmed the security alarm. "I think all our agents must be scratching their heads. Guess we'll be filled in later."

Elliot took Kate's hand in his. "I'm just grateful that Hawk is safe and this thing's finally over."

Natalie's and Clarissa's phones beeped, and each glanced at her screen.

"Well," Natalie said. "Looks like our ride will be here within the hour. We had better go pack. It's been our pleasure staying with you. You're a really special family."

Clarissa nodded. "Your faith throughout this ordeal has truly been an inspiration. For your sake, I hope you never need the FBI ever again."

The front door slammed, and Abby and Jesse came rushing in, sounding out of breath.

"Were y'all listening to what happened?" Jesse said, his face flushed. "Deputy Duncan saw that guy's gun and knocked it out of his hand just as he shot it, and then he tripped the bounty hunter, who fell flat on his face—"

"And Hawk held the bounty hunter on the ground," Abby said, "until Deputy Duncan could put cuffs on him! They're both heroes!"

"Yes, we were listening," Kate said, slipping her arm around Jesse's sweaty back. "Where were you two when it happened?"

"Jesse and I were just about to walk home. We were sitting in Flutter's, cooling off and having a Coke—"

"When people outside started screaming and running all over the place," Jesse said. "We looked out and saw Hawk sitting on the guy's back, holding him down. And then Deputy Duncan cuffed him and gave him over to the FBI. The shooter too." Jesse grinned. "My big brother is a hero. I can't wait to tell Dawson!"

Natalie shook her head. "Jesse, the rules haven't changed. This isn't going to be written up in the newspaper. Or talked about on the news. And you can't tell anyone. And why is that?"

Jesse sighed. "Because it's classified."

Clarissa tilted his chin. "It's for your brother's safety."

"I get it," Jesse said. "I just wanted to brag on him. He was awesome."

"You can certainly tell *Hawk* how you feel," Kate said. "I can hardly wait to put my arms around him."

Jesse looked at Natalie and Clarissa. "Now that it's over, I guess you'll be leaving soon."

Clarissa nodded. "Within the hour. We were just going to pack."

"We'll miss you—each of you." Natalie blinked the moisture from her eyes.

Kate, Elliot, and Buck rose to their feet.

"We can't thank you enough for making us feel safe," Kate said.

"And informed," Elliot added.

"And for being good sports when I clobbered you at gin rummy." Jesse laughed. "I guess if you really must go, I'll have no choice but to remain the champ."

"I can't thank you ladies enough for the good conversation," Buck said. "I sure won't forget you."

Abby put her arms around Natalie. "Thanks for walking me to work every morning. I would've been scared to walk alone."

In the next minute, everyone exchanged hugs and more thank-yous. And then it was pin-drop still.

"I hate good-byes," Jesse said. "This is the part where it's always sad."

"A little," Natalie said.

Clarissa brushed Jesse's damp hair off his forehead. "But I'm glad we enjoyed you enough to miss you. That doesn't happen most of the time."

Hawk sat in an interview room in the Raleigh County Courthouse, finishing up his statement and feeling eager to get home.

"Hawk, I want to thank you for a superb job," Romo said. "Special Agents Barron and Ziegler said you did as well as any agent could have done."

"I'm glad I could help." Hawk folded his hands on the table. "Can you tell me anything about the shooter? I honestly thought he was coming after me."

"We don't know anything about the shooter," Romo said. "The Bureau is doing a background check, but right now, he's a mystery. We didn't see that coming. Thankfully, Deputy Duncan did."

Hawk nodded. "That's for sure."

"I mean, what are the odds that he scheduled a few vacation days that happened to coincide with our operation?"

"Yeah, what are the odds?" Hawk said.

"And he just happened to be right there when our unidentified perpetrator pulled a gun?" Romo said. "And just happened to ram the guy just as he pulled the trigger, keeping the bounty hunter unharmed—which happened to be what my orders were?"

"Wow." A grin stretched Hawk's cheeks. "I remember you sitting in my living room, telling us that it wouldn't be necessary to rely on God, that your people are the best at what they do, and that *you* would keep me safe. But it's pretty hard to deny that God was in the details that even you couldn't plan for."

Romo's face went blank. "Well, you got me there. I'm not really a man of faith, but you make a point worth thinking about. I've got a five-year-old son, and a baby girl due in October. My wife, Annie, wants us to start going to church. Maybe this is a sign from God that we should."

"Maybe," Hawk said. "After I was grown, I really appreciated that my parents brought me up in the church."

"You didn't resent being made to go?"

"Not at all. I didn't know any differently."

"I always thought I'd let my kids decide for themselves what to believe," Romo said. "You know, when they're older."

"They *will* decide," Hawk said. "We all do. But Grandpa Buck always said, 'If you don't stand for something, you'll fall for anything.' Now that I'm grown, I understand what he meant. You have to know what you believe before you can stand firm. You need a moral compass."

"I guess that's true." Romo was quiet for a few moments. "So when Christians grow up with this moral compass, do you think they make decisions that are better than everyone else's?"

Hawk felt shame scald his face. *Lord, give me the right words.* "Not always. At least not right away. But we know things won't be right again until we turn it around. For example, how did I end up having an affair with a woman I hardly knew, after being raised in a strong Christian home to believe that sex is a gift God created for a husband

and wife, and it's meant to be expressed only within the parameters of marriage?"

"Hawk, I really wasn't talking about you. I—"

"It's okay. I'm a perfect example. I met Kennedy in a parking lot and helped her pick up a sack of spilled groceries. She was new to the area and didn't know anyone. She seemed lonely and I offered to give her a Jeep ride after work. Innocent, right? Or *not* so innocent. Deep down, I knew I was playing with fire. She was gorgeous and vulnerable and available, and I knew to guard myself against any situation that could turn sexual. But instead of helping her out and then politely walking away, I opened the door that every guy knows is dangerous, and lust exploded into a full-blown affair. That's like lighting a match and walking into a room flooded with natural gas. My point is I had a strong moral compass. I *ignored* it. I deceived myself clear up until the time she disappeared. But the truth is I was never really comfortable sinning, and I lied—even to Kennedy—to keep it secret. I disgraced myself. I broke Laura Lynn's heart. And I disappointed my family. When I realized what I'd done, I asked God to forgive me, and He has. But that doesn't erase the natural consequences I just have to live with."

"Don't be too hard on yourself, Hawk. This is the twenty-first century. Those kinds of old-fashioned values are honorable, but few people live by them anymore. You're still the same person. Sure, you have life experience you didn't have before, and you don't want to make the same mistake again. But you're still the same man."

Hawk blinked the stinging from his eyes. He wasn't the same man. There's no way Special Agent Romo would understand. Hawk didn't understand it himself.

"The point I was trying to make," Hawk said, "is that a moral compass is extremely important. If I had read mine and done what I knew was right, I would have gone an entirely different direction, and my life wouldn't be the mess it is at this moment. It's important to equip your kids with the principles found in God's Word. They work, if we use them. And we can't use them if we don't know what they are."

Romo nodded. "I see what you're saying. Maybe Annie's been right all along. Thanks for being so candid. You've given me a lot to think about. Well, Hawk, I guess this is the end of the line for us. Special Agent Barron will drive you home." Romo stood and extended his hand. "Thanks again for your willingness to help us catch the bounty hunter."

Hawk smiled and shook his hand. "I was willing. Deputy Duncan got it done. But it was a split second only God could've planned for."

Hawk walked up the steps to the front porch and waved at Gary Barron as he drove away, a cloud of dust kicking up behind his rental car. It felt as if a lifetime had passed since he had sat on the porch swing and counted the minutes until it was time to go into Foggy Ridge and give his statement to Sheriff Granger.

Now he sat on the porch swing and just listened to the sounds. The hummingbirds fighting over the feeder. The mourning doves cooing. A jet crossing the wide expanse of Arkansas sky. The hot June breeze whistling through the pines. He knew the minute he walked into the house, he'd be smothered with kisses and hugs and tears of joy from a family that truly loved him.

So why was he feeling so lost and alone? He had thought that after he helped the FBI capture the bounty hunter, he would have done all that he could to honor Kennedy and would be free to move on. She was dead. It was over. Why couldn't he let go? Why did it hurt so much to know that he would never see her again? He knew nothing true about her, except for what he had read in her heart. And yet an indefinable bond more real than the relationship itself would not let him go.

The orange-and-white kitten climbed up on the porch and sat at Hawk's feet meowing. He reached down and picked him up and looked into his bright yellow eyes.

"What are you doing out here all by yourself? Are you feeling lost too, little guy? I can't believe you're still nameless."

Nameless. How he hated that word. Her name was Kennedy Taylor. Nothing was going to change that reality in his heart and mind. It had been painful listening to her referred to as Nameless, as if she never existed, never made an impact, never left an impression. She wasn't just a vapor that disappeared.

The front door flew open and Jesse came outside.

"I saw you sitting out here." Jesse leaned against the railing and looked at Hawk. "When did you get home?"

Hawk set the kitten down. "Just a few minutes ago. I needed time to catch my breath."

"You're a hero," Jesse said. "Abby and I saw you holding the bounty hunter down on the ground until Deputy Duncan came over and put the cuffs on him. When that guy's gun went off, people were running and screaming. It was cool—in an awful kind of way, I mean. At least nobody got hurt. Natalie reminded me it's classified and I can't tell anybody. I want everyone to know you're a hero."

Hawk smiled. "You're wound up tighter than a tick."

"I know." Jesses flashed a mouthful of silver. "It's been crazy. I'll bet you're tired."

"Not really. Worn out, maybe. It's almost like I was on a movie set, and Director Romo told me what to do next. There was something intriguing and fun about it, before it got intense. I made friends with two of the FBI special agents, Gary Barron and Ryan Ziegler. They were really great guys. Romo wasn't so bad either. I respected him when he was coordinating the whole thing, telling each of us what to do. And I got to witness to him a little before I left."

"Romo?" Jesse said. "The same guy that told us we wouldn't need to rely on God because we had *him*?"

Hawk smiled. "I think he got knocked off his high horse when Deputy Duncan came in and saved the day. It all played out the way God intended."

"Come on." Jesse grabbed both of Hawk's arms and pulled him to his feet. "Everybody's been waiting for you to come home. They'll want to hear all this. Mama's been holding dinner."

Jesse picked up the kitten, draped it over his shoulder, and opened the front door. Hawk followed him inside, the smell of their mother's pasta sauce permeating his senses. He had forgotten it was Saturday. It was one week ago, almost to the minute, that he had awakened to find Kennedy gone.

"Hawk's home!" Jesse hollered.

A stampede of family members came charging out of the kitchen, and seconds later came the kisses, hugs, and tears of joy he knew awaited him. He was grateful for such lavish love but felt very undeserving. His choices had put them through an entire week of anguish, worry, and fear. And yet not one of them had complained or thrown it back in his face.

Hawk laughed and enjoyed the moment, thinking that this was how the prodigal son must have felt. They hadn't prepared the fatted calf, but Mama's spaghetti would do just fine.

CHAPTER 28

Just before ten on Saturday night, Special Agent Romo sat at his desk in the temporary FBI office in the Raleigh County Courthouse, waiting for a text. Special Agent Nadia Vaughn from the Milwaukee Field Office was the last FBI actor needed to complete this operation. But unless Herbod Abbas Jalili agreed to cooperate, everything they had worked for might be for naught.

He glanced at his watch. Special Agent Gary Barron assured him that he would get the video just as soon as the final cut was finished.

Romo got up and stood in front of the window. The courthouse grounds were lit up, and a surprising number of people were walking on the sidewalks. Traffic was heavy and noisy on Main Street. Virgil had told him that the population of the town tripled during tourist season, and got even higher on the weekends. And that even though fighting crime within the city limits was Police Chief Mitchell's responsibility, Virgil's department worked hand in hand with the police to help keep the peace, enforce the speed limit, and deal with traffic flow.

Romo's phone beeped. He had a text from Gary: *Done. Unbelievably realistic. Farsi approved by the FBI interpreter. Take a look.*

"I hope you're right," Romo murmured. "I want to get home to Annie and Timothy." Romo tapped the screen to open the video and then put it on full screen.

Jalili was looking into the camera, holding up a copy of the *Wall Street Journal* with today's date. In the background could be seen the side view of a young woman kneeling, her hands bound behind her. She was crying and looked very upset. Jalili picked up the camera and walked over to the woman. He held the camera in front of her face and said something to her, presumably in Farsi. She lifted her head, a tear trickling down her cheek. Special Agent Nadia Vaughn! She was striking, and looked remarkably like the pictures he had seen of Nameless, right down to the almond-shaped eyes. She faced the camera, her lips quivering, and spoke in Farsi for half a minute or so. When she finished talking, she hung her head. Jalili went back and set the camera down, then walked over and stood behind Nadia, who was quietly weeping. Jalili straightened his arm, held the gun to the back of her head, and fired. He turned and walked back to the camera, wearing a smug grin, then pulled up a chair and sat so his face took up the entire screen. He began talking again, this time looking arrogant and sounding bold and confident. He ranted for half a minute, then wrote something on an index card and held it in front of the camera. It was a series of numbers that appeared to be a bank account number. Finally, Jalili picked up the camera, walked over to the victim's body, and pulled her head back by her hair, displaying the exit wound, which was the size of a walnut. He said something that sounded derisive and then laughed.

Romo sat back in his chair and exhaled. He stared at the woman's lifeless face and wondered how horrible it would be for her father when he was forced to view the tape. He keyed in Gary's cell number.

"What did you think?" Gary said.

"Honestly? It took my breath away, even though I knew it was staged. Nadia was perfect and very believable. Great job."

"Thanks," Gary said. "We're all beat and ready to pack it up. But we're pleased."

"I know how you staged the shooting," Romo said. "But how in the world did you create the exit wound?"

Gary laughed. "They were two different women."

"You're kidding?"

"The first woman was Nadia. She's a dead ringer for Nameless. According to our interpreter, her Farsi was impeccable. She looked into the camera and condemned the Iranian regime, told her father she loved him, and didn't blame him for the action of these barbarians. After Jalili shot her, he went back and set the camera down. He put his face in front of the camera to hide the background and talked just long enough for us to make the switch."

"Clever," Romo said. "So when he went back and exposed the victim's face, who was it?"

"That was Molly Isaac from our office. She's a pretty gal with a similar body type and the same dark hair. And with a little makeup and an authentic-looking exit wound, she made a believable victim. Let's hope the CIA will be able to get word to Nameless's father that this was staged. He can never know what *really* happened."

"He won't," Romo said. "Okay, Gary. Get this to Langley immediately. Ask them to let me know when it's done. Then go home and hug your wife. I'm going to crash for a few hours and then head back to Fayetteville first thing in the morning. I promised to take Timothy swimming."

"Will do, Chris. Enjoy tomorrow. I'll see you Monday."

Romo disconnected the call. He sat back in his chair and put his feet on his desk, watching the slow-moving traffic on Main Street. Mission accomplished. He had brought in Jalili unharmed, and Jalili had cooperated to fake Abrisham Kermani's execution. Now, when the five million dollars was transferred into Jalili's bank account, that would signal the Iranian officials' belief in the video's legitimacy. The young woman's execution would then serve as payback for her father's treasonous act of giving Iranian nuclear secrets to the United States. What would happen to Jalili after that was classified.

A knock at the door caused him to jump. "Come in."

"I saw the light on," Virgil said. "Just checking to see if you were really here. Don't you guys ever sleep?"

Romo laughed. "About every other day. I'm just sitting here waiting for a phone call. Why don't you sit with me for a few minutes. I'm going to have a cup of coffee. Can I fix you one?"

"Since I'm up, why don't I get them both?" Virgil said. "You drink yours black, if I remember right."

Romo nodded. "Thanks."

Virgil went to the Keurig in the back of the room. "So why are you still here? You took the bounty hunter into custody hours ago."

"We had to complete a couple more steps before we leave."

Virgil handed Romo his cup of coffee, then sat in a chair next to his desk. "I suppose those 'couple more steps' are classified?"

"They are." Romo took a sip of coffee. "But I think you deserve to know in generalities what's going on."

"Thanks. I'm all ears."

"I trust you will keep this between us," Romo said. "For his own safety, Hawk can never know."

"Understood."

"Virgil, Nameless was the daughter of a double agent who works for a foreign government, one not friendly with ours. This double agent has been feeding vital information to the US. He was compromised. And in retaliation, this foreign government hired Jalili to kill the double agent's daughter and send proof of her death, after which they would have five million dollars transferred to his bank account. Jalili is more than a bounty hunter—he's a professional assassin."

"And your job was to keep Jalili from finding Nameless?" Virgil said.

"Technically, my job was to bring him in unharmed."

"I see." Virgil took another sip of coffee. "Of course, Jalili couldn't have found her anyway, because you said she was dead."

"I did say that."

"And that there was no public record of her death," Virgil said.

"Yes, I said that too." Romo stared at Virgil and studied his demeanor. "This is crazy. Give me your word that this stays between us, and I'll *show* you why we had to bring Jalili in unharmed."

"You have my word."

Romo handed his phone to Virgil. "Open the video."

Virgil tapped the screen and watched with great interest. When it was done, he handed the phone back to Romo. "I see why you were so adamant that the bounty hunter be brought in unharmed. I assume his making this video was part of the 'couple more steps' you referred to?"

"Very perceptive, Sheriff."

"That's an Oscar-winning production," Virgil said. "Very convincing."

Romo nodded, the corners of his mouth twitching. "That's the goal." Romo's phone beeped. He looked at the text message. *Congratulations. And thank you. We shall all sleep well.* He smiled. "Well, Sheriff. Everybody's happy. The operation was a complete success. When I file my report, I will make sure Deputy Duncan is given his due and make it known that your department's help was invaluable, even though you never did say just how it was you were involved."

"How? I never even said *if.*"

Romo laughed and shook Virgil's hand. "I hope our paths cross again. Just think what a good team we'd make if we could actually talk straight to each other."

"I would like that, Chris. I've enjoyed getting to know you. You've got a bright future. A beautiful family. And unusually good taste in hot dogs."

Romo smiled and picked up his briefcase. "It's been a pleasure. See you around, Sheriff."

CHAPTER 29

Virgil watched from the window as Christopher Romo's car pulled out onto Main Street and disappeared in a jungle of red lights. What a crazy and confusing few days it had been.

He owed Mitch. Without the information and personal analysis he had shared, Virgil would truly have been operating in the dark.

And Billy Gene ... how many times had his instincts been right on? Too bad Virgil couldn't brag on Billy Gene, at least to his peers, but the FBI covert operation would remain classified. There would be no newspaper article, no spot on the news, no interviews given. What had happened at Angel View today would be known only by those who were directly involved. The guests who were aware of a gun going off were told by a quick-thinking FBI special agent that it was a training exercise for law enforcement involved in crowd control, and that the gun, loaded only with blanks, went off by mistake. It was a nonissue within five minutes.

Virgil smiled. He doubted it was a nonissue at Kate and Elliot's. He knew how relieved they must be that the ordeal was over. He took his phone out of his pocket and keyed in Kate's number.

"Hello, Virgil," Kate said. "I was hoping you'd call. What a day. I can't thank you enough for sending Billy Gene up here to keep you informed. I would love to have seen the look on that arrogant Romo's face when he realized it was one of your deputies who had saved his operation."

"For what it's worth, he was humbled and very appreciative. Romo's not such a bad guy once you get past the surface."

"Really, Virgil? I'm surprised to hear you, of all people, say that."

"Opinions can change. You really never know what people are made of until you see them in action. He did an amazing job of coordinating every aspect of the operation. I prejudged him, and that was a mistake. And he was great with Hawk. He had his people watching him carefully. Hawk is the one who wanted to ramp things up and draw out the bounty hunter. He said it was less stressful than sitting around waiting with a target on his back."

"Hawk told us the same thing," Kate said. "I'll take your word for it. Maybe when Romo left, he regretted saying that there was no need to rely on God because his people were the best and they would protect Hawk."

Virgil smiled. "Oh, I'm quite sure that he ate those words."

"Did he ever tell you who the bounty hunter was and why the big effort to bring him in totally unharmed? Or who the shooter was? Or who killed Kennedy Taylor? Hawk told us that he's known about her death since he agreed to help Romo. He's been through so much, and now he's grieving on top of everything else."

"I know. I'm sorry. Romo didn't want anyone to know until they had the bounty hunter in custody. The whole operation was based on his believing she was alive and that Hawk knew where she was."

"Did he tell you how she died?"

"No, he didn't," Virgil said. "It's classified."

"So no one knows who kidnapped her?"

"He didn't say. I think we'd all like to know. But it could be for the best that we don't."

Kate sighed. "What about Brody's death? Are you going to investigate it now?"

"Several FBI special agents were assigned to investigate while the covert operation was going on. I was told the skid marks indicated only one car—Brody's. There's no evidence of foul play."

"But what about Brody's claim that he was being followed? Everything else he said made sense. Why would that be any different?"

"Kate, the young man had mental issues. The stress of seeing the drone attack and kidnapping could easily have triggered enough anxiety to make him think he was being followed. And make him restless so he couldn't sleep. It's certainly possible he got up around ten o'clock the night of the accident and just went for a drive and took a curve too fast."

"Do you really believe that?" Kate said.

"I believe that the science shows only one set of skid marks. Beyond that, I can only speculate."

Kate laughed. "Since when? Your hunches are almost always right. What's your hunch?"

"Honestly, I haven't had any mental time to give to it," Virgil said. "The FBI has one of the best labs in the world. They said there was no evidence of foul play. They were sure enough that they told Brody's parents, who were immensely relieved."

"What about Dennis? Is he buying it?"

"I haven't talked to him. Kate, there is no case anymore. The FBI told me that the men who kidnapped Kennedy were professionals and didn't leave a speck of evidence. They checked out Kennedy's house. It was wiped clean with bleach. They interviewed the people at the realty company that listed her house. It *is* owned by the FAMPRO Corporation out of Little Rock, which is what they told Hawk. They said the house has been vacant since it was listed last fall. FAMPRO had been using it as a perk for their executives to enjoy a weekend getaway, and decided to sell it and buy something closer to Little Rock. And the FBI found nothing suspicious about Brody's death."

"Good heavens, Virgil. When did this happen? Why didn't you tell us?"

"I didn't find out until this afternoon when I went back to the office, but Kevin has been working with the FBI on the case. There's just nothing there for us to justify using the manpower to investigate what's already been investigated."

"You don't find it odd that the realty company told the FBI that the house had been vacant since last fall, when we know Kennedy had lived there for at least six weeks?"

"Of course I do," Virgil said. "But the FBI also checked the post office, and they didn't show Kennedy Taylor getting mail delivered there. Or any bank in Foggy Ridge that had an account under that name."

"Maybe she used another name."

"Maybe she did, Kate. But there's no way to know that. It's as if she never existed."

"Hawk is going to be disappointed."

"Maybe not," Virgil said. "He's known since Wednesday that Kennedy's dead. It's the FBI's case, not mine. It's better not to step on their toes, especially when they have been forthcoming with their findings."

Kate sighed. "I suppose you're right."

"On a lighter note, is Hawk still up? I'd like to speak with him for a minute."

"Sure, I'll walk the phone into the kitchen. I think he and Jesse are eating the last of tonight's cheesecake."

"Riley's coming home from camp tomorrow, isn't she?"

"Yes, and I can hardly wait. I'll talk to you soon. Hawk, Virgil would like to speak to you for a minute. Here, just use my phone ..."

"Hello, Sheriff."

"How're you holding up, Hawk? You've had quite a week."

"I'm all right. I think I'm feeling the letdown after the hype. It's a lot to take in. I hope now that it's over, I'll be able to get Kennedy off my mind."

"Give it time," Virgil said. "I think we men want everything that hurts to go away too quickly. I think pain is supposed to be a symptom of something that needs to be treated. Whether it's the physical variety or an aching heart."

"I don't think there's an effective treatment for an aching heart."

"Time," Virgil said.

"I'm not sure even time will be enough for this ache. What I need are answers. And there aren't any."

"I know, Hawk. I'm sorry. I was proud of the way you handled yourself throughout this ordeal. Romo hit you with Kennedy's death right off the bat, and yet you stepped up, put your feelings on hold, and did what you had to do. You deserve a little time to be alone with the pain. The one thing I can promise you is that it won't hurt like this forever. It does get better."

"That's what I hear," Hawk said. "By the way, thanks again for letting Deputy Duncan stay at Angel View and keep an eye on things for you. Now that it's over, I realize that part of the reason I stayed focused was because I saw him hanging out around the lodge and knew that he and you were in touch."

"Thanks, Hawk. I care a lot about you and your family. I wasn't about to be shut out on my own turf. It worked out. And Romo turned out to be a nice guy after all."

"Yeah, he did."

"Well, I'll let you go. Get some rest. Be good to yourself."

"I will. Good night, Sheriff."

Virgil disconnected the call and just listened to the silence. His body was tired, but he would have to wind down before he went home.

He knew Kate was expecting him to find out the answers to all her questions. What she would have to accept is that all of them were classified. Romo had taken a big risk letting Virgil see the video, which confirmed most of what Mitch had revealed in secret. Virgil could not, in good conscience, pursue any unanswered questions. He already knew far more than he should and would never expose any information they trusted him to withhold.

Virgil felt bad for Hawk. What a whirlwind of emotions that young man had been caught up in this past week. Virgil knew Hawk was hurting more than he let on, and hoped that, in time, he would accept Kennedy's death and move on.

Hawk sat in the living room, telling and retelling snippets of the past week's saga—in no particular order. Jesse had reluctantly gone to bed after falling asleep twice, but the others were wide eyed and all ears.

Hawk finally slouched in his chair. "I'm talked out. My brain is fried."

"I'm surprised you lasted this long," Kate said. "I think I've aged ten years, realizing what you've been through."

Abby sat on the couch, holding hands with Jay. "We didn't mean to keep you so late, but Riley will be home tomorrow and we really can't talk about this when she's around."

Elliot nodded. "That's for sure."

Grandpa Buck groaned as he rose to his feet. "Well, it's already the Lord's Day. And if I'm going to be fit for church, I best get some shut-eye." He walked over to Hawk and patted the top of his head. "You're a hero in my book. Get some sleep."

Kate and Elliot said their good nights and went to their room.

Hawk got up and stretched. "See you two tomorrow."

"I should go." Jay rose to his feet.

Hawk smiled and pushed him back on the couch. "Not so fast, Romeo. The lady wants a proper good-night kiss."

Abby's face was pinker than her sundress.

Jay laughed. "Look at you."

Hawk turned around and walked toward the stairs. "Good night, lovebirds." He walked up the steps, his heart heavier than it had been all week. He guessed he was finally feeling the full force of his losses.

Hawk opened the door to his room and closed it behind him, careful not to wake Jesse. He turned around and was stopped abruptly by something pressed against his chest.

"Do not move, or you will die." The intruder's voice was deep. He spoke with an accent.

"Jesse, are you okay?" Hawk felt as if his heart had fallen down an elevator shaft.

The man turned on a flashlight and shone it on Jesse. He was bound and gagged.

"Who are you? What do you want?" Hawk said. Had they gotten the wrong man? Could this be the bounty hunter? Terror seized him.

"I am Reza Turan. You will come with me. And we will talk."

He turned Hawk around and shoved him toward the window, which was open.

"It's too far to jump," Hawk said. "We'll break our legs."

"I attached metal steps for you." Reza shined the light on what appeared to be a portable fire escape ladder. "First, you go."

Hawk turned around and gingerly stepped down until he felt a thin metal step securely under his foot, and then with the other foot, stepped down on the metal step below it. He couldn't see anything, but he was able to feel the steps and descend slowly, one foot at a time. He planned to grab Reza from behind and get the gun away from him as soon as he reached the bottom.

Hawk sensed something moving on his left. He reached out and groped the air, grabbing on to what felt like taut cloth. He heard a loud thud below, just as the cloth went limp.

"Reza?" Hawk said.

"I am down here. Why do you take so long?"

Hawk kept descending until he had both feet on the ground. "I thought you were above me on the ladder."

Reza laughed. "I am not stupid. I brought rope made with torn sheets. I go down faster. And you do not have the chance to take my gun."

"What now?" Hawk's voice was shaking. He knew full well that, this time, no special agents had his back. If this was the bounty hunter, he was a dead man.

"Now you come with me. We will talk. And if you do not talk, you will die."

CHAPTER 30

Hawk sat tied to a kitchen chair in an abandoned log cabin not far from Angel View. Reza had parked his truck down the road from the lodge and had forced Hawk at gunpoint to walk with him to the truck, and then to drive up here.

Reza set the flashlight on the table so that the beam of light was pointed toward the ceiling and lit the room. The place had to be a hundred years old. It was hard to tell how long it had been since anyone had stayed there. Thick dust covered the table and chairs. Ornately spun cobwebs connected the stove and sink. And the charred smell from the fireplace permeated the humid night air.

Reza raised a window halfway, but it seemed to be stuck. He brushed his hands together, then breezed past Hawk, pushed open the screen door, and walked out to his truck. He came back with a roll of paper towels, a bottle of cleaner, and a whisk broom.

He brushed the dust off the table with the whisk broom, sprayed cleaner on the tabletop, then wiped off the grime. He grabbed one of the chairs and brushed, sprayed, and wiped the seat and back. He repeated the process and seemed satisfied.

Reza took the gun out of his waistband and set it on the table, then pulled out the clean chair and turned it backward, straddled it, and sat with his arms resting on the back. "Okay. Now we will talk."

Hawk nodded.

"Where is Abrisham?" Reza said.

"Who?"

"Abrisham," he said. "Don't pretend you don't know her. Where is she?"

Hawk's heart pounded so hard he could hardly breathe. This had to be the bounty hunter. How could Romo have been so wrong? After all he had done to help the FBI, he was going to end up tortured and murdered after all. "I–I don't know anyone with that name."

"You do not lie to me! I know it was you. At her big beautiful house up there on the mountain."

All Hawk could think to do was stall the inevitable. "I don't know anyone named … whatever name you said. I swear."

"I said Ab-Ree-Shum. You know her. You lie badly. You own a Jeep? With a gold cross hanging from the rearview mirror? Arkansas license plate HAWKTOURS?"

"Yes. But I don't know any woman by the name you said."

"I see." Reza's tone was mocking. "So it is your little brother who is the lady's man. He stole your keys and drove your Jeep. Maybe I should go back and punish *him*?"

"What is it you want from me?"

Reza got up from his chair and shoved it with his foot. "The truth!" He reached in his back pocket, pulled out his wallet, and held up a picture. "You know her. Say it."

Hawk's heart sank. "I knew her by the name Kennedy Taylor."

Reza shook his head. "No. Her name is Abrisham Kermani."

"She told me it was Kennedy Taylor."

"Why would she lie? Maybe you are the one who is lying." Reza grabbed the gun, cocked it, and pressed the barrel to Hawk's forehead.

"I'm telling the truth, I swear," Hawk said, perspiration dripping down his temples. "I met her less than two months ago in the parking lot of a grocery store. The bottom had fallen out of her sack and groceries were all over the ground. I helped her pick them up. She told me her name was Kennedy Taylor, that she was new here and hadn't made any friends yet. She seemed very nice and a little lonely, so I asked her if she would like to ride in my Jeep sometime."

"I don't believe you," Reza said.

"I'm telling the truth. I did take her on a Jeep ride and we became friends. She told me she inherited a fortune from her parents. That they were both dead. That she came here to start a new life."

Reza put the gun on the table and straddled the chair again, his arms folded on the back. "She lied to you."

"How do you know that?" *Who are you? You're not the bounty hunter.*

"Because I met her when she was a senior at Baumar International Girls School in Cambridge, Massachusetts. I was a freshman at MIT. Her mother and father owned a restaurant in Budapest but let her attend Baumar because she had an aunt and uncle in Cambridge who promised to look out for her. We fell in love. She promised to marry me."

"Why didn't she?"

Reza rested his chin on his arms and seemed miles away. "She was everything to me. Her name, Abrisham, is Persian. It means 'silk.' Her parents gave her this name because she had a head full of dark, silky hair when she was born." Reza lifted his gaze and looked at Hawk. "We were both proud to be Persian. I think that is what drew us together. She had met my parents, who loved her. She did not want me to meet her aunt and uncle. Because of 9/11, they forbade her to make any reference to her Persian heritage. They said it was irrelevant, that she was American. I was so honored when she told me her parents were coming to America that summer and wanted to meet me."

"So did you meet them?" Hawk said.

Reza shook his head. "No. Sadly. Abrisham stopped taking my calls. I finally went to her aunt and uncle and they told me she did not love me or want to marry me, that she was too kind to face me. They were lying. I could tell. But I knew the truth of our love, and I begged them not to keep us apart. They threatened to take out a restraining order if I did not leave them alone. What could I do?"

"Why are you here?" Hawk said. "That was five years ago."

"I will tell you. I got a phone call last week. It was a man's voice. He spoke to me in Farsi. He said he was a friend of Abrisham's father, Dalir, and he knew where Abrisham was living. He said it was not her choice to leave Cambridge five years ago, that not even her aunt and uncle knew where she was, and she very much would like to see me and explain everything. He gave me her address and said if I wanted to see her, I should go right away and tell no one. Of course, I was shocked. I had no idea if this stranger was telling me the truth. But I thought it over. I still loved her. I had to take a chance."

"So you came here looking for her?"

"Yes." Reza sat up straight. "After many hours of driving, I arrived at her home around ten Friday morning, anticipating that

Abrisham would be overjoyed to see me and would greet me with warmth and affection. When I rang her doorbell, holding a dozen fragrant red roses, my heart was going crazy, like old times. When the door finally opened, her beauty took my breath away."

Hawk wasn't sure he wanted to hear any more. He had no right to feel jealous, but he did.

"And you know what she said to me? The one she had loved, the one she promised to marry? She drew in a breath and put her hands on her heart and said, 'You must be from Foggy Ridge Floral. And those beautiful roses can only be from my beloved Hawk.' I said, 'No, Abrisham, they are from me, Reza. Do you not recognize the man you promised to marry?'"

"Good grief. How did she answer?" Hawk didn't know who he felt sorrier for, Abrisham or Reza.

"I don't think she had even looked at me until then," Reza said. "She got this horrified, broken expression on her face, like she knew I had discovered something shameful she did not want me to know. But I knew. Right then. She had given herself to *you*. That she loved *you*." Reza turned his head and looked into Hawk's eyes. He picked up the gun and held it in his hands. "So I asked myself. Who is this friend of Dalir Kermani that he sent me here to break my heart all over again? I rack my brain, but I do not know. Who does something this cruel?"

"I'm so sorry," Hawk said. "I can't imagine. Abrisham never talked about herself. I never knew she had been engaged. I didn't even know her real name. To me, she was Kennedy Taylor."

"Did you love her?" Reza said, his eyes welled with tears.

"Yes, but not the way you loved her."

Reza turned the gun on Hawk. "Now back to my question. Where is Abrisham? I left her house on Friday morning a broken man. I came Saturday morning to apologize for surprising her, and your Jeep was parked in her driveway. I saw the license plate. I wanted to ring the bell, but I could not bear it. I drove around and came back. You were still there. I drove around longer and came back. But you were still there. I waited down the block. But you did not leave. I knew what you were doing! My heart was breaking in a thousand pieces. I would never have behaved this way with her, the woman I vowed to marry."

Hawk felt ashamed. Neither had he with Laura Lynn.

"So I returned on Sunday, hoping to see her face once more before I drove home. And there was a for-sale sign in the yard. The drapes were open, so I looked inside, and there was no furniture at all. Tell me, where did she go?"

Hawk shook his head. "I honestly don't know. She just up and left without saying good-bye. I was as shocked as you were." *I can't tell him she's dead. He'll have questions I don't have answers to.*

A tear rolled down Reza's face. "I lost her not only once, but two times. I will never know her the way *you* knew her."

Hawk was silent. What could he say?

"It is you she loves. You!" Reza stood and pushed the chair away. "How could you take advantage of her innocence? Tell me!"

Hawk just assumed he wasn't the first man she had been with, but he didn't dare say that, for fear of dishonoring her and enraging Reza further.

"I am waiting for an answer." Reza pushed the barrel of the gun into Hawk's chest.

"I–I was taken with her beauty," Hawk said. "Unlike you, I'm a weak man."

"You are ruled by lust. No respect for what is sacred."

Hawk blinked the sweat from his eyes. "Please understand that I didn't know she had ever been engaged or that she left you without a good-bye. All this is news to me. I didn't even know of her Persian heritage. As far as I knew, she was a lovely American woman who was lonely and needed a friend."

Reza smiled derisively. "Oh, I am sure you could hardly wait to be her *friend*. So many men want to be her *friend*. Well, your friend-ship is cheap! It is immoral! She was so much better than this. I am the only man who honored her. Who knew what was in her heart."

"I admired Kenn— Abrisham," Hawk said. "She was one of the most giving, unselfish women I've ever known. Her heart spoke volumes without her ever saying a word. I loved that about her. I miss her too."

Reza eyes brimmed with tears. He lowered the gun and started pacing again.

"I cannot hear this from you. Her heart spoke without words when she realized it was me, Reza, standing at her door. It said she was ashamed for me to know she had been with you."

"Maybe not," Hawk said. "Maybe she was ashamed for leaving Cambridge without any explanation. Maybe she was ashamed she never contacted you."

"Maybe this. Maybe that." Reza backhanded Hawk across the face. "All is moot now. Abrisham is gone again. She does not want me to find her. And I do not want to live without her. And *you* … why should you live? You took from me the only thing I loved."

"Reza, please," Hawk said. "Let's discuss this like reasonable men. How can you blame me when I knew nothing about any of this? I never hurt Abrisham. I cared about her."

"Did you? Then why did you not marry her?" Reza pressed the gun to Hawk's forehead. "I think you used her. It was obvious to me she loved you. You had no intention of marrying her as long as she welcomed you into her bed. How could you treat her this way?"

"Reza, I thought she was the most beautiful woman I had ever seen. Don't hate me for that. You must have felt the same way."

"Oh, I did. I still do. But it means nothing now. It is you she loves. I saw it in her face. She is not the Abrisham I loved."

"Of course she is," Hawk said. "But five years is a long time. She's matured. We all grow and evolve into better versions of ourselves."

Reza stepped back, his face turning red and then almost purple. He took the butt of his gun and hit Hawk over his right eye. "Who are *you* to judge what is better? There is more to love than pleasure! So much more!"

Hawk closed his aching eye, hoping to keep the blood out. It was useless to try to reason with Reza. His anger had escalated to danger-ous. *Lord, I'm so sorry I've hurt this man. How many times do I have to suffer the consequences of my relationship with Kennedy? Maybe dying is the final blow. Unless You help me, he is going to kill me and himself.*

CHAPTER 31

Kate lay in Elliot's arms, feeling herself drift off to sleep, finally able to let go of the tension of the past week. Tomorrow all of her children would be home again. No more bounty hunter. No more FBI. Riley was coming home ...

The sound of screaming shattered the peaceful night.

Kate sat up in bed, her heart pounding, her thoughts disoriented.

"It's Abby." Elliot threw back the covers. "Stay here."

Kate grabbed his arm. "I'm going with you. I'll get the pepper spray."

Elliot took a wooden ball bat from behind the door and slipped into the hallway. Kate grabbed the pepper spray from her top drawer, caught up to him, and clung to the hem of his pajama top.

"Ab-by!" Elliot hollered.

"I'm upstairs. Come quickly!"

"Kate, wait here. Let me make sure it's safe." Elliot ran up the stairs. A few seconds later he hollered, "Bring me my hunting knife! It's in my closet, third or fourth drawer of the dresser."

Kate ran into the bedroom, found the knife, and hurried up the steps. She breezed through the door and saw Jesse bound and gagged, and Elliot trying to slide the gag off his mouth.

"Jesse's not hurt," Elliot said. "Hawk's gone."

Kate handed Elliot the knife, then hurried over to the open window and saw a portable fire escape ladder. She looked over at Hawk's unmade bed and felt as if she might faint.

"Honey, call Virgil," Elliot said. "See if you can get him here right away. It's okay, Jesse. I'll have you free in just a minute."

Kate keyed in Virgil's number. He picked it up on the first ring. "Virgil, something's happened out here. We found Jesse bound and gagged, and Hawk is gone. One of the windows in their room is open, and a portable fire escape ladder is attached. As soon as Elliot gets the gag off Jesse, maybe he can tell us what happened …"

Elliot carefully cut the gag off Jesse's mouth and began cutting him loose.

"A man was in the room when I came to bed!" Jesse said. "He threatened to kill me if I opened my mouth. He had a gun. He tied me up and put a gag in my mouth and then waited for Hawk. He made Hawk go with him!"

"Did you hear where they were going?" Elliot said.

Jesse shook his head. "They just left."

"Okay, buddy. You're free." Elliot hugged him.

"That's all we know, Virgil. I'll leave the door unlocked. Come in when you get here." Kate disconnected the call and sat on the bed and put her arms around Jesse. "You okay?"

"I'm fine, but we've got to find Hawk."

"We'll find him." Abby gently rubbed Jesse's back. "Sheriff Granger's on his way."

"He said not to touch anything," Kate said. She brushed Abby's hair out of her face. "Are you okay, honey?"

"I'm all right. Halo came into my room meowing and meowing. She ran out to the steps, and I had a feeling something was wrong. I came upstairs and that's when I found Jesse."

"Thank heavens you did," Kate said.

Jesse reached down and picked up Halo, and put her over his shoulder. "I guess we have a watch cat. Good girl."

Abby sighed. She got up and stared out the window. "I'll call Jay and get him back over here. We may need his help."

❁

Reza had been sitting in the chair for ten or fifteen minutes, staring at his wallet picture of Abrisham. He hadn't said a word, and Hawk was afraid to start up a conversation again.

Hawk listened to the night sounds. A coyote howling. An owl hooting. Mosquitoes buzzing around his ears. This cabin was no more than ten minutes from Angel View, and yet it might as well be in Australia. No one would ever think to look for him here.

He hurt for Reza. He could relate to the pain Reza had suffered during the five years that followed Abrisham's disappearance. How utterly exciting it must have been when he got that phone call from her father's friend, revealing her whereabouts and insisting that she wanted to see him. And then how devastating when she disappeared again without a good-bye, after he discovered that she had loved someone else and shared his bed.

Hawk could hardly believe that he was that someone else. If only he could go back and undo the night he took Kennedy for that first Jeep ride. He knew when he lied to Laura Lynn about his plans that night that he was leaving his options open. He told himself that he was just being nice to a lonely newcomer and making her feel welcome. But that bottle of cologne and navy Ralph Lauren shirt had been in his drawer since his last birthday. He had never worn either until that night.

And looking back, he could see signs that Kennedy was growing increasingly fond of him. He kept an emotional distance because he loved Laura Lynn and never considered his relationship with Kennedy to be more than physical. But after she was taken, it was as if the blinders had been removed. The bond he felt with her was unlike any he had ever experienced. And the grief he was experiencing, knowing he would never see her again, was both intense and confusing.

"Tell me again why you did not marry Abrisham," Reza said.

"I only knew her for six weeks."

"And yet you think nothing of sharing her bed?"

"I never said I thought nothing of it," Hawk said. "Being with her changed me in ways I can't explain. I miss her. I don't think I'll ever meet anyone else like her."

"Believe me, you won't."

Hawk didn't like the finality in Reza's tone. "Didn't you ever date other women?"

"I tried," Reza said. "But Abrisham was my soul mate. I always knew it. I never enjoyed spending time with other women. At least, not for long."

"Did you ever go back to her aunt and uncle and try again to find out where she was?"

"Not after they threatened to get a restraining order. It is not popular in America to be from Iran. I do not want trouble."

"Was Abrisham Muslim?" Hawk said.

"No. Her father was raised Muslim and her mother was raised Christian. Neither was practicing. They wanted her to choose for herself. My family has strong ties to Islam, but not so strict. It is our Persian roots that makes us proud."

"Tell me about that," Hawk said. "Obviously it's very important to you." *Just keep talking.*

Reza turned his chair around and straddled it. "To be Persian is to be a descendent of the oldest civilization know to man. In fact, it predates Egypt's by five hundred years. My ancient culture gave the world poetry and art. Chess, algebra, and trigonometry. We invented money, the guitar, windmills, anesthesia. Even the use of alcohol in medicine."

"That's impressive," Hawk said. "I had no idea. Tell me more." *Talk all you want.*

"I think most of all, to be Persian is to be tolerant of diversity and accepting of change. Willing to embrace religious and ethnic differences and accept opposing points of view. Even to allow dissent. It is to carry the legacy of the first declaration of human rights in history, issued nearly three thousand years ago. Of course, many people in the United States think if we came from Iran, we are radicals. But most Persians I know disagree with what the Iranian government does. What can they do? I am glad I live here. But I can also say I am proud to the core of my Persian roots. It is a rich culture."

There was a long pause. What now? "Thanks for explaining," Hawk said. "Abrisham never talked about any of this."

"Because she knew you cannot understand. Abrisham embraced these things as I do. I know she did not leave the first time by choice. But why did she leave me again?" Reza sat and stared at nothing. Finally, he stood and shoved the chair with his foot. "Who is this friend of her father that called and told me I should come? That she wanted to explain? Explain what? That she loves someone else? That she gave him all of herself?" Reza paced, combing his hands through his hair. "It makes me crazy! I came this close to finding out why she left the first time. And now she has disappeared again. It is too much!" Reza picked up the gun. "I don't want to live without her. I cannot go through this again! The pain is too much!"

❦

Virgil stood in the upstairs bedroom at Kate and Elliot's and tried to make sense of what had happened.

"Jesse, do you remember what time the man tied you up?"

"I had just come to bed, so it was about eleven thirty."

Virgil glanced over at Kate. "And Hawk went to bed about one fifteen?"

"Yes," Kate said. "We all did, except for Abby. She went to bed after Jay left, which was roughly one thirty. She said Halo kept meowing and meowing and went out to the stairs. Abby knew something was wrong, so she went upstairs, and that's when she found Jesse."

"Okay, thanks. Jesse, can you describe the man who tied you up and forced Hawk to go with him?"

"The light was on in the bathroom and the door cracked, but the room was dark," Jesse said. "He was about Hawk's age, I think. He had short, dark hair. A little bit of a foreign accent. Oh, and he was wearing blue jeans and a white T-shirt."

"Did he have a beard or mustache?"

"No, sir."

"Glasses?"

Jesse shook his head.

"Anything else that stood out?"

"No, sir."

"Okay, thanks," Virgil said. "That should help us. Deputy Hobbs is going to dust for prints and collect fibers or anything that might contain DNA. Why don't y'all wait downstairs? I'm going to go out back and look around while Deputy Duncan tries to track the GPS signal on Hawk's iPhone."

"Do you think this is related to the FBI case?" Elliot said.

"It's certainly suspicious, but it's too soon to know." Virgil put his arm around Kate. "I'll find him."

Kate wiped her eyes and nodded. "I know you will."

Virgil went downstairs and flipped the light switch to the deck, then went out through the sliding glass door. He turned on his flashlight and looked at the back of the house and then walked slowly through the grass to see if he could tell which way they went. The dew was thick and he could see prints leading down to the path the family took when walking over to the lodge.

His cell phone rang. "Yeah, Billy Gene?"

"I've got the coordinates, Sheriff. You ready to roll?"

"I'll meet you out front."

Virgil went back inside and out to the kitchen where the family was waiting. "We've got the coordinates. Billy Gene's out front, and I'm going to ride with him. I'll call when we know something. Say a prayer."

Virgil went outside and slid into Billy Gene's radio car.

"We caught a break," Billy Gene said. "Hawk's GPS signal isn't far from here."

"Let's go get him," Virgil said.

CHAPTER 32

Hawk was sure Reza was going to start shooting at any moment. He had to talk him down or they were both going to end up dead.

"Reza, listen to me," Hawk said. "It's going to be all right. You're stronger than you think. Your emotions are just on overload. Maybe after a good night's sleep, things will look better."

Reza shook his head. "No more sunrises."

"You've seen many sunrises since Abrisham left."

"And every one has brought pain!" Reza shouted. "I am tired of pain!"

"We all are," Hawk said. "You think her leaving without a good-bye was easy for me? I have a million questions that will never have answers. There's a hole in my heart too."

Reza held the gun to Hawk's temple. "Maybe I will put one in your head to match it—like this one." Reza stuck his finger in the wound above Hawk's right eye.

Hawk cried out. The pain was excruciating. "Come on, man. Is this the way you want your parents to remember you? You're a proud Persian. You're not a barbarian."

"Maybe I *like* roughing you up," Reza said.

"You're angry. Who wouldn't be? It's not fair, what happened to you. But hurting me or yourself isn't going to change it."

"No. But it feels pretty good right now." Reza punched Hawk in the stomach and knocked the wind out of him. "I have the power to kill you at any moment."

Hawk tasted the blood that was trickling down from above his eye. "Reza, my life belongs to the Lord. If you want to kill me, there's nothing I can do to stop you. But the second I die, I'll be with Jesus for eternity. And you'll just be deeper into the hell you've dug for yourself. Why don't you let me help you? Let's work this out together."

"You cannot help me. Why would you want to?"

"For starters, because Abrisham would want me to. She loved both of us. We can't change that. But she's not some possession either of us can own. She's her own person. A kind, sensitive woman who hated violence. She would despise what's happening here. It would break her heart."

"You are right." Reza laid the gun on the table, and dropped in the chair, his arms limp.

"Her father's friend told you it wasn't her choice to leave Cambridge. Maybe it wasn't her choice to leave Foggy Ridge either."

Reza lifted his gaze and looked at Hawk as if that possibility had never occurred to him.

"It's hard not knowing," Hawk said, "but I don't think either of us is ever going to have the answers."

"You do not seem sad," Reza said.

"I am, though. More than you can possibly know. I'm just very good at hiding my emotions. I miss her. I suppose, on some level, I always will."

"What do we do now?" Reza said. "I guess we call the police. And I am going to jail."

"Not if I don't press charges," Hawk said. "What happened tonight was a case of temporary insanity. You will have to answer to the sheriff, who happens to be a good friend of my family. But he's a reasonable man."

Reza buried his face in his hands and sobbed. "I am so ashamed. I have never before in my life hurt anyone. Forgive me, Hawk."

"I forgive you. How about cutting me loose?"

The screen door flew open. "Get down on the floor!" Virgil shouted. "Put your face down, and lock your hands behind your head. Do it!"

Reza obeyed without saying a word.

Billy Gene grabbed Reza's left arm and pulled it behind him, and then the right, finally putting on the cuffs. He stood him up. "What's your name?"

"His name is Reza Turan," Hawk said. "He's a friend of Kennedy's. We've both had a really bad night."

"Get him out of here," Virgil said.

Billy Gene led Reza away, reading him his Miranda rights.

"How did you find me?" Hawk said.

"We got the GPS coordinates for your phone."

"I didn't think I had it. It's not in my pocket.

"We found it on the floor of Reza's truck." Virgil cut the rope and freed Hawk, looking closely at his eye. "You're going to need stitches." Virgil took a clean handkerchief out of his pocket and handed it to Hawk. "Hold this over your eye and apply some pressure. You want to tell me what this was about?"

Hawk shrugged. "Just another piece of the puzzle. He and Kennedy, or I should say Abrisham Kermani, were engaged to be married five years ago. She disappeared without a good-bye. He never believed she left of her own volition."

Hawk highlighted for Virgil everything that had happened to Reza from the time he got the call that Abrisham was in Foggy Ridge, until tonight when it all came down on Reza and he had a meltdown.

"Put yourself in his shoes," Hawk said. "After five long years he thought his beloved was waiting for him. That's all he could think about as he drove from Cambridge. And when finally he got here, the bottom fell out of his dream and she disappeared again. He lost it, Sheriff. But he's not a criminal."

"I've got half a dozen charges to throw at him that say he is."

"I'm not going to press charges," Hawk said. "He's already spent five years in an emotional prison. I know he won't get off without probation and/or community service, but putting him behind bars won't serve anyone."

"He could've killed you."

"He didn't."

"The DA may decide to file charges, Hawk. It's not entirely up to you."

"Well, I'd like to talk to the DA."

"Why do you want to help Reza?" Virgil said. "You don't even know him."

"I understand how tortured he feels. He lost Abrisham without a good-bye and with no understanding of why. So did I. Only I believe their love was real and true—the kind that almost never comes around again."

"She's dead, Hawk. Doesn't he deserve to know?"

Hawk sighed. "Probably. But not tonight. Besides, I couldn't tell him without raising even more questions—and I don't have any answers."

The flash of red lights outside caught Hawk's attention.

"That's Hobbs," Virgil said. "He and Billy Gene are going to take Reza down to the jail and process him. I'm going to take you to the ER. Your family's waiting."

Hawk glanced outside and saw Reza, his hands bound, being put into the back seat of the deputy's car.

"You ready?" Virgil said.

"Just a second …" Hawk's voice cracked, and he turned away and swallowed the emotion, blinking away the tears that threatened his composure. Finally, he said, "Sheriff, I did everything in my power to help Romo catch a despicable man who wanted to kill Kennedy. Can't you do something to help a broken man who just wanted to love her?"

CHAPTER 33

Hawk sat on the porch swing, having a cup of coffee and watching the sky turn pink in anticipation of Sunday's sunrise. His family had gone to bed a couple of hours ago, hoping to get some sleep before they went to late church, after which Riley's bus would arrive from camp.

Virgil must have filled them in because no one in the family had asked him questions at the ER or on the drive home. Not that there was anything he wanted to talk about. They already knew from Jesse how and why he had left the house with Reza. They could clearly see from Hawk's cuts and bruises that it had gotten violent.

They would never understand that being with Reza had made him miss Kennedy more than ever. But it had also exposed again the shallow nature of his relationship with her. It wasn't until after she disappeared that Hawk began to sense that something had changed in him. That the relationship he thought was merely physical had bonded him to Kennedy on an emotional level. He had no frame of reference for it, and he didn't even know whom to ask.

He breathed in slowly and exhaled. What was going to happen to Reza? Hawk couldn't pretend that he hadn't feared for his life when Reza raged out of control. But how much pain can the human heart bear before it erupts? Hawk had played over and over in his mind the picture of Reza standing at his true love's door, holding red roses and thinking she was going to welcome him after five long years, only to have her dismiss him as the florist and declare her love for another man. And then disappear again.

Hawk blinked the stinging from his eyes and took a sip of luke-warm coffee. He felt so lost. What direction did he have for the future? He had been building on his relationship with Laura Lynn for almost two years. He had money in the bank, ideas for building a house, and now no one to share it with. And no one to blame but himself. He had traded a few weeks of pleasure for a dream. What a fool.

The front door opened and Elliot came outside holding a mug. He breathed in deeply and let it out.

"Why are you up already?" Hawk said.

"Probably for the same reason you are. Do you mind if I sit? If you'd like to be by yourself, I'll go for a walk."

"No, I'm fine," Hawk said. "Come sit."

Elliot sat on the swing. "Reza really clobbered you."

Hawk smiled. "Yeah, for a short guy, he packed a wallop."

"I remember the first time I came home with a face that looks like yours," Elliot said. "My dad stayed out of it. But Mother lectured me for days on the virtues of not fighting."

"I've already had that lecture," Hawk said. "I've stayed away from it whenever I can."

Elliot nodded. "I did too. But some big ape on the football team thought I'd make a good punching bag."

"Did you tell your mother that's what happened?"

"No. I didn't want her running to the school, trying to defend me. It would've made things worse. I went out for the track team and built up my strength and speed until no one could catch me." Elliot laughed. "Believe it or not, it worked."

"Hard to run when you're tied up," Hawk said.

Elliot patted his knee. "I know. I felt tied up, until I didn't."

"Meaning what?"

"Hawk, I know you relate to Reza's pain. But you're not responsible for it. As long as you think you are, you're going to feel tied up."

"I know that in my head. But last night, his pain was so real. So personal. I wasn't even mad when he lashed out. I understood why he did."

"It's one thing to understand. It's another to excuse it. If he gets by with it this time, what happens next time he has a meltdown? He could have killed you."

"I know," Hawk said. "A couple of times I thought he might. Maybe I felt I deserved it."

Elliot took a sip of coffee and seemed to be thinking. "Hawk, did you confess your affair and truly lay it at Jesus's feet?"

"Of course I did."

"Then He showed grace by forgiving you, which you didn't deserve. And mercy, by not giving you hell, which you did deserve. We all *deserve it* for something. That's why we need Him."

Hawk nodded. "Thanks for reminding me. It's easy to fall into that trap of feeling like we deserve to be punished and forget that He already took our punishment once and for all time."

Elliot smiled. "Now remember to remember."

"I will. I really hope the judge shows Reza a little mercy and doesn't incarcerate him. He's already been in an emotional prison for five years."

"We can pray that God will see that true justice is done. How can we ask for more than that?"

"Fair enough. I'm really sorry, Elliot. I didn't mean to wreck Riley's homecoming."

"Are you kidding? After the stress of the past week, all of us can hardly wait for her happy chatter to fill the house!"

Hawk laughed. "Yeah, our pipsqueak is never dull. What are we going to tell her about this week? About my face?"

"We can't tell her about the FBI operation," Elliot said.

"And we shouldn't scare her by telling her a man broke in and tied up Jesse and took me at gunpoint."

"How about we just tell her that you tried to help a man work through his anger, and you learned what not to do?"

Hawk laughed. "That'll work."

That afternoon, while the family was sitting around the kitchen table, eating chocolate-chip cookies and listening to Riley's wonderful camp adventures, Hawk slipped away to make a phone call.

He sat on the porch steps and keyed in Dennis's number. He hadn't had a chance to talk to him since they gave their statements to Sheriff Granger.

"Well, if it isn't the Hawk Man," Dennis said. "What's up?"

"Oh, you know, same old." *You wouldn't believe me if I told you.* "The sheriff finally called to tell us that the FBI didn't find any evidence of foul play in Brody's death."

"That's what they said."

"You're not buying it?" Hawk said.

"They had no reason to lie about it. My aunt and uncle are relieved."

"I'll bet," Hawk said. "It's been an emotional roller coaster."

"For sure. I miss Brody. I know he was quirky, but we grew up together. He was the brother I never had. I really thought he'd been murdered. It's going to take awhile for my emotions to shift gears."

"But truthfully," Hawk said, "it's very feasible that Brody got paranoid after he witnessed the drone attack and imagined he was being followed."

"I know. I had my doubts at first. I'm moving past it. No one's bothered me, and I know everything Brody knew. Does the FBI have any leads on Kennedy's disappearance?"

"That's part of the reason I called," Hawk said. "Kennedy didn't make it. Special Agent Romo told me himself."

"I'm sorry, man. What happened?"

"That's classified. I was just told that she's dead. I knew you'd want to know."

"How are you handling it?" Dennis said.

Hawk looked up at the hummingbirds dive-bombing the feeder. "Not that well. I only knew her for six weeks, and yet I think about her all the time."

"You think some of it could be survivor's guilt?"

"Sure," Hawk said. "I'll probably wonder for the rest of my life why I got to live and she didn't. I hope someday I'll be able to shake the horrible images I see when I think about her being kidnapped by eight men. But I honestly think there's more to it than survivor's guilt. I just have a big hole inside right now."

"Well, you lost Laura Lynn at the same time. A double whammy."

"That's probably it," Hawk said, knowing it wasn't. "So are things getting back to normal at the garage?"

"Yeah, pretty much. I still think a lot about the drone attack. It freaks me out that we don't know who was behind it."

"I know what you mean," Hawk said. "If I never hear the word *classified* again, it'll be too soon. But some things are just not ours to know. At least we can put aside our suspicions about Brody's death."

"Hawk, I've never thanked you," Dennis said.

"For what?"

"For being nice to Brody. You're about the only one of my peers who accepted him the way he was."

"I grew up with him too," Hawk said. "He was different, but he wasn't hard to like. I never gave it much thought."

"I did. But I never said thanks, so I'm saying it now. I know Brody was a handful. At least in heaven he'll be whole …" Dennis's voice cracked. "Sorry, it's still so fresh."

"I guess we're both grieving for different reasons," Hawk said. "When my dad was killed, people told me the only way to deal with grief is to walk straight through it, that if you try to sidestep it, it'll come back with a vengeance somewhere down the road."

"Oh, great."

"Seriously, man. Let yourself feel whatever you feel, and don't worry about it. Thankfully it doesn't last forever. It really will get better."

"I'll take your word for it," Dennis said. "I hope you take your own advice."

"I will. What choice do I have?"

"Don't be a stranger, Hawk Man."

"Never a stranger. Always a friend. We'll talk again soon."

Hawk leaned his head back and let the warm sun melt over his face. It felt more like years than days since Romo told him that Kennedy was dead. He knew that never seeing her again, never having the chance to tell her the truth about himself, was just something he would have to live with. But he was unprepared for the insight he'd had this morning after his family left for church.

He had sat for a long time on the porch swing, his mind playing over and over again last night's dramatic encounter with Reza, in an effort to understand why he felt so compelled to help him. Hawk prayed for wisdom and understanding. It was as though his eyes were opened for the first time, and he had a painful and sobering insight about his affair with Kennedy.

From the beginning, Hawk sensed that Kennedy was much more invested in the relationship than he was. In those intimate moments when Kennedy gave herself to Hawk as if he were all that mattered—unselfishly, unashamedly, as if she were letting go of pent-up feelings for which she had no other means of expression—he had concluded that sadness over losing her parents had filled her heart with emotion. That was true, but not for the reason he had thought.

It was suddenly clear to Hawk that, from somewhere deep in the heart of Kennedy Taylor, Abrisham had been expressing her love for Reza, a love she knew would never be consummated, but a love that kept her from falling into crippling despair at their forced separation. That was why she looked horrified and ashamed when she saw Reza on her doorstep. She had never expected to see him again and didn't want him to judge what he saw at face value.

Hawk wiped away a tear that trickled down the side of his face. Reza had correctly judged Hawk's intentions at face value. Lust had been his sole motivation. Reza's intentions toward Abrisham had always been unselfish and honorable. Hawk was ashamed that his had been shallow and self-serving. Even so, that intensely intimate experience had changed Hawk. It had bonded him to Kennedy, and now it was difficult to let her go. At the same time, it was impossible not to feel Reza's gut-wrenching sorrow as his hopes were dashed a second time.

Lord, I am so sorry. I had no idea how complicated this would be and how much it would hurt.

"There you are," Jesse said.

Hawk quickly sat up and wiped his eyes. He rose to his feet, then turned around, facing Jesse. "I just got off the phone with Dennis. I hadn't had a chance to talk to him since we gave our statements."

"Are you okay after last night?" Jesse said.

"I'm getting there. Did the sheriff tell you that Reza and Kennedy were engaged five years ago?"

Jesse nodded. "I guess that's why he did a number on your face."

"It's complicated," Hawk said. "She disappeared without telling him good-bye, and he always knew she didn't leave by choice. Then last week, a friend of her father called and told him that Kennedy was here and wanted to see him and explain. Reza came with great hope that they would get back together."

"And she disappeared again."

"Right," Hawk said. "He lost it. He took his anger out on me, but I think his heart was broken."

"Maybe hers was too," Jesse said.

"You're probably right. But you usually are." Hawk climbed the steps and pinched Jesse's belly. "Did you leave any cookies for me?"

Jesse laughed. "I can't be held responsible for what gets eaten if you're not there to protect your share."

The front door flew open and Riley appeared on the porch, her dark hair tied back in a ponytail, summer freckles sprinkled sparingly across her nose and cheeks. "Hawk, where have you been?"

"Right here waiting for you." Hawk bent down and let Riley get on his shoulders, then he stood. "My goodness, you've grown in a week. Your head almost touches the ceiling."

"I think I'm getting long legs, just like Abby."

Hawk smiled and winked at Jesse. "I think you are. I've got the two prettiest sisters on Sure Foot Mountain."

Riley gently patted the bandage above his eye. "Does it hurt much?"

"Just a little."

"Next time," Riley said, "if you want to help someone who's angry, you should get him a *real* punching bag."

"Yes, ma'am. I think you're right. Okay, tell me what I missed after I left the table."

With Jesse at his side, Hawk carried Riley on his shoulders to the end of the long driveway, listening to her describe the fun things they did at camp and the new friends she had made. He loved her honesty, and the sheer joy that seemed to fuel her energy. And Jesse ... what a treasure his little brother was. So perceptive. So trusting. So full of light.

Hawk wanted to keep them just the way they were for a lot longer than time would allow. Soon Jesse would start noticing girls with different eyes. And Riley would beg to wear fashions that wouldn't pass the scrutiny of his mother and Elliot. How he wished he could keep their pure hearts untouched by the world. He wondered if that's how our heavenly Father feels when He sees sin crouching at our door. He wants to keep us from getting hurt, and has already laid out commandments that will protect us—if we listen and obey.

Hawk felt a scolding pat on the top of his head. "Hey, are you listening?" Riley said.

"Of course I'm listening. You said that Pamela Sue Something-or-other invited you to come for a sleepover, but she lives in Eureka Springs."

Riley hugged his neck and didn't let go. "I know someone who could drive me to Pamela Sue's ..."

"Oh, *now* she's nice to me," Hawk said. "It's my Jeep she wants."

Jesse looked up at Hawk and flashed a silver smile. "I think they're born that way."

Hawk laughed. "You're always one step ahead of the class, Jesse."

CHAPTER 34

Hawk slept off and on all day Monday. But on Tuesday morning, he was ready to go back to doing what he loved most: taking guests on Jeep tours across Sure Foot Mountain. He told Connor he would be there by one o'clock and work the late shift. His cell phone rang and he glanced at the screen.

"Hello, Sheriff."

"How're your wounds healing?" Virgil said.

"Better than the rest of me. But I'm anxious to get back to work this afternoon."

"I wanted to let you know that the judge released Reza. He's to appear before a judge in Cambridge on Friday at eight a.m. He'll be on probation for two years. And he'll be required to complete two hundred hours of anger management. I doubt if he'll ever be issued a real firearm. The one he used was a pretty impressive fake."

Hawk smiled. "So no jail time?"

"None. I thought you'd be pleased."

"I am. I'm just shocked. Is he still there? I'd like to see him before he goes."

"I think he's already left town."

Hawk stood for a moment in stunned silence. "You put in a good word for him, didn't you?"

"Hawk, I made it clear to him and to the judge that it was you, the victim, who felt strongly that Reza had been pushed over the top, and this violent act against you was a crime of passion, resulting from cruel and deeply gut-wrenching circumstances. I reported that his background check was clean. He's never had as much as a parking ticket. I didn't think he was a danger to society."

"Thanks, Sheriff. In my heart, I knew it was the just and merciful thing to do. What changed your mind?"

"I thought about what you said. I decided Reza could use a break. Let's just hope we're right."

"I can't thank you enough. I appreciate the call."

Virgil sighed. "You're a brave man, Hawk Cummings. You remind me so much of your dad. He'd be proud of you."

Hawk swallowed hard and blinked the stinging from his eyes. "Thanks for saying that. It means a lot."

"Tell your mother that Jill Beth wants a rematch on Mexican Train."

Hawk laughed. "I'll tell her."

Hawk showed up thirty minutes early at the Jeep tours office. The "out to lunch" sign was on the door. He sat on the log porch and inhaled the smell of pine. The fragrance reminded him of family camping trips when he was a kid. He sensed someone standing in front of him and looked up.

"Reza!" Hawk stood. "I heard the judge released you. I'm so glad."

Reza's eyes glistened. "I understand you are the reason. That you did not think I am a criminal."

"I don't."

"But what I did to you … it was unthinkable. I am so sorry."

"I know that. There's only so much a human heart can stand. You broke. Reza, in my Christian faith, the Bible teaches us to show mercy. I honestly don't think you started out to hurt me. What happened to you was over the top. You just wanted answers. Given the same circumstances, I might have done the same thing."

"But you also saw truth in me instead of the evil, which did terrible things."

"I saw the man Abrisham really loved. It was always you, Reza. When she was with me, she saw you. That's how she stayed alive. How she survived without you."

"How can you say this?"

"I just tell it like I see it." Hawk put his hand on Reza's shoulder. "I forgive you. And I ask your forgiveness too."

"Mine?"

"Yes. I'm ashamed that I took so lightly what you held as sacred. My intentions toward Abrisham were self-serving, not unselfish like yours. I was not seeking a marriage covenant, and I had no right to share her bed. I have confessed my sin, and God has forgiven me. I hope someday you can too."

"You are a big man, Hawk. My heart is still broken. Forgiveness will come. But for now, I cannot say it."

"That's okay. Thanks for being honest," Hawk said. "I'm glad you came by before you left. I really wanted to see you and tell you how I feel."

"I will go home now. My heart is very heavy. But I'm grateful not to be in jail, and I will gladly do whatever the judge orders."

Hawk looked into Reza's eyes. He held out his hand to shake Reza's, and the next thing he knew, they were embracing.

"Thank you again for seeing truth in me," Reza said. "And for telling me what you saw in Abrisham's heart. It helps my pain to think that she never forgot me."

"Believe me, she never did." Hawk reached into his pocket and handed Reza a business card. "Call me anytime if you want to talk. I am praying for my Jesus to heal your heart."

"I think only time can do that," Reza said. "But I appreciate your prayers. You have mine as well."

Hawk watched Reza walk through the ground cover to his truck. He got in, started the engine, and drove off, leaving a trail of red dust behind him.

❧

Hawk got home from work just before dark. He took the roast beef dinner his mother had saved and put it in the microwave.

"You're home," Kate said. "I didn't hear you come in. How was your first day back?"

"Good. Connor was asking me when the landscaping project would be finished. Not sure what to tell him."

"Elliot already thought of that," Kate said. "He did hire a landscaper today, and they'll get right on it. We won't miss a beat."

Hawk smiled. "He's such a great guy, Mama. I'm so happy for you."

Kate kissed him on his left cheek, taking care not to touch the stitched cut above his right eye. "I'm happy for me too. How are those wounds feeling?"

"Not so bad. At least I don't have headaches anymore. Where's Elliot?"

"He went into town to talk to a friend of his. He should be home soon. I have cherry cobbler for dessert."

Hawk smiled. "You're the best. You need to get busy canning. I noticed your stash of pasta sauce is dwindling. Savannah is really pushing it, and you don't want her to run out."

"I'm going to get busy as soon as we can get fresh tomatoes at the farmer's market. Abby's going to help me. She's getting to be quite the homemaker."

"Have she and Jay set a date for the wedding yet?"

"Not specifically, but it'll be next year, probably in October. They want to get married up on the slope at sunset. She wants a white gazebo with the lake as the backdrop."

"Makes sense," Hawk said. "They spent hours up there the summer they met, and that's where Jay painted her portrait."

"I know. It's perfect. I've already contacted the couple that owns the property, and they insist on letting us use it free of charge. But it'll be challenging to get a white gazebo positioned just right on a hillside. Elliot says we can have a platform built to level it. We've got plenty of room for two hundred chairs and the white pavilion she wants for the reception." Kate laughed. "Oh, listen to me going on and on. I do this all the time here at Angel View. But setting up on the slope will be fun and different. Abby and Jay are excited."

"They are such a great match," Hawk said. "I love watching them together. She adores him, and he treats her with such respect. That's how it should be. That's how you and Elliot are too."

Kate was quiet for a moment and then said, "Hawk, I know you've been through the mill, but I also see that you had feelings for Kennedy. I know I reacted poorly in the beginning, but I really don't want you to shut down. I want you to feel free to talk about her. She meant something to you. And having her die after being taken so suddenly … well, it's a lot to handle by yourself. I want you to know Elliot and I and Dad are here for you. I know Abby and Jay are too."

"Thanks, Mama. That means a lot. I'm going to finish eating and go take a shower. I may turn in early. Seems all I want to do lately is sleep. You heard Reza was released, didn't you?"

"Yes. What you said to Virgil changed his perspective about Reza. The kind of mercy you showed doesn't come in the natural, Son. God is speaking to your heart."

Hawk nodded. "I know. And I'm listening."

Kate cupped his cheek in her hand "Your mercy toward Reza really touched me too. That was the kindest, most unselfish thing I've ever known you to do."

Hawk felt his cheeks burn at his mother's kind words. "I had an insight Sunday while you were at church. I'd like to tell you about it."

"Then I'd like to hear it."

Hawk articulated for his mother what he knew only God could have shown him. But somehow, putting it into words made it sound more like a soap opera than an insight that had changed his thinking.

Hawk sighed. "I can't explain it very well, but I know in my heart it's true."

"That's what counts," Kate said. "Often the things God shows us are just for us because it's what we need to understand at a given point in time. The important thing is that *we* know and respond to His Spirit's leading. I may not understand it the way you do, but I can already see the fruit in your life."

"So God has given you insights before?"

"Yes," Kate said. "And I was just as frustrated as you were, trying to make the words I came up with do it justice. I'm convinced there are times when the understanding is just for us and can't be adequately explained."

Hawk smiled. "Thanks. At least you don't think I'm nuts."

"Hardly."

"Oh, before I forget to tell you—Reza stopped by the Jeep tours office just before I started my shift. He wanted to thank me for what I said that helped to get him released."

"I'm glad," Kate said. "I think. Seeing him must have been awkward."

Hawk shook his head. "It really wasn't. I told him what I told you, only it came out better then. He said it helped his pain to know that she never forgot him." Hawk sighed. "He still doesn't know she's dead. I can't tell him because it would raise questions I can't answer.

I thought the sheriff was going to tell him, but I guess he changed his mind."

"Maybe you both felt it's better for him to have hope."

"Well, hope is a good thing. I have enough guilt and regret to keep me humble for a lifetime. It cuts me to the heart that I didn't hold tightly to my values the way Reza did. Especially when I really do believe in the sanctity of marriage and saving ourselves for our future spouses …" Hawk paused at the unexpected surge of emotion, then pulled himself together. "It's so ironic that the very thing I believe in so strongly, I defiled. I ruined everything. And I can never go back. No matter who I marry, she will never be my first. I can't change that …" Hawk buried his face in his hands and muffled his sobs.

Kate laid her head on his shoulder, linked arms with him, and cried too.

No more words were necessary. He knew his mother couldn't deny the truth. But he was so relieved and grateful that she empathized with his pain. He felt loved and not judged. What more could a prodigal son ask for?

CHAPTER 35

One hot Saturday night in July, Hawk sat on the porch swing, listening to the nearby energetic children splashing and playing in the water at Angel View's swimming pool. He loved the sound of happy guests and remembered his boyhood days when his parents let Abby and him play in the pool right along with the guests. Such a carefree time that was.

Suddenly, he had no idea what to do in his free time. For over a year, he had spent nearly every Saturday evening with Laura Lynn, enjoying spaghetti night around his family's table before meeting up with friends at Coffey's Grill House for more lively conversation and laughter. Some nights they got into philosophical or political discussions that went on for hours, fueled by specialty coffees and plates of Coffey's homemade cookies. Other nights they just had fun playing Mexican Train or Scrabble and munching corn chips and salsa. In the warmer months, they moved the fun out to the back patio among trees that were strung with festive colored lights.

It was four weeks today that Kennedy had disappeared from his life. Despite his sincere desire to leave her in his past, Hawk still thought of her every day and couldn't understand why he was having such a tough time letting go. Especially when he knew that the tenderness she had shown him was really meant for Reza. Not that it really mattered. Hawk had never intended for the relationship to be anything more than physical. Why couldn't he leave her in the past and move on?

Elliot came outside and stood at the top of the steps where there was a decent cross breeze. "Aren't you getting hot out here?"

"Not really. I work all day outside in the heat. I'm used to it."

Elliot smiled. "I knew that."

"You want to sit?" Hawk said.

"Sure." Elliot sat on the swing next to Hawk. A comfortable silence passed before he said, "I'm guessing that this isn't the way you'd like to spend a Saturday night."

"You'd be right."

"Your mother's worried. She thinks you shouldn't cut yourself off socially. That you've got friends you could hang out with and not run into Laura Lynn."

Hawk shifted his weight, his arms folded across his chest.

"I don't think Laura Lynn is the problem," Elliot said.

"Then tell me what the problem is, because I sure don't know."

"Can I talk to you man to man?" Elliot said.

"You're not going to lecture me on the evils of premarital sex, are you?"

Elliot smiled. "No lectures. But I found something online that might explain exactly what's been happening to you. It was totally new information for me. If you've heard it already, stop me at any time. Deal?"

Hawk nodded. "Deal."

"Quite unexpectedly," Elliot said, "I found myself on a website called Moral Revolution. I don't even know how I got there, but once I did, something caught my eye. I'm going to try to explain what I read. It made a lot of sense. It was an article talking about the *invisible* effects of sex before marriage."

"Okay."

Elliot pulled some index cards out of his shirt pocket. "I made some notes so I don't just ramble. This is the opinion of a whole team of people, including doctors and counselors. Okay, I'm quoting now, '*We can't stop our bodies from doing what they were created to do.* What were they created to do? Bond. We were created to connect with another human being in such a way that we would become one unit, together, for life.'"

"Go on," Hawk said.

"'This happens because our hormones cause us to glue, so-to-speak, with our partner. No amount of consent or informed decision making can change that. There's a bonding that occurs that supersedes a mere skin-to-skin connection. Scientifically, we know that sex engages us hormonally, neurologically, psychologically; it forms intense bonds mentally, emotionally, and physically, especially when we do it over and over again.'"

"I've never heard any of this before," Hawk said.

"I hadn't either. Okay, still quoting, 'Quite simply, any kind of sexual activity that takes place releases chemicals in our brains. For women, it is primarily the hormone *oxytocin*, and for men it is *vasopressin*. Oxytocin allows a woman to bond to the most significant people in her life. It eases stress, creating feelings of calm and closeness, which leads to increased trust. It also causes her to want to nurture and protect the one she's bonded to.'"

"And what's the chemical in men called?" Hawk said.

"Vasopressin. Here's what it says: 'It's similar to oxytocin, except that it is primarily released in the brain of men. This hormone causes a man to bond to a woman during intimate contact. Some call it the commitment hormone or monogamy molecule. This hormone generates a desire for commitment and rouses loyalty. It inspires a protective sense over one's mate, and can create a jealous tendency.'"

"Interesting," Hawk said.

Elliot nodded. "There's more. There is a third set of hormones called endorphins released during sexual activities, and they affect both genders. Endorphins are what we call *happy hormones*. They are highly addictive and cause us to want to experience the rush again and again and again. What makes things even more interesting is that these hormones are values-neutral. Whether it's a one-time encounter or a lifelong commitment, we bond the same way. It also crystallizes these emotional memories in our minds, making these encounters and experiences difficult to forget.'"

Hawk blew out a breath. "Wow. This really hits home. So if I'm understanding this, having sex with Kennedy released all these hormones that caused us to bond, whether we wanted to or not. And the longer we were in a sexual relationship, the more those hormones bonded us. All those feelings of contentment, happiness, calm, and trust were present. But the part that hit me was that sexual intimacy forms intense bonds mentally, emotionally, and physically. And those hormones make emotional memories hard to forget. I guess that explains what's going on with me and why I can't let go."

"I think you're right. Hawk, God designed sex exclusively for marriage because it binds a couple together at a depth they don't have with anyone else."

"So am I trapped with these feelings forever?"

"Not necessarily," Elliot said. "But you do need to be intentional about doing some things that help to rewire your brain."

"What things?"

"According to Cole Zick, the codirector of Moral Revolution, the first is repent. I believe you've done that. But you might be having problems believing you're forgiven. The second thing is accepting your forgiveness. Zick suggests thanking God out loud for your forgiveness and telling Him you believe in His grace. Each time you do this, you will be rewiring your brain to believe God has forgiven you."

"What's the third?" Hawk said.

"Create a statement of change. Prayerfully create a statement that addresses the broken paradigm. For example, a statement of change might be 'I find my value in who Christ has made me, and I don't need casual sexuality to discover my self-worth' or 'I believe that marriage was ordained by God and that, by the blood of Christ, I can start fresh and keep myself pure for the woman who will one day be my wife.' Name how it is you want to change."

"That's seems like a great step," Hawk said. "What's the fourth?"

"The fourth is to find loving support. To identify someone in your life that you trust and who will commit to you. Ask them for a twenty-one-day commitment to help retool your thinking. They will be your support when you don't feel forgiven or struggle with temptation and will pray for your freedom."

Hawk looked over at Elliot. "Would you do that for me?"

Elliot patted Hawk's knee. "I'd be honored. I was hoping you'd ask. I'm eager for you to take a look at the website: moralrevolution-dot-com. It's categorized so that you can pick the subject you want to read about. You should finish reading the 'Invisible Effects of Sex before Marriage' article and learn what happens to our ability to bond when we're sexually active with multiple partners. As we bond and break, bond and break, bond and break, we lose our ability to properly bond, and it can really mess with future relationships."

"Well, that's not going to be me," Hawk said.

"The really good news is that by changing the way you think and behave, you begin to rebuild a foundation of purity that will prepare you for the kind of marriage I know you want."

"I really do. That I even *can* rebuild a foundation of purity gives me hope. I was really feeling defeated. I should've known better. Just because we mess up doesn't mean we can't start over."

"That's right. First John 1:9 promises, 'If we confess our sins, he is faithful and just and will forgive us our sins and purify us from all unrighteousness.'"

Hawk smiled. "It does say that. I like the *purify us* part. Elliot, thanks. I think this is what I needed to hear. I've been so confused about why I can't get Kennedy out of my mind and heart. There's a lot here to think about."

"You're a lot deeper person than you let on," Elliot said. "I've known you and watched you grow for the past eight years. I knew when you confessed your affair to your mom and I and Buck that the consequences were going to be painful."

"You called that right," Hawk said. "This is great information. I'll check out this website."

Elliot rose to his feet and stretched his lower back. "You want to come play Mexican Train with us?"

"You know, I'm just going to sit here awhile and think."

Elliot held out his hand and he and Hawk did their fancy handshake.

"I love you like you were my son," Elliot said.

Hawk got up and put his arms around Elliot. "I'm beginning to realize that I love you like I loved my dad."

CHAPTER 36

December brought the first snow of the season to Foggy Ridge, and evening shoppers were out in droves, admiring the elaborate window displays and choosing gifts for the people on their Christmas lists. The traditional lighted silver bells had been strung across the main avenues, where the trees on both sides of the street glistened with millions of twinkling white lights. Salvation Army bell ringers could be heard on every corner. The huge manger scene that had survived a failed ploy to ban Christmas was prominently displayed on the front lawn of the courthouse. And First Methodist Church, First Baptist, and Praise Chapel had each turned on their sanctuary lights, so their gorgeous stained-glass windows would shine for the outside world.

Hawk brushed the snow off his black London Fog dress coat and red plaid scarf, then pushed open the glass door and went into Markle's Specialty Gift Shoppe, where a wonderful spicy citrus fragrance permeated the air. He loved shopping here for all the women in his life. He wanted to get Abby a silver charm to represent her engagement. Jay had told everyone except Abby that he was going to officially propose on Christmas Eve and that he had saved and bought her the ring she had admired at Long's Jewelers. Hawk hadn't decided yet what to get the others, but he loved to browse through each of the rooms at Markle's and was bound to find something just right.

As he perused the items on a shelf, he heard a familiar *clip clop* sound and glanced through the window in time to see a horse-drawn carriage go by. He hadn't missed taking a carriage ride at Christmastime since he was old enough to remember. He returned to his hunt and studied the collectibles on the lighted shelves before working his way around to jewelry. He was intently eyeing a pair of amethyst earrings he knew his mother would love when someone bumped him from behind. He turned around—and stood facing Laura Lynn Parks, whose face was as red as the tassel trim on his plaid scarf.

"Hello, Laura Lynn," Hawk said.

"Uh, sorry I backed into you. I–I wasn't paying attention." Laura Lynn's thick blonde hair fell perfectly over her shoulders. She looked stunning in black velvet pants and an ivory cowl-neck sweater.

"It's late in the season for *you* to be Christmas shopping," Hawk said.

"Oh, I'm done," she said. "I just wanted to get Abby a silver charm for her engagement."

Of course you did. "What a great idea," Hawk said. "Are you enjoying the snow?"

Laura Lynn smiled. "I am. In fact, I'm getting ready to go on a carriage ride."

Hawk glanced over her shoulder at a decent-looking guy holding what appeared to be Laura Lynn's red coat over his arm.

"I see you brought your warm Red Riding Hood coat."

She stared blankly and then looked behind her, motioning for the guy to come.

"Hawk Cummings, this is Michael Cooper. Michael and I sing in the choir at Praise Chapel and we've been hanging out together for a while now. Hawk is Abby's older brother."

Hawk extended his hand and shook Michael's. "Nice to meet you. I hope you two enjoy your carriage ride." Hawk was surprised that he didn't have to fake his sincerity. "Better bundle up or Jack Frost will be nipping at your nose."

"Well, pretty lady, our carriage leaves in fifteen minutes," Michael said, holding up her coat so she could slip her arms in. "We'd better head over to city hall. It was nice meeting you, Hawk."

"Same here." Hawk looked at Laura Lynn. "I guess I'll be seeing you at all of Abby's engagement festivities."

"I'll be there," she said. "Merry Christmas."

"Merry Christmas."

Hawk went back to admiring the intriguing amethyst earrings, which were a definite maybe. He glanced over his shoulder and watched Laura Lynn and Michael get into a black Land Rover. They seemed suited.

Hawk was glad that he'd run into them and gotten the awkwardness out of the way, especially since Jay had already asked Hawk to be his best man, and he assumed Abby had chosen Laura Lynn to be her maid of honor.

Hawk, carrying two shopping bags full of gifts, walked up the hill toward Salisbury's Market, the snow falling ever so softly. He wondered if he might be the last shopper in town to go home. The sidewalks were empty and there were few cars on the road. He turned around and said in loud voice, "Will the last one to leave please turn out the lights?" He laughed and continued up the hill, his heart filled with Christmas cheer.

When he shopped at Salisbury's earlier, he had decided to back his Jeep into a space in the far back row and walk to downtown to avoid the holiday traffic.

He walked over to his Jeep, one of just two vehicles left in the lot, and opened the door and put his bags on the floor in back.

The other vehicle, a black Suburban, had pulled out and was coming toward the exit. Its brights were on and Hawk wondered how people could be so inconsiderate.

He stood on the driver's side, waiting for the Suburban to slow before it exited so he could tell the driver to dim his lights. But instead of exiting the parking lot, the Suburban pulled in next to him. His heart pounded. Suddenly this didn't feel right. There wasn't another person in sight. He was on his own.

He quickly got inside his Jeep and locked the doors. He turned on the motor and started to put it in gear when he realized his windshield was iced over. He couldn't see anything. And he knew his defroster wouldn't clear the thick frost off the windshield for at least ten minutes. *Lord, I need Your help!*

Maybe they were thieves who wanted the gifts he had bought. Certainly his life was worth more the contents of two shopping bags. He would gladly surrender them.

The Suburban driver's window rolled down. It was definitely a man. He had on a stocking cap and his lips were moving, but Hawk couldn't understand him with both car motors going.

Hawk cracked his window and listened, but the man was already getting out of his vehicle.

Hawk looked down on the floor, even his ball bat wouldn't help him right now. *Lord, give me wisdom, quick. Protect me!*

The guy knocked on the window. "Hawk! It's me, Reza."

Hawk looked up and recognized Reza's face. He rolled down his window.

"Man, you scared the fire out of me," Hawk said, trying to calm down. "What are you doing here?"

"I'm sorry. I did not mean to scare you. I want you to meet someone. Please, come."

I almost had a stroke, and he wants me to meet someone? Hawk left his Jeep running with the heater turned on high. He got out and moved next to the Suburban.

Reza opened the back door. "Please come in and get warm."

Hawk slid into the back seat and didn't see anyone. Reza opened the door to the driver's side and got in.

Hawk tried not to sound as irritated as he felt. "Reza, what's going on? There's no one here."

Reza smiled. "But there is."

From out of the darkness behind Hawk, a woman spoke. "Hawk, it's me. Don't be scared."

"Kennedy?" Hawk's heart pounded. It couldn't be. But it had to be. Her voice was unmistakable.

"I'm coming up there," she said.

The smaller middle seat folded down, and the woman climbed through and sat on the other side of the back seat, opposite Hawk. She took out her cell phone and turned on the flashlight.

Hawk stared at her in disbelief. Was this some kind of cruel joke? Then again, why would Reza be a party to that? "I–I thought you were dead! Romo told me you were dead. That it was classified."

"It is classified. But you found out from Reza that I had disappeared once before. I wanted to explain, and then I have to disappear again, but permanently this time. You can never, ever speak to anyone about this, Hawk. Promise me."

"I promise," Hawk said.

"Tell me what you know," she said.

"I know your real name is Abrisham Kermani. I know your mother was American and your father, Dalir, was Iranian. I know you and Reza were engaged to be married when you disappeared the first time. He tried to find out from your aunt and uncle where you were and why you left, until finally they threatened to get a restraining order if he didn't leave them alone."

"All of that's true. Tell me what you *think* you know."

"I think you and Reza were cheated. I think you belong together. I think your father is or was involved in something big and had enemies. I thought those enemies had kidnapped you, but here you are. How about telling me why you had to disappear without telling me."

"I'll start at the beginning, but I have to talk fast because we can only stay a few minutes. I won't be able to tell you everything, but it's for your own safety. My father worked for some people who wanted him to get involved in things that violated his conscience. He refused. So these people killed my mother to force his hand. Of course, I knew nothing about this and believed her death was an accident. My father sent me away to school in Cambridge, where my aunt and uncle lived, and they agreed to be my guardians. Then after some time, these same people wanted my father to do even worse things—dangerous things—and threatened to kill *me* if he didn't comply. Reza and I were engaged then, but I was forced to disappear by my father's closest friend, who feared for my life. He moved me without telling anyone and supported me in secret."

"She could not contact me," Reza said, "because I was being watched by the people her father worked for. She knew they would have tortured me to find out where she was."

"I'm sorry, Hawk," she said, "but I can't reveal how or why I came to Foggy Ridge. But there's no record of Kennedy Taylor anywhere. The house was provided for me, and there could be no trail leading to me."

"So that's why you were so mysterious," Hawk said. "You never told me anything about your background."

"Oh, I wanted to. I wanted so much to tell you everything. I trusted you. I still do. But it would only have put you in danger. On the day we watched the sailboat races, some very good people used a drone and drugged us so they could kidnap me and erase any evidence that I was ever there. When I came to and they told me what had happened, it hurt so much because I knew I couldn't contact you and explain. And God knows, I'd left Reza again without a good-bye or an explanation. I regretted so much that my reaction when I saw Reza after all those years sent him away in tears. But the fact that he found me had put his life and mine in danger. I knew then that I would be moving again. I didn't know where or when, but that's why I was overjoyed when you called and said you had Saturday off. I wanted to spend every moment I had left with you."

"Where have you been all this time?" Hawk said. "I have grieved your death every day. I couldn't tell Reza because it was classified."

"And I can't tell you, for the same reason. Believe me, it's for your own safety. I shouldn't even be here now."

"Then why are you?"

Kennedy's face suddenly looked radiant. She reached up and took Reza's left hand and shined the light on two simple gold bands.

"You're married?" Hawk said.

"Yes," she said, exchanging a loving expression with Reza. "We've been married for some months now."

"I'm thrilled for you," Hawk said. "I really am. Wow. This is such great news."

"Reza told me everything," Kennedy said. "I'm so sorry about what happened. But thanks to you, Reza didn't go to jail or I would never have known where to find him."

"So you went back to Cambridge?"

"Hawk, this is another of those areas I can't comment on," she said. "But I want you to know how grateful I am for all you did for Reza because you understood his love for me and mine for him."

"It was the right thing to do," Hawk said. "But I'm not the great guy you think I am. I know you must have figured out that I wasn't really looking for a long-term relationship. The truth is I was *already* in a relationship that we hoped would end in marriage. I betrayed her when I got involved with you. After you disappeared, I told her the truth, and we've since broken up, but I never thought I would have a chance to tell you the truth. I'm so sorry I deceived you. I hope you can forgive me."

"Hawk, I knew," Kennedy said. "I was in Bella's Bakery one morning and overheard a pretty blonde talking on the phone to 'Hawk.' How many other men do you know with that name? I suspected she was your girlfriend or fiancée. I never asked. I guess I didn't want to know. What we had together met a need for both of us. I knew it was wrong. It went against everything I believe, and it bothered me for a long time. I've asked God to forgive me. Reza said you have too."

"I have. I *know* I have the Lord's forgiveness. I guess I wanted yours too."

She leaned across the seat and kissed his cheek. "You have it."

"Abrisham and I have decided to pursue Christianity," Reza said. "You may be a sinful man, as am I. But, Hawk Cummings, we also saw much light in you. We want this light."

Hawk felt so unworthy that he didn't know how to respond. He blinked the stinging from his eyes and wiped away the disobedient tear that trickled down his cheek. He blew out a breath, and said, "So this is the last time we'll see each other?"

"It has to be," Kennedy said. "I will always be grateful that you were in my life."

"Let me say a prayer for us before you go." Hawk reached out and took Kennedy's hand and then Reza's. "Lord God, we're so grateful that You're bigger than our sin. That Your plans for our lives can't be thwarted. Only You could take our sin and brokenness and use it for Your glory. I pray blessings on Reza and Abrisham as they depart now and go live their lives in peace. I pray that You would protect them and keep them invisible to anyone who would seek to hurt them. That You would bless them with good health, new friends, and children to love. I ask that You make Yourself known to them with the same loving-kindness and faithfulness that you have shown me. Draw them to Your Son, Jesus, the Light of the World who lives in the heart of every Christian, and bring them into a personal saving relationship with Him. I ask these things in the holy name of Jesus Christ, Your Son and our Savior. Amen."

"That was beautiful." Reza put his arms around Hawk. "Thank you."

Hawk smiled. "Merry Christmas."

Kennedy reached over and embraced him with what felt like her whole heart and soul. "Merry Christmas, dear friend. We will never forget you." She dabbed her eyes. "Hawk, we have to go. I need to ask you not to follow us. Not to try to find us. To do so could put all four of our lives in jeopardy."

"Four?"

Reza put his hand on her middle and laughed. "See how fast the Lord answers you?"

CHAPTER 37

Kate rummaged through her jewelry box, wondering if she looked as flustered as she felt. She went out into the living room where the family was milling about, waiting to leave for Abby's wedding ceremony.

"Has anyone seen my amethyst earrings?" she said.

Hawk shot her a devilish grin. He reached in his pocket and put something in his palm. "You mean these?"

"My earrings!" Kate said. "Where did you find them?"

Hawk walked over to her and handed her the earrings. "Mama, you gave them to me after church last Sunday and told me to keep them in a safe place, remember? You said you'd lose your head if it wasn't screwed on."

Kate smiled sheepishly. "Thanks. I've been so focused on the wedding details that everything else is suffering."

Elliot laughed. "Sweetheart, do we look like we're suffering?"

Kate looked around the room at all the handsome men outfitted in black tuxes, white pleated shirts, and purple bow ties. And Riley, the junior bridesmaid, looking so grown up in a long dress of rich purple peau de soie.

"Oh my, you're all gorgeous," Kate said, her eyes filling with tears for the hundredth time today. "I can't believe Abby will be married before the sun goes down."

Elliot went over, put his arm around her, and kissed her cheek. "Which is why we need you to finish getting ready so we can get moving." He gently nudged her back into the bedroom.

"I'm glad you finally talked me into getting a wedding planner," Kate said. "I thought it would be hard to let someone else take over, but it's been a blessing."

Elliot sat on the side of the bed. "I went up the mountain to see how things look. Kate, it's magical. I think Abby and Jay are going to be thrilled ... Do you ever regret that we had a small family wedding at the church?"

"Not at all," Kate said, fastening one earring. "It was perfect. And the snow floating down, ever so slowly, almost poetically—talk about magical."

Elliot got up and stood behind her, his arms around her. "I love you so much. I can't begin to tell you how happy I am to be a part of all this. I can hardly believe I'm the stepfather of the bride and she's asked us both to walk her down the aisle."

Kate leaned back in Elliot's arms. "I feel blessed beyond measure. I guess a little like Job. After enduring so many tragedies and near tragedies, the Lord is pouring out His blessings on this family. I've wondered what this day would be like from the moment I first held Abby in my arms. If Micah is watching from heaven, I know he must be as proud as I am that you are a true father to the bride, and to all of our children." She turned around and put her arms around his neck. "I love you."

"I love you more."

She smiled. "I love you most."

He started to kiss her. She giggled and pushed him away. "Don't even start. You'll mess up my makeup. I need to finish getting ready or we're going to hold up the wedding. Why don't you go round up the kids, and I'll be ready in five minutes."

Elliot stood smiling at her.

"What?"

"You might want to put on the other earring." He laughed and left the room.

Kate smiled as she fastened her other earring. She powdered her nose. Freshened her lipstick. Sprayed her newly highlighted hair just a little more on the left side. Picked a piece of lint off her jacket and then slipped it on. She went over and stood in front of the full-length mirror.

She scrutinized the mother of the bride. She was pleased with the feminine drape of the long raspberry lace bolero jacket dress she and Abby had shopped for together. The silk heels were a perfect match. Her earrings went beautifully with the diamond and amethyst necklace Elliot had bought her for her birthday, and the gem color was even more stunning with her dress than she had envisioned. She turned slowly from side to side, confident that her outfit was appropriately elegant, but not overstated, and would complement the dark purple dresses of the bridesmaids. Well done.

Kate's eyes suddenly brimmed with tears … again! This was Abby's day. All eyes would be on the bride and her groom. Kate needed to stop worrying about how she looked and just enjoy the moments, memories that would be pasted in the scrapbook of her heart. She wanted everything to be perfect and memorable. How could it be anything else with so sweet a couple, totally smitten, committing their lives to each other?

"Honey, are you about ready?" Elliot said. "Jay, Hawk, and Jesse have already left, and Riley and Buck are chomping at the bit."

"I'll be right there."

Kate opened her top drawer and took out the picture of her holding Abby when she was a day old. What a beautiful baby she was. *My sweet girl, this is your day. You and Jay are about to become one new creature in Christ. I am so proud of the lovely woman you've become. I love you so much and hope you and Jay will live on Sure Foot Mountain and raise your children here, but wherever you are, you'll always be my daughter.*

Kate held the picture to her heart and then put it back in the drawer. She grabbed her purse and went out to the living room.

Elliot whistled. "Wow, you look stunning."

"So do all of you," she said.

A smile appeared under Buck's white mustache. "The grandfather of the bride is ready to roll. I didn't put on this monkey suit for sheer comfort, you know."

Riley laughed and locked arms with Buck. "Come on, Grandpa. We've got a wedding to go to."

Kate stood with Abby and Elliot in the staging area, looking down at the guests who had filled two hundred white chairs neatly placed in rows on the green slope high above Beaver Lake. In front of the chairs near the bottom of the slope stood a white gazebo that had been leveled on the hillside to accommodate the wedding party and Pastor Windsor. The lighted center aisle was carpeted in deep purple.

The tree-covered hills surrounding Beaver Lake wore rich autumn hues of crimson, rust, gold, and orange and were reflected in its calm glassy water. The photographer took notice and didn't miss the opportunity to capture it.

The huge white pavilion where the reception would take place had been set up behind the staging area, where the ground was more level.

Abby looked as if she had stepped off the cover of a bride's magazine, dressed in a long-sleeve, slender column gown of soft, white silk and a crown of white spray roses and lavender, which accentuated her long auburn hair. Her bouquet was a simple mix of white and purple spray roses, and lavender.

Kate leaned over and whispered to Abby, "Are you nervous?"

Abby smiled, her eyes twinkling with joy. "Not really. It's so beautiful. My eyes can't get enough of it. All that planning ... all those details ... and just look at how perfect it is. I can't thank you and Elliot enough."

Elliot bent down and kissed Abby on the cheek. "It's magical."

"It *is*," Abby said. "Everything I dreamed of, and more."

The wedding planner, Samantha Bouvier, appeared out of nowhere. She straightened Kate's jacket and then moved to Abby.

"You, sweet angel, are perfect," Samantha said.

She moved over to Elliot and straightened his bow tie and brushed some lint off his sleeve.

"Okay, everyone," Samantha said. "Remember how we practiced. As soon as you hear Pachelbel's Canon, the bridesmaids will begin the descent. When I give the signal, Abby and her parents will lock arms and slowly descend the steps, heads held high."

Kate took a deep breath when the music began, and when it was their turn to go, she held tightly to Abby and descended the steps, her head held high as instructed. But as she neared the bottom, one face held her attention, and that was Jay's. The way he looked at Abby nearly took her breath away. He was as radiant as she was, and just as pure, having saved himself for her alone. For a split second, Kate got a glimpse of Jesus as our Bridegroom, His face radiant and overflowing with love when He finally comes for His church.

Kate glanced over at Hawk, his eyes brimming with tears. Did he see it too? Was he feeling the sting of regret in the presence of such innocent love?

Kate and Elliot kissed their daughter and gave her hand to Jay, then stepped back and took their seats in the front row.

With Elliot's hand in hers, Kate entered into the ceremony with every fiber of her being. She would never again hear the parable of the Bridegroom without seeing the radiant purity that had emanated from Jay's face.

CHAPTER 38

Inside the white pavilion, a string quartet played just loud enough to add to the festive celebration. All the guests had been served in the buffet line, many remaining seated and visiting at tables, others mingling as they moved around the room.

Hawk mingled with the wedding guests as he made his way around the pavilion. Abby was gorgeous. She and Jay looked so happy. Laura Lynn looked beautiful too. He was happy to hear of her engagement to Michael.

Hawk kept moving through a sea of people—and then he spotted her. He politely elbowed his way through the guests until he caught up with the tiny spirited brunette in a simple black dress.

"There you are," Hawk said. "I've been trying to catch up with you."

"The wedding was wonderful," Jordan Bryan said. "Abby looks amazing. You look pretty handsome yourself. I rather like the tuxedo look on you."

"You do, huh?"

"It's *almost* as becoming on you as jeans and a T-shirt."

He laughed. "It's crowded in here. You want to go for a walk?"

"Definitely," she said.

Hawk took Jordan's hand and led her through the crowd to the nearest exit, and out into the clean mountain air. A full moon lit up the landscape.

Hawk took off his tux jacket and put it over her shoulders. "I'm glad you came. I told you it would be okay."

"I'm not in the habit of crashing weddings," Jordan said.

"You're hardly crashing it when I invited you. Abby insisted."

Jordan laughed. "And some escort you turned out to be."

"I'm free now," Hawk said. "I'm all yours until you tell me to get lost."

Jordan looked up at him, the corners of her mouth twitching. "Did I say anything about you getting lost?"

"I want you to meet my mom and Elliot," Hawk said. "We can't keep putting it off. Abby figured it out. I don't want them finding out about us from someone else."

She nodded. "You're right. I just know how much they loved Laura Lynn. I'm nothing like her."

Hawk stopped and cupped Jordan's face in his hands. "They'll love you. How could they not? *I* love you." Hawk let his lips melt into hers, then gently pulled back and looked into her eyes. "I've never been so sure of anything in my life."

"You really don't think they'll gasp when you tell them I'm a jockey?"

"A winning jockey. And no. I don't."

Somebody came outside and announced that the bride was going to throw her bouquet.

"Come on," Hawk said. "Let's go watch. I already know she's going to throw it to Laura Lynn."

"That doesn't bother you?"

"Not at all," Hawk said. "Come on. Abby's feelings will be hurt if the family's not there."

He took Jordan's hand and went inside. He saw Abby standing with her back to a bevy of ladies, each eager to catch the bouquet. She kept looking over her shoulder.

"See," Hawk said. "She's going to throw it straight to Laura Lynn."

Hawk walked to where the giggling females were waving their arms. He stood over to the side, getting a kick out of Abby looking over her shoulder.

"Here she goes," Hawk said.

"One, two, three ..." Abby flung the bouquet over her shoulder. It went high into the air, over to one side, and right into Hawk's hands.

He stared at it in disbelief, aware that the room was suddenly quiet. Then came a round of applause and laughter.

Jordan laughed so hard she had tears coming down her face.

"Okay, babe, let's give them something to talk about." Hawk reached down, sat Jordan on his arm, and lifted her up. Waving the bouquet with the other hand.

The room erupted in more cheers and laughter.

Hawk looked over at Abby, who was red faced and smiling from ear to ear. She winked.

CHAPTER 39

On Thanksgiving Day, Hawk sat out on the porch swing, wearing his warmest jacket, his hands in his pockets. His mother, Riley, and Jordan were in the kitchen, up to their elbows in piecrust, and having a ball. He could hear them laughing, clear out here. Jesse, Grandpa, and Elliot were watching football. Abby and Jay promised to be there around two o'clock, with a double batch of Abby's homemade dinner rolls.

On this day of heartfelt reflection, Hawk had been counting his many blessings and marveling that God had given him a new love. Jordan was everything his heart desired. And his family had fallen in love with her too. Jordan knew about Hawk's affair with Kennedy. She had made a similar mistake several years ago. Together, over the past ten months, they had sought God's healing and committed to a different course for their current relationship. Hawk had every hope that someday he would stand at the altar and look at Jordan the way Jay had done with Abby. It was never too late to do the right thing. He frequently recited the words from Isaiah 1:18 as a reminder: *Though your sins are like scarlet, they shall be as white as snow.*

Hawk reached in his pocket and pulled out a photo that had arrived in yesterday's mail, the only contents of an envelope that had been run through a postage meter. It was a picture of a beautiful baby girl, maybe five months old. She had a head full of dark, silky hair and happiness in her eyes. On the back was written: "June 12, the second happiest day of our lives." He stared in awe at the picture, wondering what her name was and if she would ever know her parents' story.

Hawk smiled. *I'm thankful for you, my friends. You showed me what real love is.* He put the picture back in his pocket.

The door opened and Jordan came outside, bundled up in a navy down jacket and a pink stocking cap. "I just put my first cherry pie in the oven. And I cannot tell a lie, it was so much fun."

Jordan sat next to him and pulled his arm around her. "I love Kate. She actually taught me how to make a piecrust. I never did anything like that with my mother."

"Mama's an amazing cook," Hawk said. "She loves doing it. She's been teaching Abby since she was old enough to hold a spoon."

"It's weird, but I feel more out of control in the kitchen than I ever have riding a horse."

Hawk grinned. "I feel out of control doing either."

"Then let me teach you to ride," Jordan said.

"Why?"

"Because I love it, and I want you to love it too."

"Okay," Hawk said. "But only if you let me share with you something I want you to love."

"Sounds fair."

"Me first. Come on." Hawk took her hand and hurried out to his Jeep. He opened the passenger side door and she hopped in. He ran around to the driver's side, got in, started the motor, and backed out of the driveway."

"Where are we going?" Jordan said.

"You'll see."

$$\maltese$$

Kate looked out the kitchen window and saw Hawk's Jeep pull out of the driveway. She wiped her hands with a towel and went out to the living room.

"Does anyone know where Hawk and Jordan just went?"

"I don't," Elliot said.

Jesse looked over his shoulder. "Not me."

Buck shook his head. "I didn't even know they left."

"Hmm." Kate went back in the kitchen.

Riley shrugged. "I was with you."

"I hope they're back by the time these pies are ready to come out of the oven. I thought Jordan would get a kick out of taking hers out."

Kate smiled. It had been so much fun making pies with Jordan and Riley, both of them so eager to learn. She had known Jordan for only six weeks, but it felt as if she'd always been part of the family. Hawk didn't talk much about his intentions, but number-one son was smitten. Kate had never seen him this way with any woman before and wondered how he'd kept her a secret for the past ten months while the two of them went through an intensive recovery workshop.

"Well, Riley. How about helping me make the sweet potatoes? We've got to keep the momentum going if we're going to eat at three."

⚜

Hawk stopped the Jeep and turned to Jordan. "Promise you won't peek."

"I won't peek. But I may die of curiosity if you go any slower."

He hopped out and ran around to her side and opened the door. "Keep your eyes closed. Now give me your hand and step down. That's it. Okay, you can open your eyes."

Jordan's eyes flew open. "I see beautiful trees. What am I supposed to be seeing?"

"A big log house with a covered front porch. And a barn. You don't see it?"

"No, I don't, David Copperfield."

"But it's right there."

Jordan's eyebrows came together. "Is this supposed to be something like a snipe hunt?"

"Absolutely not. I've never been more serious in my life," Hawk said. "Look really, really hard. Imagine the future. See those eight acres there—between that red flag and that sign way down there? They're mine."

"You never told me you had land. Nice. Great view."

"Can't you picture that big log house, with the front porch facing those rolling hills and the lake?"

"What happened to the barn?" she said, a grin tugging at her cheeks.

"Oh, it's there. Can you picture it?"

"Yes, I can imagine horses in that barn," Jordan said.

"There are! Now you're getting it."

Jordan got a serious expression and seemed to look deep inside him. "Hawk, what are saying? What's this about?"

"Babe, this is about you and me and everything we love."

"Could you be a little more specific."

"As a matter of fact, I can."

❧

Kate stood at the sink rinsing off the celery stalks she planned to chop for her dressing.

Elliot came up behind her and put his arms around her. "Smells terrific, honey. Can I do anything to help?"

"Not yet," Kate said, "but when I get closer, I'm sure I'll have something … Oh my, is Hawk doing what I *think* he's doing?"

Elliot looked out the window. "That would be my guess. Oh, definitely. That's what he's doing, all right."

Kate wiggled out of Elliot's arms and rushed to the kitchen door. "Everybody outside on the porch! Hawk is proposing to Jordan! Come on, Riley!"

The entire family poured out onto the porch. Off in the distance, Hawk was kneeling on one knee, holding something in his hand.

Riley's face beamed. "Does this mean Jordan is going to be another big sister?"

"No, she'll be your sister-in-law," Jesse said, "but only if she says yes."

⚜

Hawk looked up at Jordan, whose eyes glistened. "I love you more than anything on this earth. And I've dreamed of building a house on this land ever since I was old enough to understand that I never wanted to leave it. Sure Foot Mountain is in my blood. And you're in my heart, in my soul, and on my mind, with every breath I take. You are, in the deepest sense of the word, a pure gift from God. I can't imagine a future here that doesn't include you. Will you marry me?"

A tear trickled down Jordan's face. "And that includes the barn, right?"

Hawk laughed. "Yes, that includes the barn."

"Then yes! I'll marry you." She threw her arms around him.

Still laughing and completely flustered, Hawk said, "Wait, babe, I forgot to give you the ring." He opened the tiny black box and revealed a marquise solitaire.

Jordan put her hands to her cheeks and drew in a breath. "It's perfect!"

Hawk smiled, and slipped it on her finger. "It's a size four. I'm so glad I guessed right. I love you."

"I love you too."

❀

"Hawk, just kiss her, for heaven's sake," Kate said. "There, *finally*. Oh, I'm dying to know what they were laughing about. Jordan's got such a quick wit."

Elliot pulled Kate close and kissed her cheek. "I'm sure you'll manage to pull every detail out of them before you've served dessert. I'm so happy for Hawk. There's no doubt in my mind that he's ready for this. And Jordan's going to fit right in."

"So she said yes?" Riley said.

Jesse grinned. "Looks to me like she's *still* saying yes."

Buck took Jesse's arm. "Come on, boy. Let's give them a minute to themselves. We still have a ways to go before this football game is decided."

Kate waited to speak until she and Elliot were alone in the kitchen. "You've been so good to mentor Hawk. I wondered if he would ever recover after his affair with Kennedy. But he's allowed God to use it to make him stronger."

"I'm so proud of him. He's going to make a good husband," Elliot said. "He appreciates on a much more mature level the decision he's making and what a blessing it is to love a woman who shares his values and his dreams. He and Jordan seem perfectly suited."

"They do, don't they?" Kate giggled and wiped her eyes. "I just love that girl. She's added so much to our family already. And she loves my son. Really loves him. Only God could have turned Hawk's life around this way."

Elliot pulled Kate into his arms and smiled. "You're right. Well, unless you need help, I'll leave you alone with your thoughts."

"Thanks." Kate brushed his cheek with back of her hand. "You know me too well."

Kate went over and stood at the sink. It looked to her as if Hawk and Jordan, hand in hand, were walking the perimeter of the acres that Hawk had chosen. How excited they must be at this moment in anticipation of planning their future together. It had been two years to the day since Elliot had gotten down on one knee and proposed to Kate, right there in the dining room with her dad and all the kids present. She remembered how gloriously happy she was, and it had just gotten better and better since they married.

And now Abby and Hawk had tasted that same joy. She had no doubt that Jesus was the Lord of their lives and would direct their steps through times of joy and times of sorrow. She wished she could make an easy way for them, but only He knew the path they needed to take in order to grow into His image.

Kate wiped a tear off her cheek. How she loved each of her children. How blessed she was that Abby and Hawk wanted to stay on Sure Foot Mountain. She hoped that Jesse and Riley would make that decision too, when the time came. And she hoped with all her heart that one day her grandchildren would carry on the legacy of this mountain resort called Angel View.

As for Kate, her roots had grown deep and strong, and she couldn't imagine living anywhere else. She was content to share her life with Elliot and looked forward to many more happy years as they grew old together.

... a little more ...

When a delightful concert comes to an end,

the orchestra might offer an encore.

When a fine meal comes to an end,

it's always nice to savor a bit of dessert.

When a great story comes to an end,

we think you may want to linger.

And so, we offer ...

AfterWords—just a little something more after you

have finished a David C Cook novel.

We invite you to stay awhile in the story.

Thanks for reading!

Turn the page for ...

- **A Note from the Author**
  - **Discussion Guide**

A NOTE FROM
THE AUTHOR

*"O, what a tangled web we weave, when first
we practise to deceive!" Sir Walter Scott*

Often we're so skilled at deceiving ourselves that it's not until
the Holy Spirit shines His light on our sin that we realize how
ugly it really is. Anytime we take the pure truth of God's Word
and water it down with worldly values, half-truths, and excuses,
it becomes something else entirely—a treacherous mix full of
spiritual poison.

Hawk would probably never have outright "chosen" to have
an affair. Instead, he deceived himself into believing his motive
in giving Kennedy a Jeep ride was just wanting to help a lonely
newcomer to Foggy Ridge not to feel so isolated. It wasn't until
after Kennedy disappeared and the Holy Spirit began to expose
Hawk's sin and the true motives of his heart that he admitted

he had known from the beginning that he was playing with fire. Kennedy was gorgeous and vulnerable and available, and he knew to guard himself against any situation that could turn sexual. But instead of helping her pick up the spilled groceries and then politely walking away, he opened the door that every guy knows is dangerous, and lust exploded into a full-blown affair.

But it's not as though it just "happened." In hindsight, Hawk could see, when he deliberately failed to tell Laura Lynn about his plans that evening and wore the new Ralph Lauren shirt and cologne that had been in his drawer since his last birthday, that he planned to keep his options open. He had a strong moral compass—but he ignored it, and with serious consequences. Kennedy was just as guilty of sinning, but she wasn't yet a believer in Christ and didn't have the same moral compass or the power of the Holy Spirit to help her appropriately deal with her deep grief over losing Reza.

It's important that we don't point only to sexual sin to find examples of moral compromise. Most employee theft starts small, and usually leads to more and more stealing, often with the thief feeling justified because they "aren't paid enough." And then there's taking sick days when you're not sick because you think you deserve more vacation time. And then there's cheating on tests because you're too lazy to study or just didn't make the time. Not returning something you didn't get charged for. Or taking something that isn't yours. We all make moral compromises of some kind. But the point is that every grave sin starts out with something small and deceptive. If only we would listen to our moral compass, we would avoid so much heartache. Few people start out compromising with the belief that one day it will cause heartbreak. Most think they'll never get caught. Some don't. But a believer in Christ will come under the scrutiny of the Holy Spirit, who will not turn a blind eye. Who will not allow us to deceive ourselves for long. Hawk learned that the hard way. And were it not for the mercy and grace of God, he might never have fully recovered.

We believers have a strong and accurate moral compass—the very Word of God. Let us fill ourselves with His truth and refuse to blend it with the lies and deceptions of the world, lest it become for us a treacherous mix.

Oh, friends, it is bittersweet having to say good-bye to the characters I have grown to love and respect. Perhaps with this series, more than any previous, I have delved more deeply into their hearts and minds and exposed their true motives, both good and bad. I was so proud to see them grow.

I've loved every moment spent in Foggy Ridge, and at Angel View, high atop Sure Foot Mountain, where Beaver Lake, like a million blue sapphires, sparkled beneath the lush Ozark hills, forming a maze of inlets and islands as far as the eye could see.

This series was born out of my love for that region and my many happy experiences there with my late husband, Paul, with my mother-in-law, my sister Pat, and several friends over the years. For anyone who has ever looked out over the Ozark Mountains, especially at sunrise when the billowy fog that settles over the White River turns the color of lava—and a handful of sunrays fan out across the pristine expanse of earth, water, and sky—there is no doubt that it was God breathed.

I would love to hear from you. Join me on Facebook, where you can find me at www.facebook.com/kathyherman, or drop by my website at www.kathyherman.com and leave your comments in my guest book. I read and respond to every email and greatly value your input.

In Him,

Kathy Herman

DISCUSSION GUIDE

1. These words spoken by Hawk's pastor stuck with him: "Just remember you can't have it both ways. If you walk in the pure light of God's Word, you know the truth. But if you start compromising what you know is right, your truth becomes an ugly, watered-down shade of gray. It's a treacherous mix." Hawk had taken them to heart, and yet he still fell into the trap. What are some things he could have done to avoid falling into sexual sin? Once it happened, what might he have done to lessen the consequences?

2. Galatians 6:7 tells us clearly, "Do not be deceived: God cannot be mocked. A man reaps what he sows." Do you know Christians who have deceived themselves into believing that premarital sex is okay because times have changed? That it's old fashioned to think people actual remain virgins until they marry? That experience will make them better spouses? Do you think people who think they are the exception eventually realize they've cheated themselves? What are some of the consequences they have shared or you have observed?

3. Do you know any couples who, like Abby and Jay, took a vow to save themselves for marriage and didn't fall into the trap of compromising? Did their wedding day seem more special to them? More special to those who were privy to their choice?

4. Why do you think young people in our culture, even many who are Christians, tend not to see the value of waiting until marriage to engage in sexual relations? How does that balance up with what Scripture says about sex and marriage? What factors in our culture seem to speak more loudly than the Word, the parents, the church?

5. Why does it seem that adulterers and homosexuals are the only groups of people who are publicly singled out for their sexual activity? Is fornication just as offensive to God? Why do you think it's not as offensive to most people anymore? In a culture where people live together before they marry, what are some of the justifications they give for choosing to do so? Is it possible that this is one of the most watered-down shades of gray in our society today? Has it been further watered down with each subsequent generation?

6. Why do you think God ordained sexual intimacy to be enjoyed only in a marriage relationship? Was God wrong? Then why have people since the beginning of time rebelled against Him on this issue? Why do you think surveys consistently show that Christian married couples are the most sexually adjusted? How important do you think it is to have the right premise about what sex is and why it was created?

7. Do you think it's harmful that so many kids today just want to get their virginity "out of the way"? That for many, sex has become

merely entertainment void of rules or commitment? Where did this thinking come from? Do you think many of these kids carry their sexual baggage from relationship to relationship? How might that affect their marriages?

8. An increasing number of single senior adults today have adopted this blasé attitude about sex. The very values they taught their children they are abandoning and adopting values more like their grandchildren's generation. What are some of the excuses they use to justify their behavior? How has society influenced their thinking?

9. Do you think pornography has become a watered-down shade of gray for a lot of people today—in other words, if you're not physically involved in fornication or adultery, does it really matter that your mind is completely immersed in it? Do you think this would affect more than just a person's mind?

10. What are some other ways people in our culture today compromise and water down their values in the workplace? At school? In politics? In Hollywood? On social media?

11. How closely do you think the world watches the behavior of Christians? Are we judged by a different standard? Should we be? Which do you think has more power to influence: our behavior or our words? What should this tell us?

12. Finish this sentence: If I could go back in my life and change any one thing I've done, it would be _____ _____. Do you, like Hawk, believe it's never too late to do the right thing? How different would a believer's life be if he or she consistently took to heart the words of

Isaiah 1:18 as a reminder: "Though your sins are like scarlet, they shall be as white as snow"?

13. Which character in this series did you relate to the most? What was your takeaway from this story? From the series as a whole?

DON'T MISS THE SOPHIE TRACE TRILOGY!

The Great Smoky Mountains are the backdrop
for another series from Kathy Herman—filled with
high-tension suspense that will tug at your heart.